CENTRAL OUTBREAK RESPONSE:
GENESIS

RJ KENNETT

Published in the United States by Richard J. Kennett.

www.rjkennett.com

ISBN-13: 978-0-9899850-0-0

To my family for their love, encouragement and infinite patience in humoring my crazy dreams.

CONTENTS

ACKNOWLEDGMENTS

A special thank you to my friend Craig Spearing, for the fantastic cover art. I promise I'll pay you for the art for the sequel.

To Fletcher Haymes, for advice and service as a reading guinea pig, over and above what was required to avoid physical harm.

To Jeff Bezos (who I recently found out attended the same elementary school as myself) and Amazon, for creating such a wonderful platform for readers and authors alike.

To Google, for being a nexus of valuable research.

And of course, to independent authors everywhere, who together broke down the walls of convention to unleash the creativity of millions.

1

The distant crackle of gunfire pierced the quiet of the afternoon. Max Newsome's head snapped upright, his eyes alert.

The Professor, a tall, bear of a man in his late fifties or early sixties with unkempt white hair and a proud, unshaped beard worthy of Grizzly Adams, droned on about Hesiod's "Theogony" in a deep, gravelly voice. The other students frittered about, taking notes or lost in thought, daydreaming. It seemed no one else heard the shots.

Max quietly set his pen down.

Crack. Crack. It was just at the edge of his hearing, and difficult to discern. He closed his eyes and cocked his head, straining to listen more closely. He knew the distinctive sound, having served his country as an infantryman in combat, but it was eerily out of place at a college lecture.

Crack.

To Max, the sound was unmistakable. He wasn't surprised that no one else heard it; hypervigilance was but one keepsake bestowed upon him by war, and perhaps the only one in which he could find value. It was preferable to other mementos that came from his time in combat, like the deep scars that laced his back and shoulder, or the nightmares which tormented him nearly every night.

His pulse quickened as he slid his compact frame out of his seat and glided quietly to the window. From the second floor at the corner of the Bate building, he could see over the grassy Mall that was the heart of the university. A number of squat, two and three story red brick buildings – a mix of dormitories, lecture halls and

1

administrative buildings – crowded its edges.

It was a warm spring afternoon with a flawless azure sky. The dogwood trees were in bloom, painting the campus a glorious white, accented with broad strokes of pinks and reds. Students ambled along the lush, tree lined walkways on their way to late afternoon classes, as if they either hadn't heard the shots or didn't recognize them as such.

Max saw one of the students below gesture wildly toward several others nearby. He was a pale, lanky young man wearing a red and white striped rugby shirt. With the striped shirt, Max thought the kid resembled Waldo, from the "Where's Waldo?" picture books he'd enjoyed as a child. Though his sense of style might be questioned, his common sense could not. Waldo knew what gunshots sounded like.

"Mister Newsome!" the Professor bellowed, displeased that Max ignored or hadn't heard his first several protests. "Would you like to share what is so interesting outside? Or would you rather take your seat and explain the significance of the titan Perses?"

Max continued to scan the Mall and the street below, heedless of the Professor's righteous and growing annoyance, as well as an immature, tittering snicker from a classmate. Dryly, he mumbled "I heard gunshots."

The Professor gave a placating grunt. "I'm sure it was just a car backfiring or something."

Max looked squarely at his instructor. "Or something. Specifically, multiple gunshots."

"You're imagining things," the Professor said curtly, frowning. His face was flushed behind his thick white beard, making him resemble a large, angry Santa Claus. His temper was the stuff of legend on campus, and Max was testing it. "Return to your seat. You're disrupting my class."

Max ground his teeth, a nervous habit he picked up in war, and glanced out the window again. Waldo was ushering his small flock into the Flanagan building, across the street from Max's own.

"Perhaps you're right, Professor," he said, forcing an uneasy smile as he yielded and slid back into his seat. "Maybe it *was* just a car backfiring." He couldn't blame the Professor. Even if he believed Max, there were systems in place. If there were a gunman on campus, they would learn about it from official channels, and there was no point in frightening the other students. The shots were still far off, and therefore not an immediate threat.

Content with having reasserted his authority, the Professor returned to his lecture, but Max wasn't listening. His gaze was focused on the window and the blue sky beyond, which was all he could see from his seat. He was thinking about the shooter, wondering who he was shooting at, and why. His thoughts drifted to his girlfriend, Aimee. She would worry about him when news got out.

Aimee and Max had taken a picnic lunch together by Trustees Fountain earlier that afternoon. They had met almost a year earlier, when he accidentally slammed a door in her face at the Student Union. Hard. He apologized profusely, and bought her lunch to make up for it. They had been dating ever since. But that afternoon as they talked about the future – their hopes, their dreams, their fears – he knew for sure that she was the girl for him. He'd considered asking her to marry him right then, but thought better of it. Aimee would appreciate him doing it right, picking a memorable and romantic time and place. That's just the way she was; everything should be done properly, and in order. Max had decided it was time to start saving money for an engagement ring.

Aimee was in medical school. She had a laser-like focus, mapping out her career path and following it as if it were dogma. Her professional ambition ruled her above all else, and Max felt honored that she made room in her life for him.

While he admired Aimee's ambition, Max was her polar opposite. He was a drifter and a dreamer by nature, who saw life as a journey rather than a destination. Experience in war reinforced that by driving home the point that life can change in the blink of an eye, that it was best lived for the moment. He was majoring in English, and if he could make a living as a poet or a writer, that would suit him – as long as he had Aimee to share in that life.

Crack. Crack. Crack. The gunfire was getting more frantic, and louder, which meant closer.

Max arched his eyebrows and looked expectantly at the Professor, who had stopped lecturing mid-sentence and was instead biting his lip. He heard. He *knew.*

Crack. Pop. Pop. Pop. Crack. The shots were unmistakable. Several students glanced about nervously. The change in report told Max there was more than one gun involved, but whether it was return fire from the authorities or a second shooter, the gunfire alone wouldn't reveal. More disturbingly, it occurred to Max the gunfire might be coming from multiple locations, but he couldn't be certain it was not just an echo. He drummed his fingers loudly on his desk, taking advantage of the stifling silence in the room to goad the Professor into action.

"Uh, Professor?" came the tiny, quaking voice from a petite, bookish brunette behind Max.

"Yes, Jennifer, I hear it," the Professor said with a hint of false bravado in his voice. "Everyone move away from the windows."

The room bustled with activity as students crowded towards the center of the room, murmuring to one another in hushed tones punctuated by the screeching of steel on tile as they slid their desks with them – all except for Max, who stepped to the window for another look at the Mall.

Waldo was standing sentry outside the Flanagan building, directing passing students inside. Max admired the kid's clear headedness in a dangerous situation, and his raw guts for helping others rather than heading for safety himself.

The Professor turned off the lights and locked the door.

"Yep, lockdown," said Arthur Poole in his nasally, rapid-fire staccato speech, while scrolling through a message on his smartphone. "There's a text from Administration. Says there's a gunman on campus and everyone is to stay put and lock their doors until further notice. Well duh. Glad they could clue us in." Arthur was the prototypical nerd, and either proud of it or oblivious to the fact. He wore red canvas high-tops, jeans that were pulled up too high, and thick glasses that magnified his eyes to a nearly cartoonish level. Missing from his nerd accoutrement were a pocket protector and slide rule, likely because he had opted instead to wear a green tee shirt with an image of copulating cartoon pigs that read "Makin' Bacon."

"Okay, everyone just sit tight," said the Professor, trying too hard to look calm and reassuring. "The police will handle it. When it's safe, they'll let us know. Remember that we practice for this type of thing."

Across the street, Waldo made his way inside the Flanagan building, with what appeared to be a janitor locking the door behind him. Max knew that his own building was being similarly locked. They'd been through a drill only a few weeks before, with an assigned staff member locking the building and collecting attendance records from each class, so they knew who was sheltered there.

"Max! Get away from the window!" the Professor hissed.

Grudgingly, Max slid his desk to the center of the room and joined the other students. He wasn't comfortable following the herd. He would rather be doing something. Anything. Standing at the window, he felt informed, which gave him a sense of having some control over the situation. Sitting with the other students was like sticking his head in the sand.

"This is too weird," Jennifer whispered to no one in particular. "What is this world coming to?"

"Why are you whispering?" Arthur boomed in a far louder voice than was warranted. "Think the shooter can hear us talking, all the way out there?"

Jennifer blushed. "No, I guess not," she shouted, trying in vain to match Arthur's volume. Then more conversationally, "I was just thinking about some stuff I saw on the news. Did anyone else see the story about those homeless guys biting people around town? They put a bunch of people in the hospital, and that was just yesterday."

"Yes. They killed some of them. The police did," interjected Roberto in a thick accent. He was a chubby foreign student; Max thought he had once said he was from El Salvador. "And not just here in Greenville."

"Yeah," nodded Jennifer. "In a bunch of cities. Then there were some guys who released animals from the Asheboro zoo. Now *we* have a shooter on campus. Things have just gotten too weird."

Arthur shrugged. "Same kind of crap that's been in New York and Los Angeles for years. Now it's in North Carolina is all. Hell, Virginia Tech had that shooter a few years back. People suck. Accept it and get over it."

What a sniveling little prick, Max thought. To her credit, Jennifer just rolled her eyes and actively ignored Arthur, who set about playing a game on his phone. Max wondered if some life experience had made Arthur callous, or if he just acted that way because he thought it made him look cool.

The minutes ticked by in uncomfortable silence, punctuated by blips and bleeps from Arthur's game. Several other students fiddled with their own cell phones, texting or trying to find information on the shooting.

Jennifer picked up her quietly buzzing phone and answered it, speaking softly. "Hey. Yeah we're in lockdown. No, we're all okay, don't worry." The person on the other end of the call spoke at length. "Oh, no! That's just... unbelievable! I hope everyone is okay. Did they say what started it?"

Several other students were also chatting quietly with family or friends on their phones, offering assurances that they were fine. Max's cell phone, however, stayed quiet. He considered calling Aimee to reassure her that he was safe, but doubt wriggled like a worm in his gut. He didn't *feel* safe, and he'd learned to trust his gut.

"Wow," Jennifer said after ending her call. "Now there's *rioting* in the Medical District!" She looked at Arthur. "Still think this is all normal?"

"Okay, it's weird," Arthur admitted, shrugging. "One might even say it's odd. Happy now? Does it change anything for you?" He returned to his game.

Jennifer sat back hard in her seat, lips pursed and arms crossed.

"The Medical District? Riots?" Max asked. Aimee was in class there.

Jennifer nodded.

Muttering a curse under his breath, Max pulled his phone out of its belt clip and scrolled to Aimee's mobile number. Her laughing blue eyes sparkled from the screen as he hit the button to dial. After several rings, her voicemail message played. "Aimee, it's Max," he stated simply. "Give me a call when you can. I need to know you're safe. Love you, bye." He slipped the phone back into its clip. *That's just great. Rioting there and I'm trapped here.* There could be any number of reasons she didn't answer, he knew, but Max's mind drifted to the worst possible scenarios. He shuddered.

Distant sirens wailed and grew nearer, the sound reverberating off the buildings around the Mall before abruptly shutting off. Adrenaline-fueled, overlapping and ambiguous shouts from police barking fervent commands drifted up to the classroom, punctuated by the crackle of gunfire.

"Everyone stay in your seats," said the Professor, looking at Max but preempting any student from dashing to the window to check out the action.

"Man, I'd hate to be that gunman," Arthur laughed nervously, setting his phone down on his desk. "Cops are gonna be all over him like white on rice. Like a duck on a junebug. Like a—"

"Can it," Max interrupted. Arthur seemed to have no concept of the inappropriateness of his comments or their effect on others. "Now's not the time," he scolded. People were being hurt, possibly killed. Arthur didn't seem to get that.

Arthur continued to babble. "Right right, I was just saying that—"

"*Can it,*" Max glared at Arthur, willing him to shut up. Jennifer smiled smugly and winked at Max. Arthur just crossed his arms and slouched in his chair, sulking.

"Like white on rice," Roberto mused, stroking his chin. "I do not get it. Not all rice is white. Some is brown."

"There's even black rice," Jennifer chimed in.

"*Can it!*" Max exploded. "What the hell is wrong with all of you? No one cares about the goddamn rice!"

"Now children, play nice," the Professor warned in a half interested tone, his attention focused elsewhere. He was gravitating to the window himself, perhaps to see specifically what was going on outside.

A helicopter roared low overhead, shaking the building with the mighty thumping of its rotors, driving the Professor back into his seat. Max could feel its power reverberate in his chest. It circled the Mall just above the treetops, drowning out the sounds of battle. Jennifer plugged her fingers into her ears. It was a warzone, and Max's class had a front row seat.

Except they couldn't see anything. They were huddled up in the middle of the room like a herd of sheep. For Max, just hearing the violence unfold was worse than seeing it. He felt horrifyingly out of control. It took all of the self-discipline he could muster to keep from rushing to the window. He ground his teeth in frustration.

After circling several times, the helicopter flew off, its thunder quickly fading. Once more, Max heard unintelligible yelling and gunshots. Then screams, the kind that told of primal pain or fear, screams with which he was all too familiar from war. More gunshots. More screams. To Max, the fight seemed to be raging for hours, even though it could only have been minutes. Jennifer had her hands clasped and her head bowed, praying. Even Arthur sat speechless, eyes wide in awe.

Stress, and the aural assault triggered something in Max. His vision blurred. He blinked hard, trying to clear his sight. His heart began to beat rapidly and his breathing became ragged. Cold sweat broke out on his brow and his head pounded fiercely. Max could feel both panic and rage welling up from a dark pit in his soul, where evil memories were buried but never forgotten. An incident from the war forced its way into his consciousness. The firefight where he lost his friend Riggins, and nearly his own life; the nightmarish memory that invaded his slumber nearly every night. He'd experienced the sensation a few times before when under stress, and recognized the warning signs. An Army psychiatrist he spoke with had diagnosed it as post-traumatic stress disorder, or PTSD. It was one of his most unpleasant keepsakes from the war. He knew he had to get out of the room, and fast.

"Professor, I need to use the restroom," Max mumbled as he got up and darted for the door. He was vaguely aware of the Professor's protests, as if they were drifting across a great chasm, muted by the void. Max didn't stick around for a debate. He unlocked the door and flung it open. He had to alter the sensory input he was receiving before his PTSD took over. His blurry vision danced in rhythm with his frantic heartbeat.

Max bolted into the hallway. The door swung closed behind him and muffled the sounds of the chaos reigning outside to a ghostly echo stealing through empty halls. He ran trembling fingers through his short brown hair as he scurried to the men's room and rushed inside.

The bathroom was blissfully silent, save for the steady hum of electric lighting. None of the sounds of the fight outside reached him in his cocoon of serenity. He glared at his reflection in the cheap, polished metal mirror that slightly distorted his features.

The firefight came flooding into his mind like a black riptide, tugging at his sanity. *Get it out of your head, idiot*, he thought. They were on patrol in the city. Sergeant Sommers made the decision to head down an alley in pursuit of a suspected insurgent, rather than wait for the engineers. *Stop thinking about it!* Riggins was perhaps twenty yards ahead of Max, on the right side of the grimy, trash-strewn alley as they moved in staggered formation. He was a good guy, who made the boredom of the barracks bearable with his practical jokes and quirky sense of humor. He and Max had grown to be close friends. *Focus on something else, dumbass!* Riggins turned to Max with concern etched into his face. "Hey, Combat," he whispered. It was slang sometimes used for an infantryman, but Riggins had taken to using it as a nickname for Max. *Focus on something else!* Something clicked or snapped near Riggins. The alley exploded in a blast of light and heat–

"Focus, Combat!" Max shouted at his reflection and slapped himself, a stinging blow hard across his cheek. The slap sparked his anger with adrenaline, and enraged, he slammed his fist into the mirror wildly. Again and again he pounded the mirror, each blow echoing like thunder in the tiled bathroom. It focused him on the pain shooting through his battered knuckles, until they could take no more. He stopped punching and gripped the sides of the sink hard, closing his eyes tightly. He rocked slightly back and forth, focusing on his breathing; heavy at first, easing into shallow, regular breaths. Gradually, the sense of panic that gripped his chest lessened its hold. He let out a deep, soul-filled sigh, and quietly, calmly, opened his eyes.

"Assess the situation," he said aloud to his dented reflection. *I'm done playing the sheep.* The rooftop seemed his best option for a good vantage point, so he shouldered open the door and stalked purposefully back into the hallway. The sounds of battle drifted ethereally into the building as Max made his way down the empty corridor.

He bounded up a flight of stairs to the third floor and saw a door to which was glued a small red sign with white lettering that read "utility." Written just underneath it was "roof access." He tried the door, but found it locked. It was a typical, cheap interior door, not half as sturdy as some Max had encountered while raiding insurgent safe houses in the war. He glanced down the hallway each direction to make sure it was empty. "Screw it," he mumbled and, bracing himself, kicked the door hard below the doorknob. The doorframe splintered with a loud crack as he muscled his way through.

The utility room was narrow and dingy, cluttered with old rags, rusty buckets, mops, brooms and other miscellaneous junk. A musty odor thick with chemicals hung in the air and stung his nostrils. He threaded his way through the jumble of cleaning supplies, old projectors and dusty boxes, then up a rickety metal ladder bolted to the wall. At the top was a hatch. He pushed it up and clambered onto the flat rooftop, bathed in the golden glow of the late afternoon sun. Sounds of the fighting that raged on the Mall again assaulted his ears full force.

He kept low, more out of habit than necessity, and slipped nimbly over a cluster of piping before making his way to the edge.

Although thick tree cover obscured parts of the Mall, Max could see dozens of bodies scattered about the grassy areas. Some lay still. Others crawled, wounded. Many students were running haphazardly around the campus. Some were screaming in terror, while others raced after them in pursuit. Still more were wandering aimlessly, seemingly in a state of shock. Curious huddles of eight or ten were randomly scattered around the Mall, their activity obscured.

Groups of students were gathered at the entrances of several buildings, trying to get inside. They were panicking, and from the bloodshed around the Mall, Max couldn't blame them. Some of the buildings, including the geology building Max could see clearly, had opened their doors to let the panicked students in to shelter. It was a violation of lockdown procedures, Max knew, but this was no ordinary lockdown – if there were such a thing. Other buildings, including Max's own, hadn't opened up. Thirty or forty students were clustered around the entrance to the Flanagan building where Waldo had taken refuge, with more bloodied and battered students swelling their ranks. A cacophony of screams drifted up to Max as they pounded on the wooden doors with such force, Max thought they would splinter. A dozen more were banging on the wall length glass windows and doors below Max at his building.

Two police cruisers were parked at Trustees Fountain at the near end of the Mall. One officer was seated on the ground, his back braced against one of the cars. He wasn't moving and appeared to be in bad shape, as a dark smear of blood on the pavement showed where he had dragged himself. The other three officers were stationed around him, warning students away. Judging from the number of bodies near them, quite a few students failed to heed their instructions and discovered too late that the officers were deadly serious about protecting their fallen comrade.

At one corner of a dormitory across the Mall, Max spotted a gunman – though it was obvious there were quite a few around campus – and he momentarily entertained the possibility it was a terrorist attack. But this gunman looked to be a student, thin with a yellow tee shirt, jeans and purple ball cap. A large camouflage backpack hung from his shoulders. He had a handgun that he was waving wildly at anyone near, popping off horribly inaccurate shots. It was hardly the work of a hardened terrorist. Most students ran away; two others ran at him and were gunned down. One of the wounded crawled into nearby bushes, while the other lay deathly still in a spreading pool of blood.

A crowd of eight students rounded the corner of the dorm, in a full sprint towards the gunman. He saw them and screamed, emptying the clip at them, the report of the pistol echoing off of the buildings.

To Max's astonishment, none of the students fell. He'd seen bullets hit flesh during the war, and he'd seen it with the two students only moments before. He knew the expected and normal result, but the students didn't even slow down. They surged pack-like towards the gunman. He fell backwards, screaming, and they descended upon him. The gunman's screams rose in pitch and intensity, and were suddenly silenced. The students remained crowded around him, forming yet another curious huddle.

"Holy shit!" Max exclaimed aloud. He'd seen combat. This wasn't it. This was slaughter. The "gunmen" on campus were a mix of Greenville police, campus cops and other students – and they were losing badly.

The hellish scenario was playing out all over campus, and Max's thoughts drifted to Aimee. He felt helpless. *If the riot in the Medical*

District is anything close to this level of mayhem—

"Thought you might have fallen in," came a nasally voice behind Max.

Max whirled about, startled. He'd been so focused on the carnage below that he hadn't heard Arthur coming up the ladder behind him.

"Damn, Arthur, you scared the crap out of me!" Max exclaimed. "What are you doing here?"

"When you didn't come back, the Professor sent me to check on you," Arthur said in his typical rapid-fire staccato. "You weren't in the bathroom downstairs, so I tried upstairs and found that door smashed open. I figured that could be you, so I came on up here. So what's going on?"

Max gestured at the Mall. "See for yourself. I don't get it."

Arthur moved next to Max, and peeked over the edge. His face grew paler than usual.

"Yeah, that's about what I thought, too," Max said. "Looks like the gunmen are defending themselves. A whole lot of unarmed students are attacking them. Attacking other students, too. And look over there," Max said, pointing at the Flanagan building. "There's a bunch just smashing into those doors. It's like they're crazed."

"Okay. So. Good guys and bad guys. How do you tell the difference?"

It was a sensible enough question, given the circumstances. The roles were reversed. The gunmen were defending themselves, and among their number were the authorities. They were being attacked by riotous students, seemingly impervious to bullets.

No, Max thought. *Not all.* Many fell before the police, and to their fellow students, reacting normally to gunshots, dying immediately or crawling away bleeding. It was pure chaos. "I guess if they're attacking you, they're a bad guy," Max replied. It was the obvious, if not exactly helpful answer. "That's all I can figure. And someone attacking you, and someone running to you for help, look very similar. That's a bad combination." The two of them quietly watched the drama unfold for a few minutes.

Arthur broke their silence. "This sucks."

Max grunted in agreement. Whatever his flaws, however much he babbled, the nerd had a gift for plain talk when he wanted.

A sudden cracking sound from below alerted them to the pack of students assaulting the Flanagan building where Waldo and company were sheltered. The wooden doors splintered under the ferocity of the assault. With exultant shrieks of victory, the mob surged inside, disappearing from view.

Max heard a high-pitched scream by the fountain. He looked back at the police cruisers to see the wounded officer on his feet, biting into the neck of his nearest fellow officer, taking him to the ground where they wrestled ferociously. The other two officers desperately tried to separate them, but failed when they were overrun by several of the rioting students. Their screams didn't last long. The students and first, wounded officer formed a huddle over their bodies, as others had over the student gunman killed by the dorm.

"Oh, man! Look at that!" Arthur exclaimed, pointing to the Flanagan building again.

They watched in horror as a number of students dove from windows, many bleeding so profusely it was visible even from a distance. Those falling from first floor windows ran or staggered away. Some fell victim to crazed students, while others escaped, disappearing into the chaos enveloping the campus. As the carnage spread to higher floors over several minutes, more students made dramatic plunges from the windows. A young man in jeans and an untucked flannel shirt climbed out from a third floor window and hung from the gutter, trying to work his way the length of the building. He made it about five feet before it gave way, sending him plummeting three stories amidst a shower of debris. Other panicked jumpers also hit the ground hard. There was no certain fate of the people inside the building, but it seemed that jumping was preferable. Those injured from the fall dragged themselves with broken limbs, screaming in terror and agony until brutally silenced by rampaging attackers.

Even more riotous students began to gather around the entrance to the Bate building where Max and Arthur were, joining the dozen or so that were already there.

"Oh, shit," Arthur whispered. "They're coming here."

"We've got to warn the people in this building," Max said. "Those classrooms are deathtraps!" He slid down the ladder to the utility room.

"Wait! Uh," Arthur complained as he scrambled down after. "What are we going to tell them to do? I think they've got the don't-open-the-door-for-packs-of-psychos thing down pat. They practice it!"

Max spun to face Arthur. "Yeah? They did that in the Flanagan building, too. It didn't work out so well, did it?"

"Well, no…."

Max knew he was operating more on gut instinct than a plan. He knew only that they needed to get everyone out of the rooms to have any chance, and with floor to ceiling glass at the entrance, they didn't have much time to do it. The students in the Flanagan building who escaped, ran off. Those that remained met a grisly end. He was determined that the people in *his* building wouldn't likewise be massacred.

"Let's get this floor first," Max said to Arthur. "We'll work our way down."

Reaching the first room, Max tried the door, but it was locked. He beat on it with his fist, eager to get them on his side, excited to be *doing* something. He felt more in his element acting against a threat, rather than waiting with the herd as he had done in class.

A face peered at them from the darkened room behind the wire mesh reinforced window, that of a middle aged woman with dark brown hair pulled back in a tight bun, and deep brown eyes rimmed by thick glasses. Max had seen her in the hallways a few times before, but didn't know her, or even what subject she taught.

"Miss, open up," Max panted excitedly. The woman shook her

head. "Miss, you're in danger here! The gunmen aren't the threat! You need to get out!"

The woman stepped silently away from the door without saying a word.

"Miss! Miss!" Max screamed, pounding the door again. "If you don't open up, you'll be trapped! Listen! At least barricade the door!" He was met with silence, and slapped the door hard, grunting with frustration.

"Well *that* went over like a turd in a punch bowl," Arthur said. "May I suggest a polite knock instead?" He rapped sharply on the door with his bony knuckles and waited a few moments. He knocked again. Waited. Nothing. "Well, they're gonna die. Let's move on to the next one." He started down the hall.

"Not so fast," Max said, squaring himself to the door. Like the utility room door, it gave way to one well-placed kick with the loud pop of splintering wood, but it took a second kick to smash it fully open. Max forced his way inside, looking and feeling every bit the Viking raider, and was greeting with surprised gasps from within.

"Lady, I'm not the threat," he insisted, showing his palms to prove he was unarmed in an effort to build confidence and trust.

The woman just blinked at him, speechless. Three of the larger boys got up to confront Max.

Damn it. He didn't need a fight, especially with several fairly large young men and only Arthur for backup. He quickly decided to go aggressive and try to scare them off. "*Sit your asses down*," he commanded, doing his best imitation of a drill sergeant. Much to his surprise, two of his would-be attackers did. The third, a stocky black student with short-cropped hair, tee shirt and military-issue digital camouflage pants, wasn't so easily intimidated.

"I don't answer to you," he said as he advanced, fists up in a boxing stance.

There was no back-down in his body language or his eyes. His determined grin made it appear as though he were looking forward to a rumble. But he was willing to put himself at risk for his classmates, and Max respected that. While a part of him wanted to test the young man's resolve, he knew it wasn't the time for machismo. Since his adversary wasn't going to back down, Max figured he'd better. A fight then would be counterproductive.

"You win, big fella. I'll go."

Max's capitulation caught the young man off-guard. He stood motionless, brow furrowed in confusion and perhaps a little disappointment.

Max pushed his advantage.

"But listen first. I just broke open this door by myself. It would not have held against the crazed mob that's about to come storming in here. They did it to the Flanagan building, and they'll do it here. This isn't a joke. Look out the blasted window if you don't believe me. That's all I ask."

Max ducked quickly from the room. Behind him, he heard a murmur of voices, and hoped he had given the first class enough of a chance. Debate had begun. If any of them looked out the window, they'd see the bloodshed on the Mall, and that would almost certainly bring them around.

"You like to break stuff, huh?" Arthur said from the safety of the hallway, leaning against the wall with his hands in his pockets.

"Thanks for the backup," Max sneered sarcastically.

"I'm a lover, not a fighter," came the practiced retort. "Well really, I'm more of a–"

"Can it."

"Right right. I was just gonna say I'm more of a thinker."

Max sighed heavily, shaking his head. They headed to the next class, across the hall and down about twenty yards.

He approached the next room more calmly, hoping to get a better reaction from the faculty gatekeeper inside. Of course, Arthur was right. Beating on a door, then kicking it down probably wasn't the best way to introduce oneself. Max knocked politely.

The door was unlocked from within, and swung partially open. A bookish-looking man in his thirties thrust his goateed face out.

"What was that noise?" he demanded before Max could speak.

"Huh? Oh, nothing," Max blurted. "They wouldn't open up across the hall, so I kicked in the door."

Concern etched the man's forehead as he considered the futility of locking the door to a man who had proven he could kick it in.

"Listen, you can't stay in the classroom. The shooters are defending themselves. The threat comes from packs of lunatics." Max thought the calmer approach was working, as the man hadn't slammed the door in his face. "You should be ready to flee, or barricade the hell out of this door. Just locking it isn't enough. I think your best option is not to stay in the room. You could be trapped."

"Thank you," the man said calmly. "We'll take it under advisement." He closed the door and locked it, vanishing back into protocol.

Max was three steps away before he realized he'd been had. The man didn't believe him and had no intention of taking any serious action. The door was likely going to be barricaded against Max though, and he figured that it might help them against the mob as well.

"Well, this is going swimmingly well," Arthur muttered, rolling his eyes. "Perhaps we should start with our own class? Just a suggestion."

At an innate level, Max didn't want to acknowledge that Arthur had a good idea, but he did. Arthur was a thinker after all. "Okay," Max said. "Let's get the Professor on board."

The pair headed to the second floor, and on to their own classroom. The Professor's bushy beard materialized from the shadow of the room. Upon seeing them, he opened the door. "We've missed you gentlemen," he stated in his best calm and collected voice that failed to mask his annoyance. "You were gone quite a while."

"Yeah. Listen, Professor," Max continued, whispering confidentially. "I went up to the roof. Things aren't what you think. The shooters are defending themselves against packs of crazed students. It's those students who are the threat, not the shooters."

"I don't understa—"

"They smashed into the Flanagan building," Max interrupted, his voice rising and cracking from the stress. He felt like Chicken Little, and the Professor was taking him about as seriously. "They killed everyone. It was a massacre! They're attacking our building as we speak!" Max continued, enunciating each word for effect, "Get… everyone… out!"

"The campus police will handle it," the Professor replied.

"*The campos aren't coming, Professor!*" Max blurted out, anger growing. "They're overrun! All dead, or will be soon!" Max grabbed the Professor by the elbow and led him forcibly to the window. "Look out your blasted window! See for yourself!" he bellowed, pointing. "This is real! This is happening! Right here! Right now!"

The Professor stared out the window in disbelief.

"Dead cops! Dead students!" Max continued, spraying spittle from his lips, veins popping out in his neck. He knew he looked like a raving lunatic, but the Professor simply *had* to listen. "Sometimes protocol is wrong! I need you to face reality and help me *deal* with this situation! These classrooms are deathtraps!"

The Professor was ashen as he took in the scope of the nightmare playing out on the Mall before him.

"He's not kidding, Professor," Arthur interjected softly. "This is serious."

Max was glad to have the backup and validation from Arthur. When it mattered, the little nerd came through.

"O-okay," the Professor stammered. He'd relented, though it wasn't in his nature to do so. "So what do we do?"

Max's mind raced. He'd succeeded in getting someone to listen, yet had no viable alternative prepared. He'd seen the carnage on the Mall. He knew that between the roving bands of crazed students and panicked gunfire, running out of the building was almost certain death. Staying put would result in a massacre similar to what happened at the Flanagan building. Rescue wouldn't be coming soon enough. In Max's mind, that left them with but one option. From what he had seen of their attackers it was suicide, but at the end, it was all he had.

"We fight."

2

"Bullshit!" exclaimed an instructor. Max thought he looked like a 1960's-era hippie who grew old but never grew up, having wrapped himself in academia to hide from responsibilities in the real world. His salt and pepper hair was long and scraggly, his face pockmarked with acne scars.

It was a response Max could have predicted. Classrooms with windows were easy to win over to their cause, as the situation on the Mall and elsewhere on campus was on graphic display. Some classes had already seen it, and until Max and the Professor came by, had simply been paralyzed by bickering or indecision. The big lecture halls and other interior, windowless rooms were another matter. Without a visual aid, even with the Professor in tow, other instructors were disbelieving. They were angry, tired and scared. They had been told there was a shooter on campus, and as bad as that was, Max and the Professor were telling them it was worse.

The activity from other classrooms, shuffling chairs and desks into the hallways for the barricades, helped pique their interest as it was obvious that something was going on. The impatient crowd that followed Max and the Professor down the hall wanted to see for themselves. It was a simple human equation, proven many times in social studies: stand in a line, and people will line up behind you even though they've no idea why they're in line. It was the Professor's idea, and Max thought it brilliant. The more they collected for what Max termed a "field trip", the more others were willing to join for a look. While they could go to a classroom with a window, Max wanted to survey the enemy up close, to know more about who or what he was up against, and to check the first floor layout for ideal barricade positions. It didn't hurt, in his opinion, that a close examination would almost certainly win over any reluctant instructors. They were to head for the main entrance.

"I understand," said the Professor in his gravel-tinged voice. "Why don't you pick three students and come with us for a closer look." Max had insisted that students be included in the groups, to bring the message back to their classes from a peer's perspective. "Just leave another student in charge of the classroom until you get back. It will only take a few minutes."

The scraggly-haired instructor was the last they needed to convince. With a class of nearly two hundred, he could provide significant manpower to their defense. Seeing the others waiting for the field trip, the hippie instructor relented. He selected three student volunteers to accompany him.

"Lead on," he said, shaking his head in resignation. A wry grin of doubt twisted his face. "Let's see this 'pack of crazies'."

Max let the Professor take the lead. He was the face of the faculty for those wishing to defend, and therefore a voice of authority. As the group neared the main entrance, the thudding sound of fists on glass rang sharply through the hallway. The faculty and students along for the field trip chattered nervously. Rounding the final corner, the group stopped in silence, their mouths agape.

Several dozen attackers were frantically attacking the glass. Their number included students and faculty, many sporting what appeared to Max to be severe, life-threatening injuries – gunshot wounds, missing limbs, evisceration, missing eyes, multiple savage and bloody wounds – and yet they attacked relentlessly, with fearsome power.

Max walked up to the glass, and upon seeing him the mob's aggression was amplified tenfold. He noticed that they weren't focused solely on the doors, which were locked and chained, but attacked them equally with the entirety of the thick, floor-to-ceiling glass. It was as if they couldn't acknowledge the doors as a weak point. The rest of the building was windowless brick on the first floor, so activity was focused at the corner with the main entrance.

"See here," Max said, pointing at one attacker in particular. It was an instructor wearing a bloodstained shirt and tie, battering a bloody stump against the glass. "This guy's missing his arm. *His whole arm is gone*. He should have bled out, but he looks pretty energetic. This is wrong."

"I know him!" gasped a stocky blonde instructor with a bobbed haircut. "That's John Carmichael. He's got a wife. Kids." Eyes wide with shock, she approached the glass for a closer look, placing her hand upon the glass before her friend. He went berserk, slamming his stump of an arm against the glass, trying to bite her hand as others crowded around in a frenzy equal to his own.

"Does he look like someone with whom you could reason?" Max asked contemptuously. *Why can't they see this for the danger that it is?*

She shook her head quickly. "Not at the moment, no. He's... well, he's looked better. He looks sick or something."

"Sick or not, he wants to kill you," Max said flatly. "Do you think you could kill him?" he asked softly.

"What? No!" the blonde exclaimed incredulously.

Max inhaled deeply and steeled himself for what he had to do next. Quick as a flash, Max grabbed the woman by the back of her neck. He shoved her roughly into the glass before her insane colleague. "*He wants to kill you!*" Max yelled in her ear, painfully aware of her terrified screams echoing off the glass as the instructor with the missing arm licked and bit at her face, little more than an inch away on the other side of the thick glass. "Do you want to live?"

"What!?" she shrieked, struggling futilely against his firm grasp.

"*I said do you fucking want to live!*" Max felt sick to his stomach, terrorizing the poor woman, but felt she and the others needed a graphic, impactful lesson. The crazies might very well be sick, but they were also a dire threat that had to be dealt with at all costs.

"*Yes!*"

Max released her, and she stumbled backwards, away from the

glass and into the arms of her colleagues, rushing to confront Max. He turned to face them, flanked by a visual aid of the crazed horde outside, fists thundering on the glass. "Good! So you have some fight in you after all! Then you have to be ready to *kill!* You'll need it if—"

An enormous, crashing thud reverberated from a pane of glass to Max's right, where a new attacker ran full speed into an unoccupied pane. The glass bowed from the impact, but held. The gathered instructors and their selected students gasped in horror.

"We're under siege, people," Max glowered. "Defend, or die." He stalked back up the stairs, glancing sidelong at the Professor as he passed. The big man gave him a grim nod as he passed.

The other classes joined soon after the instructors returned from their field trip to the entranceway. Max found he had more defenders at his disposal than he knew what to do with.

Some of the students and faculty protested, but were quickly slapped down by others who had seen reason. Seventy-six students and teachers unwilling or unable to join the fight were moved to a lecture hall with two entrances on the first floor near the back exit, with fewer attackers, where they would at least have a chance to escape and flee if the main entrance was breached. Their spokesman was the goateed professor from the third floor, who had sought to fool Max. The room was also barricaded from within at Max's insistence, in the hopes it would hold off any attackers. Max selected for them a room near a back entrance, as far as possible from the main, Mall-facing entrance that was under the heaviest siege.

Max had identified leaders to serve as his lieutenants in the defensive preparations.

Curtis, the young black man on the third floor with whom he had nearly come to blows, was a former Marine, tough and dependable. He was a warrior like Max, vetted by combat. Matthew was a linebacker for the football team, a very strong and popular figure around whom others would rally. And there was the Professor, Max's own teacher, who had helped garner the support of most of the other classrooms in the building. They knew that they were asking a lot of mere students and faculty, to violently defend against people not so different from themselves, some of whom they may know. All agreed that they themselves would take the biggest risks, to start the killing once the fight started, to serve as examples for the other faculty and students.

"We're gonna need weapons," Curtis stated.

"You're right," Max replied. "Grab some volunteers, willing or not. Break open any utility rooms for materials to make improvised weapons."

"Oorah!" Curtis barked, slipping into his military persona, and headed off to the third floor.

"Matthew, you and the Professor handle the barricading. Get all the entrances and stairwells. Draft whoever you need for it. All the crap you need should already be in the hallways."

"I'm on it," Matthew said, and grabbed team members from the crowd of onlookers in the hall.

"Is anyone here a medical student, by chance?"

"Oh! Me! I am!" Jennifer shouted, bouncing up and down excitedly. "Pre-med!"

"I guess that'll have to do. Get to the third floor. Set up a triage location, near the stairwell. We may have some injuries, and I want to make sure they're taken care of as best we can. See if you can find something to use as bandages. Rags, duct tape, whatever you can find. Make do. Collect any aspirin or other pain killers, and some water." He pulled her close and whispered in her ear, "When you triage, send any that are mortally wounded to a different room. We don't want those with survivable injuries to watch them die."

Jennifer looked at him gravely, and nodded, understanding the severity of his request. He squeezed her arm to reassure her.

"Roberto!" Max grabbed his classmate from the crowd. "Go with Jennifer and help her set up a triage station. Smash into the vending machines. We're mostly looking for water, but hey – any liquid will do." They hustled off.

The Professor approached Max from the crowd. "We have a

motivational issue," he said slyly. "A lot of students more interested in looking, than working. They're curious, watching the mob at the entrance. We need to get them to focus on the task at hand."

"Well, get back to the first floor," Max said. "Stand watch at the front entrance. Don't let them rubberneck." The Professor headed to his post. As faculty, the Professor's commands to get back to work on defenses would have more impetus for the students to continue working productively.

Curtis had recruited several other students, and they were busy making their improvised weapons. Max looked them over approvingly as Curtis explained the arsenal.

"We've got broomsticks we're cutting in half, to make short clubs. Then we're driving nails in at different angles and reinforcing with duct tape," he said, holding a wicked looking example. "It's top-heavy, so you get decent velocity." He whipped it hard through the air a few times, producing a whooshing sound as it sliced the air. "The grip sucks, but it should still do some damage. We can make about a dozen or so."

He then hoisted a large silver fire extinguisher. "We've got a couple of these things. We're gonna dump whatever's in here, fill it with water and bleach, and spray it in their eyes. Might blind them."

"How are you going to pressurize it?" Max queried.

"Huh?"

"You have to pressurize it, dumbass," Max scolded. "Or it won't spray."

"Will a bicycle pump do?" Arthur asked. "Because I've got one in my backpack, back in class."

Max thought a moment, remembering his youth, filling his own bicycle tires with air pumps at gas stations. "I don't see why not. It'll take some elbow grease, but it's definitely worth a shot."

"Yeah, I always try to keep a pump handy," Arthur smiled, obviously pleased with himself for his contribution. "One time I was riding my bike over the railroad track just over Memorial – you know where that is? Anyway, I ran over some glass and didn't h–"

"Just… go with Curtis and get it," Max interrupted.

"Oh. Yeah," Arthur said dejectedly as he and Curtis began walking down the hall.

"Curtis!" Max yelled after them, over the din of students preparing defenses. "Add some soap to that mixture! Might make the floors slick!"

Curtis gave him a wave and a nod to show he'd understood.

Max toured the halls, observing his desperate forces with their makeshift weapons. A jock was showing a group of students how to use their keys as brass knuckles, with the keys protruding between their fingers. Max observed that it gave the students some apparent comfort, that they had a weapon at hand, and thought he should tell others to do likewise as he headed for the first floor.

For being in a lousy situation, Max was starting to feel a bit more confident as he watched the students hurrying about their tasks. Other student leaders emerged, taking the initiative. A neat pile of books was placed near each barricade, with which to pelt any attackers. While it wouldn't stop anyone, it might slow them down.

Fear can make individuals surprisingly efficient and cooperative, Max realized. *It can be a phenomenal motivator.* Within about forty minutes, the finishing touches were being put on the barricades, and Max was taking his position at the main entrance. The mass of attackers had swelled to such a horde that the light from outside had visibly dimmed. The hollow pounding on fists on glass was deafening, like being on the inside of a drum.

The Professor came up to him, a grim smile across his face. "You know, I have to hand it to you, Max," he said, leaning in close to be heard over the din of the attackers. "I have trouble getting students to read a book, and here you've motivated them to rip this building to pieces and reassemble it in short order." He gave Max an approving pat on the back.

Max nodded a quick thank you, but fear gnawed at his gut. Fear that their preparations wouldn't be enough. Fear of failure. Fear of not seeing Aimee again. In Iraq, when Riggins died, Max had blamed

Sergeant Sommers. It was Sommers who made the call to head down that alley before backup had arrived. Now, Max understood the weight of command. Worse, it was informal command. These people were trusting him, and if the plan failed, they would lay the blame at his feet. Max felt queasy. He couldn't let them down, but he also knew that even under the best outcome, not everyone was going to survive. His thoughts drifted to Aimee. Was her building under attack? Was she manning a barricade, ready to fight a horde of maniacs, armed with only car keys or a nail-studded broomstick? Or was she already dead?

Max swallowed hard. He couldn't allow himself think that way. He tried his cell phone again, punching up Aimee's number. Her profile photograph smiled back at him from the small screen. Her sparkling blue eyes and beautiful smile gave him some sense of peace, even as the recording played an "all circuits busy" message. He tried 911 with the same result. With a deep sigh, he clipped his phone back onto his belt.

Standing in front of the barricade, Max could see the horde of attackers through the floor to ceiling glass, raging outside the Bate building. They were a motley lot, many with savage-looking injuries. One student who looked a lot like Max, had a bloody and ripped shirt, revealing a purplish bit of intestine poking out of a wicked looking injury to his gut, but in his madness it didn't even slow him down. They were relentless. Their expressions were disquieting; dull, almost lifeless. The rage was in their actions, not their faces. The dichotomy was unsettling.

Max was with the frontline defenders, along with Curtis, the Professor, Matthew, and three more large boys recruited by Curtis. Their job was to blunt the initial wave as long as they could, armed with cruel, nail-studded broomstick clubs, then fall back. The Professor also wielded one of the silver fire extinguishers, filled with a foul mixture of water, soap and bleach. It wasn't fully pressurized, but test sprays were effective enough. Arthur's pump had worked. Given their time constraints, Curtis had wisely opted to pressurize both extinguishers partially rather than fully pressurize one. The second extinguisher was with the second barricade, at the stairwell. Glancing back over his shoulder, Max saw their impressive wall of desks and chairs, carefully interlocked, shored up with backpacks, cushions and anything else they had been able to find to help hold the haphazard structure together. At the Professor's insistence, each barricade had a narrow pass through the center for retreat. Defenders behind the barricade had chairs and desks prepositioned to quickly fill it in, should the need arise. Among those students behind the barricade, Max could see both Arthur and Roberto from his class, among a number of students wielding books to use as projectiles. Arthur nodded at Max and gave a nervous grin.

BANG!

The sound was like a gunshot. Max looked back at the entrance and saw a nasty crack in the glass. His heart raced in anticipation of battle. "Runners! Main entrance is active!" Max yelled. Several students raced off to alert other barricade defenders that the fight had begun. Max had organized a system of messengers to keep all defenders abreast of developments, and a pool of reinforcements from which any barricade in danger of falling could draw support. If any barricade fell, the others had to know quickly in order to avoid being flanked and overrun. They were to retreat to the second floor and help defend the stairwell barricades.

"Man, what the hell were we thinking, sitting out front," Curtis grumbled to Max. "This is gonna put us deep in the Suck."

"It won't be long now," Max yelled, trying to rally the defenders and instill confidence – in himself as much as in his ragtag group. "Remember that these are *not* your friends! It is them or us! So stand ready! Stand strong! Stand and *fight!*" he bellowed.

The defenders answered with a deafening chorus of enthusiastic cheers.

Hey, it worked! he thought. He'd never truly appreciated Sergeant Sommers' gift for rousing speeches before a fight. His own was the best he could do, even if he thought it weak.

Another loud bang announced a new crack in the glass.

Max caught a glimpse of a pair of desert fatigues on a man forcing his way through the mob, to the front of the window. He saw the blond hair and the winning smile of his dead friend from Iraq pressed eagerly against the glass, jostled by maniacs. It did nothing to dim his apparently cheery demeanor.

"Hey Combat!" he yelled from the other side. The friendly, familiar smile twisted into an enraged frown. "Knuckle up, bitch!"

"Riggins."

"What'd you say?" asked Curtis.

"Oh. N-nothing." Max shook his head and blinked rapidly. Riggins was gone. The sudden and unexpected hallucination left Max shaking, his adrenaline pumping, ready for battle. "Just be ready," he growled, gripping his club tightly. Subconsciously, he began hyperventilating, flooding is muscles with oxygen for the upcoming fight.

Another loud bang splintered through a glass pane. And another. The raging mob outside was smashing the glass with bloodied, bare hands, stumps, even their heads. There were so many, they blocked any view of Founders Drive or the Mall beyond.

"There must be hundreds of them," Matthew said, his voice quivering with fear.

Max took a deep breath. "Stand tall, brothers. Stick to the plan."

Seemingly in slow motion, an entire pane of glass that was spider webbed with cracks peeled away from its frame as the mob's exultant shriek of victory roared deafeningly down the hall.

The first adversary forced his way inside, then clumsily fell, where he was crushed underfoot by the mob that surged through the breach.

Wielding the fire extinguisher, the Professor boldly stepped forward, spraying the sudsy mixture on the tile floor in front of the onrushing horde as well as in their faces. The slippery concoction caused the onrushing attackers to fall over each other in a heap, but the mass of writhing bodies crept ever closer as more windows gave way to the assault. The fire extinguisher sputtered, emptying the last of its contents. The Professor shifted his grip and swung it like an enormous club, smashing it into attackers' heads, driving them back into the slippery mess. It chimed like a bell at each impact; music to the ears of the cheering defenders beyond the barricade. By sheer numbers and the absorption of water in their clothing, the crazed students were making inexorable progress, approaching the frontline defenders. The Professor stepped back to rejoin Max and the others.

"Nice work," Max said. "Now it's our turn."

The Professor nodded, his chest heaving from the exertion of battle. His eyes flashed with a fierce rage and determination.

"Volley!" Max yelled. An avalanche of books fluttered over his head and pelted the oncoming horde. Max had expected it to slow them, even if only momentarily. Instead they continued to press forward, oblivious to every impact, their advance slowed only by the slick footing.

"Brace yourselves," Max told his frontline defenders. "Stick close and work together!"

From the mob emerged a bloodied figure in a torn black uniform. Max noticed a badge and a gun, but the policeman's pistol was harmlessly in its holster on his hip. He clawed his way over the writhing mass of struggling bodies, towards the edge of the slick buffer, no more than ten feet away.

"Gun! Gun! Gun!" Curtis yelled, breaking ranks and charging the policeman, eager to seize the officer's sidearm.

"Curtis! Get back... damn it!" Max cursed.

Heedless of Max's protestations, Curtis charged the police officer. He swung his broomstick club, wickedly studded with nails, and caught his target in the throat. With a roar born of battle rage, Curtis pulled hard, ripping his weapon free and tearing out the policeman's throat. Unfazed, the officer crawled forward and grabbed Curtis' legs, pulling him to the ground. As Curtis wrestled and grasped for the officer's sidearm, two more attackers, a scrawny kid and a heavyset young woman, also fell upon him. Curtis dropped his club and grabbed the kid by the throat, keeping his head up. The woman grabbed his other hand and bit into his forearm. Curtis screamed in pain and surprise.

"Jesus!" exclaimed Matthew, on Max's other side.

"Get him out of there!" Max yelled. The gun would be a prize, to be sure, but it wasn't worth a life. Max charged the trio attacking Curtis, dislodging the police officer with a swift kick to the side of the head. The scrawny kid grabbed Max's plant foot and pulled, sending him crashing to the ground. Max's head bounced hard on the tile floor. White sparks exploded in front of his eyes, and his vision blurred. He felt his foot twist awkwardly in the kid's grip, and something popped. Max groaned as pain lanced through his ankle. The kid's grip felt like a bear trap. Refocusing, Max brought his club down hard, slamming nails deep into the kid's wrist. It served to weaken his grasp. Max released his club, leaving it embedded, and kicked his legs free. Reaching out, he managed to hook his arm under Curtis'.

Curtis' eyes rolled in panic and pain as Max, Matthew and the Professor pulled him towards the barricade in a tug of war with his attackers. His arm had several large chunks missing. Blood flowed freely from the wounds. Max was vaguely aware of other students struggling with attackers, of the barricade being hit by someone and chairs collapsing around them, but he had his hands full. More hands grasped for Max, but failed to find purchase as he rolled and twisted his body, trying to leverage Curtis free. The attackers were successfully reaching the edge of the slippery buffer. Another volley of books sailed overhead, ineffectively pummeling their targets.

Curtis, slick with his own blood, was suddenly wrenched from his rescuers' grip and pulled into the seething mass of bodies. Matthew uttered a cry of fear and revulsion as he saw Curtis torn apart by bare hands. He bolted through the narrow pathway they had built into the barricade for escape. In a panic, he and several other students hurled chairs and desks into the breach, filling it in, trapping Max and other frontline defenders on the wrong side of the barricade.

"No!" Max shouted. "You son of a—"

He didn't have time to curse Matthew further, as a blonde student lunged at him. Snatching up Curtis' nail-studded club from the floor, he jabbed it in her face, ripping out a sizeable chunk of flesh. The blow momentarily knocked her off balance, and Max desperately crab walked backwards, fear and adrenaline masking the pain searing through his injured ankle. A strong pair of hands gripped him from behind and hoisted him in the air, hurling him over the barricade. As Max crashed to the ground on the safer side of the barricade, he saw the Professor, his savior, battling the mob singlehandedly. The bearded giant roared with rage, swinging hammer-like fists futilely as no less than five attackers pulled him down.

Through the barricade and a mass of legs, Max saw that several attacking students were fighting over Curtis's entrails, and that's when he realized – they were eating him. The Professor's hoarse screams told Max he was facing a similar fate.

"Let's get out of here!" screamed Matthew, his face white as a sheet as he fled down the hall. Several other students manning the barricade needed scant encouragement by his example and were quick on his heels. Others looked at Max expectantly as they pushed back hard on the failing barricade, trying in vain to keep their attackers at bay.

Max groaned in frustration. His ankle felt like it was on fire. "Fall back to the stairwell! Support the defenders there!" He muttered a heartfelt apology to the Professor, whose screams were suddenly and brutally cut short. He chose to die so that Max might live, and valiantly fought his killers to the bitter end.

"Let me help you," Roberto said as he waddled over to Max and helped him to his feet.

Max leaned on Roberto for support as he hopped quickly down the hall to the stairwell. The first barricade, now unmanned, began to crash down behind them. It had fallen only minutes after the initial breach. Max was injured and several defenders were dead – including two of the bigger, stronger defenders in Curtis and the Professor. The classroom of noncombatants, led by the goateed instructor, came under attack by a half dozen lunatics. Max heard the sound of splintering wood almost immediately. Attackers were chasing down students who had fled the first barricade, making the mistake of running the wrong way in their panic, which cut them off from the stairwell barricade. Several made it out the back entrance to face an uncertain fate on the open campus. Others didn't. Their lives bought time for the stairwell defense, if only minutes.

Leaning on Roberto, Max hobbled up the stairs and through the barricade entrance, grimacing from the pain exploding through his ankle. He propped himself against a wall and looked at the stairwell barricade defenders. They had heard the first barricade fall, seen the primary defenders flee, and their faces betrayed their fear. These were students, not soldiers, and Max knew they had no chance. They looked at him expectantly.

"Are you okay?" Roberto inquired.

Max nodded.

"Then I will help here, at this station." Roberto boldly took up a position with the other defenders. Max could see the fear and concern in their faces morph into resolve when they saw Roberto's steadfast determination.

"You get to triage," barked a little redheaded spitfire whose confident air of command told him she had taken leadership of the stairwell barricade. "We'll hold them here."

"It's bad. It's like they feel no pain. They don't stop," Max told her. He thought of Curtis and the Professor being torn apart. *Except to eat you*, he told himself, but couldn't vocalize it. With Roberto's willingness to defend the second barricade after seeing the first fall, her team was newly resolute, and fear would only undercut them. The only alternative to fighting was dying. "Try to take out the legs of the ones in front," Max advised. "The ones behind will trample them. Use the fire extinguisher, too; that was pretty effective at messing up their traction and will buy some time. Also, you've got a narrower choke point than we had and a better height advantage with the steps. Use it." It was all the advice he had.

The spitfire nodded sharply and began to rally her troops, who wielded sharpened broomsticks and metal poles as makeshift spears. Max admired her confidence and courage, and her fellow defenders' show of resolve.

Max clapped Roberto on the shoulder reassuringly as he passed. "Gracias, amigo. I wouldn't have made it back here without you." Roberto nodded in acknowledgment. Max doubted they could hold much better than he did in the entranceway, but for all of their sakes, he hoped he was wrong. He hobbled up the stairs and into the triage station to get his ankle wrapped. It wouldn't do anyone good to have him limping about at the second barricade; he would just get in the way.

Jennifer looked at him as he entered and smiled. "My first customer," she said, trying to look cheerful. "Who would have guessed it'd be you?" She had pulled her hair back in a ponytail, and for the first time, Max realized what a beauty she was, with finely chiseled features and a warm smile. "So how're we doing?"

"The first barricade is breached and the first floor is lost," Max grunted in pain as he hopped onto the table. "The Professor is dead. A bunch of others, too."

Her smile vanished. "The Professor is dead?" she asked incredulously while removing Max's shoe.

"My number was up. He saved my life."

"Grab some acetaminophen behind you. It'll dull the pain." She grabbed a roll of duct tape and hurriedly set about tightly wrapping Max's ankle, causing him to wince.

"I don't think we held them for more than a couple of minutes," Max continued as Jennifer worked on him. "The stairwell barricades are probably a little stronger due to their position, but not by much. I'm sorry. I'm so, so sorry. Be ready to run."

"Run? Run where?" Jennifer asked in a squeaky voice laced with panic. Tears of fright welled up in her dark eyes. "If you're right, they'll run us right up to the roof, and off!"

The roof. Max wanted to slap himself for being so stupid. The roof was the ultimate choke point, up a ladder – they could engage their attackers one at a time, from an extreme height advantage. If the helicopter came back, they could signal for help.

"That's it! The roof!" Max exclaimed. "Don't waste time, get everyone you can to the r–"

A loud crash and terrified screams roared down the hall, heralding the fall of the stairwell barricade. Max hopped into the hallway in time to see bloodied defenders and their equally bloodied pursuers spilling into the third floor hall. One thin young attacker had been run through, impaled on a sharpened broomstick, and still chased his screaming prey down the hall. Panicked, some defenders bolted into classrooms, sealing their fate with the slam of a door.

"No! The roof! Get to the roof!" Max yelled, but his voice was lost in the cacophony of screams. Jennifer was right behind him, clutching his shirt in fear. *"No, Goddamn it! No!"* Max raged as students fell helplessly before their attackers. He took a deep breath through gritted teeth. "We can't help them, Jennifer," he sighed, shoulders drooping. "We have to go."

The tape job Jennifer did helped him move a little faster, but his ankle was still searing in agony. She helped him limp down the hallway, towards the utility room with roof access. Tears streamed freely down Max's face as he watched student after student fall before the onslaught, powerless to help them. As they reached the utility room, Jennifer gave forth a surprised yelp and was violently wrenched from Max's grasp. Whirling about, he saw Waldo, bloodied and battered, gripping Jennifer tightly by one arm.

Before Max could react, Waldo bit into her shoulder. "Max!" she screamed in surprise and pain as a ragged chunk of flesh was torn free. Blood streamed down her arm.

"Let her go, asshole!" Max screamed, and hopped over quickly to separate them. He desperately tried to pry Waldo's fingers off of

Jennifer as she struggled against her attacker, but his grip was like iron. Waldo went for another bite. Max swept his bad foot under Waldo's legs and tripped him, sending him sprawling backwards. Max's ankle exploded in pain from the effort, but Waldo lost his grip on Jennifer as he fell to the ground. Max hurried her into the utility room, looking back to see Waldo struggling slowly to his feet.

Three more attackers spotted them and poured into the utility room, howling like mad dogs. Max kicked over a metal cart to block their path, but it barely slowed them down as they kicked it to one side.

"Get up the ladder! Move your ass!" Max yelled, roughly shoving Jennifer towards the ladder while he turned his attention to their attackers. He pulled a filing cabinet down to block their way, then a metal shelving rack, which he wedged against the cabinet in the narrow room. It slowed their advance as they struggled to remove the obstacle. One would push while the other pulled; Max noted that they seemed incapable of working together. It bought him precious seconds. Turning, he saw Jennifer halfway up the ladder, and limped quickly to it himself. A loud metallic crash behind him signaled that his last, desperation barricade had fallen as he stepped onto the ladder. If he made it to the roof, he could keep pushing them down the ladder, but for how long? He focused on climbing the ladder, hopping up with his one good leg to keep his injured ankle free. One hand slipped off a rung slick with Jennifer's blood, but he held on with the other. In his mind's eye, he saw the grubby hands of his attackers grabbing his flailing ankle and pulling him down. He refocused his attention on the climb, never looking back, trying not to think about the psychopaths climbing up behind him.

He reached the top. Arthur and Jennifer peered over and helped him onto the roof, bathed in the amber glow of dying daylight.

"Arthur!" Max exclaimed. "Help me push them off the ladder!" Max whirled about, ready to battle to the last.

Their attackers were joined by several others, including Waldo. They howled around the base of the ladder with their devilishly empty eyes gazing up at Max. Every now and then, one would grip a rung but would almost immediately slip off, or be pulled from it by the scrabbling hands of the others.

"They don't look like they're coming up," Arthur said.

"What the hell?" Max said. "Can't climb?"

The aural nightmare of doors shattering, followed by triumphant howls of the attackers and screams of students dying drifted up past Waldo and his compatriots as they roared in frustration at Max and Arthur above them.

"Yeah, looks like they can't climb," Arthur confirmed. He hocked up some snot and spat down the ladder. "Fuck... *you!*"

Max limped over to check on Jennifer, who was sitting on the ground, rocking back and forth, hissing in pain. Waldo had torn away a large chunk from her left shoulder. She gripped it tightly, blood running through her shaking fingers and down her arm.

"I'm gonna piss on them," Arthur said, unzipping his pants.

"Arthur! Can it!" Max scolded. "Jennifer's hurt. Just keep an eye out and make sure they don't figure out how to climb. If they do, kick them off!" Max pulled his tee shirt off and used it to stanch the bleeding from Jennifer's shoulder. She grimaced in pain as he pressed it to the wound. "I'm sorry. But this will help stop the bleeding," he said, trying to reassure himself as much as her. "It may not exactly be sanitary, but it's the best I can do right now. It's reasonably clean. I did laundry just last month."

Jennifer nodded her assent, even managing a brief smile at his bad joke as she groaned in pain.

Max pondered their situation for a few moments. "What were you doing up here, Arthur?"

"Hey man, I saw the Flanagan fall, too," he said with his palms facing Max as if telling him to back off. "I gave your plan one chance. When that first barricade fell, I came up here. Call me a coward if you like, but I'm fucking alive."

"I'm not judging today, Arthur," Max sighed. He had to hand it to the nerd. He acted within himself. He wasn't a warrior or a hero.

He didn't try to be, and perhaps that was why he survived. Max and Jennifer, on the other hand, were just lucky. He thought remorsefully of the Professor's sacrifice.

"Dude! What the fuck was that!" Arthur spat, trying to change the subject. "What is wrong with them?"

"I don't know," Max lamented, still maintaining pressure on Jennifer's wound. "It's like the world has gone mad."

3

Max looked over the edge of the roof, contemplating the gruesome scene of the Mall and events of the day. Night had fallen. Gunfire rattled in the distance, and several large fires glowed on the horizon. Greenville was dying; a grand old lady torn apart in an orgy of violence by her own children. She had stood longer than the nation, but wouldn't survive the night. There were no gunmen left alive nearby. The only movement was of the shadowy forms of several hundred crazed students meandering about under the cold, dim glow of street lamps, or the strobe effect of the emergency lights from the police cars near the fountain. Hundreds lay on the ground, wounded or dead, some little more than dark stains and tattered clothing.

Waldo and his new friends were still at the base of the ladder. Other than periodically banging into the toppled metal shelving or filing cabinets, they were silent, agitated only by Max or Arthur peering down the ladder. The lights in the utility room were off, but Max was sure there were at least eight crazies waiting below, with an unknown number still prowling the halls of the building.

"So what do we do now?" asked Jennifer. Her face had grown waxen, and sweat broke out on her forehead despite the rapidly cooling night setting in.

"I don't know," Max sighed heavily. He felt the weight of the day pressing upon him. He had convinced them to fight and as a result everyone was either dead, fled, or just as insane as their attackers. "Do either of you have suggestions? My bright idea didn't pan out. I got everyone killed."

Jennifer looked at him blankly.

"Well, I did!" Max continued, his voice rising, choked with emotion. "I screwed up! I should have sent everyone to the roof right off the bat!"

"Stop it!" Jennifer scolded. "You did the best you could. You got everyone out of the classrooms. *You* got everyone organized. *You* gave everyone a chance, when they had none. The three of us are alive because of *you*. And I for one, *thank you*." She looked at Arthur, who nodded his head in agreement. "So stop blaming yourself, or thinking that *we're* blaming you. We're not."

"But your question still stands," Max said softly. "What do we do now? We're stuck on a roof, surrounded by murderous freaks. We don't even know what we're dealing with."

Arthur sighed, gazing thoughtfully at the crescent moon hanging majestically, nonjudgmental in the ebon sky. "I think it's like cooties. I mean, what else could make people go all nutso like that?"

"Cooties," Jennifer chuckled derisively. "Some form of rabies, maybe." She shivered against the chill of the night air. She had lost a lot of blood, and still clutched Max's tee shirt against her shoulder.

Arthur snorted. "Cooties I say. It's got a ring to it."

"Whatever," Jennifer mumbled.

Max's gaze drifted to the west, where he could see the taller buildings of the Medical District looming over the treetops, only a couple of miles away. Was Aimee taking refuge on a rooftop, too? How could he hope to find her in the madness? He absently ground his teeth, and swore he'd do everything in his power to find her. *She's alive. She has to be.*

"I bet a lot of religious nuts are feeling stupid right about now," Arthur said.

"Hey, *I'm* one of those 'religious nuts' Arthur," Jennifer defended. "You don't believe in God?"

Arthur rolled his eyes. "Not even before all this. And if he exists, he's a total dick for letting this happen."

"Well *I* believe. And what about you, Max?"

"Never met him," Max shrugged. "Don't get me wrong; I prayed a few times in the war, when I was scared for my life." He shrugged, "I guess I just never got an answer."

"But you lived, Max," Jennifer said. "You survived. Maybe your prayers *were* answered."

"Have you ever seen a child detonate a suicide vest? Ever seen friends blown apart? I have. Don't talk to me about God until you've seen that kind of–"

"Guys! We didn't come up on the roof for a theological discussion," Arthur interrupted. "We came up here to escape a mob of raving whack-job psychopaths."

"Arthur's right," Max concurred. "And I'm more than a little concerned about how we're going to get out of this. I'll tell you what; if God will miracle us out of this mess, then I'll believe. Until then…" Max shrugged. The conversation made him uncomfortable, and he already had enough on his mind. If belief in God kept Jennifer going through the crisis, who was he to tell her any different? In truth, he wished he could believe. If God could forgive him for the things he did in Iraq, and relieve his guilt over failing to protect his classmates, then maybe he could forgive himself, too.

"We'll get out of this. They'll come looking for us soon," Jennifer said assuredly.

"Who is 'they', Jennifer? The police? The Army? Look around us," Max motioned to the multiple infernos burning around the city. "We're stranded on a roof. Humans can survive three days without water. Three days, and we're trapped on a roof. No shelter. Under a burning sun all day tomorrow. I doubt we'll *make* it three days under the conditions we're going to have. If we go down there we die. If we stay here we die. Basically, we die."

"Well that's a cheery pep-talk," Arthur mocked. "But you're right. Nobody's coming."

Jennifer brooded in silence.

"Arthur, you got your phone?" Max asked.

Arthur nodded.

"Try nine-one-one. It's probably a waste of time with all they've got on their plate, but it can't hurt to let someone know we're here."

Arthur dialed the emergency response number. "Busy."

"Damn it. I guess it's to be expected," Max growled, grinding his teeth. "Impending death by dehydration or not, we need rest after all we've been through. Let's sleep in shifts. One of us needs to watch the ladder at all times."

"Man, I can't sleep!" Arthur exclaimed.

"Then you have first watch."

"But Max, if we're right, and it's cooties–" Arthur continued.

"Rabies," Jennifer interrupted.

"–then isn't Jennifer infected? I don't think I can sleep with her here."

Jennifer went ashen.

"I don't think we need to worry," Max said. "That Waldo looking guy down there was in the Flanagan building when it went down. I saw him there. If he got infected, it moved fast. Maybe twenty, thirty minutes at most. Fast enough that if Jennifer was infected, we'd know it by now."

Jennifer looked a little more at ease, leaning back slightly, but her concern was nevertheless written in the crease of her brow.

Max needed to keep the three of them on the same side. Arthur's suspicion may have been well-grounded, but it also drove a wedge between them. All they had left was each other, and Max didn't want paranoia to endanger that last bond. "Wake me in a few hours, Arthur, and we'll switch. Jennifer, you don't take a shift on watch. Your job is to sleep. That's a nasty wound." Max hugged himself tightly, rubbing his arms quickly to generate warmth. "Come morning, maybe we'll have clearer heads, and a better grasp of the situation."

"What happened to your back?" Jennifer asked, noticing his deep scars. She saw Max's expression droop. "I'm sorry. It's none of my business."

"Iraq," he said, grinding his teeth. He vividly remembered the pain he felt when the blast wave knocked him backwards, sending him skidding through broken glass. Shards the surgeons couldn't reach still moved about in his flesh. There were too many, and removing them all would have caused even greater trauma. Most of the time, they didn't hurt too much as they were surrounded by scar tissue. The real pain was in his memories. "I got them in Iraq." He smiled at Jennifer. "But I was lucky. I still have my arms and legs, fingers and toes. And my Kevlar vest protected more of me that would have been shredded. Don't worry about it, Jennifer. What's done is done." He put his arm around her, hoping that their shared body heat would keep them both warm as the cool of night descended.

They fell into an exhausted sleep while Arthur stood watch at the ladder.

†

Arthur zipped up his pants after relieving himself. He just couldn't hold it anymore, and didn't want to waste an opportunity to make a statement. Sure, a rooftop drain or scupper would have sufficed, but it would have lacked the editorial impact of urinating on the mob below. He looked down the ladder to see his victims, but they were shrouded in inky blackness. They saw him, though, evidenced by the growls and groans wafting up the ladder. They weren't as energetic as they had been earlier. Arthur thought that perhaps they were growing tired and slowing down. He worried that their desperate growls might wake Max and Jennifer. He glanced over at his companions as he sat back down by the hatchway.

Both were asleep, and had been for a couple of hours. They began sleeping while hugging each other, and Arthur had felt a pang of jealousy. He wished he were so confident as to put his arm around Jennifer, to console her or to warm her, either would suffice. But he felt a little better since Max's fitful sleep had pushed her several feet away. Max would occasionally swat at the air, mumbling nonsense in his sleep. Arthur could almost make out words or names amidst the soft gasps and babble, but nothing was quite clear. Jennifer was curled up in a little ball and looked uncomfortable, which Arthur figured was understandable, given her wound. Despite it, he found he couldn't keep from giving her sidelong, appreciative glances as she slept. He hoped that didn't mean he was creepy.

Still, she didn't look well. She was pale and shivering more than the cool night warranted, and sweat had matted her dark hair to her forehead. Arthur was worried. If it were a form of rabies, what would they do if Jennifer woke up as crazy as the lunatics at the base of the ladder? What if Max was wrong about the speed of infection? He glanced over the edge of the hatch and into the darkness below, to a chorus of groans. *We could push her down there, if we have to*, Arthur thought. *I like her, but if it's her or me, I choose me. Besides, the head cases below don't seem to attack each other, so she'd probably be fine, if she… becomes one of them.* He swallowed hard, hoping that Max was right, that she was indeed in the clear. Maybe she just looked sick from blood loss or shock.

Arthur withdrew his phone from his front pants pocket and scrolled through a national news website. It was the site with the most recent information, but there had been no updates to any of their stories for several hours. Similar riots had been reported in several dozen countries, but as the article stated, that was just from those that would admit it. Giving up, he slipped the phone back into his pocket.

Arthur gazed up at the moon for a long while. He shivered, longing for the morning sun to rise and bathe him in its warmth. He could see over Greenville and hear the occasional crackle of gunfire in the distance. He could see three helicopters buzzing like angry hornets several miles away, in the direction of the airport. He thought he saw muzzle flashes from one of them, though he'd never seen a muzzle flash to know for sure. A large plane thundered overhead, lazily circling the city several times before landing at the airport under the watchful eye of the helicopters. A short while later, another – or perhaps it was the same plane, Arthur couldn't tell – took off, its distant rumble fading to the southwest.

"This sucks," Arthur grumbled under his breath. He checked the news website on his phone again, but again found no new articles or information. He sighed and slipped it back in his pocket. "Useless."

"Arthur," mumbled Jennifer weakly.

Arthur climbed to his feet and padded across the roof to sit next to her. "How're you feeling?"

"I'm scared. My shoulder hurts." She looked pleadingly at him with dark circles under eyes, bloodshot even by the dim light of the moon.

Arthur could see she was shivering, with cold, fear or fever, and perhaps a little of each. "I'm sorry. I wish I could do something to help." He meant it, but felt powerless to do anything.

She paused a moment, sucking on her lip, then reached out to take his hand. His heart skipped a beat. "Maybe you can. Pray with me?" she said. Arthur opened his mouth to speak, but she interrupted. "I know you don't believe in God, but I do. It would help me. Pray with me? Please?" she squeezed his hand. Her fingers were cold, her grip weak.

"Sure, okay," he stammered. *If her faith keeps her focused, if it keeps her going through this nightmare, then it's a good thing,* he thought. *I can do this.* "What do I do?"

"Just hold my hand, close your eyes and listen to my voice," she croaked weakly. "You don't have to say anything." With Arthur's help, she struggled to her knees and faced him, holding his hands in hers. "Heavenly Father," Jennifer began, "We don't always understand your ways, but trust in your love for us through your Son, Jesus Christ. Whatever your reasons for allowing all this to happen, we accept them without question. Help us to find the strength..." she paused to swallow. "The strength to persevere, and by our struggles, grow closer to your majesty. Please help... Arthur and Max... overcome their preconceptions and... and grow to know you.

Lord, I know… that many of your folloshm… died todesh… grhgh….” Jennifer’s grip on Arthur’s hand suddenly tightened.

Arthur cracked his eyelids open and peeked at Jennifer. Her eyes were wide with an eerie emptiness to them. A tremor wracked her body.

“Aghh… Arth–” Jennifer gurgled as vomit exploded from her trembling lips, splashing on Arthur’s “Makin’ Bacon” tee shirt. Her grip tightened to an almost crushing power as she sputtered and heaved again.

“Ow, ow, now this… not good. Jennifer, I need… let… *go!*” he shouted, wresting his hand from her icy grip and jumping to his feet. She collapsed forward and vomited again.

Instinctively, Arthur pulled his phone from his pocket and dialed 911. For the first time in the crisis, the phone rang, and Arthur’s spirit soared with hope. *Come on, come on, at least get me someone who can talk us through this.* After about a dozen rings, he hung up. He bit his lip, dejected. *I’ve gotta wake Max.*

†

Max awakened with a start as Arthur shook him. “Huh? Whazzit?” he asked, looking around groggily. It was still night, but the city had grown quiet. Concern was etched onto Arthur’s face.

“Max, wake up! Jennifer’s sick.”

Max saw Jennifer laying on the rooftop. Bile was trailing down her chin and a pool of vomitus was next to her.

“For crying out loud,” Max muttered. It was yet one more problem to deal with, and Max had no resources, no ideas – not even his shirt. “What happened?”

“She woke up for a while. We talked. She asked me to pray with her. I mean, it doesn’t mean anything to *me*, but who was I to say no if it gave her comfort?”

Max smiled at him. “That was a good thing, Arthur.” He yawned and wiped crusty sleep from his eyes, then knelt beside Jennifer.

"Anyway, she was praying, and then mumbled a bunch of gibberish I couldn't understand. I thought maybe she was speaking in tongues or some shit, but next thing I knew, she barfed on me!" he pointed to a large stain on his shirt.

Jennifer mumbled something that was mostly incoherent. Max could only make out the phrase, "put the dog outside."

"She must be hallucinating," Arthur commented.

Max felt her forehead. "Oh man, she's burning up. Try your cell phone again," Max told Arthur.

"Already did," Arthur said. "No answer."

"You called nine-one-one?"

"Yeah, dumbass. Who else would I call?"

"Wait a minute. You called the emergency number, and no one answered? Not just busy, but ringing with no answer?"

Arthur nodded.

"Crap."

Max had seen everyone in his building massacred. He did not want to lose Jennifer, too. "Maybe I can make it to the triage room. We've got acetaminophen in there. It should help to knock her fever down."

"Past Waldo and company? Don't be stupid."

Max peered down the ladder to a chorus of guttural screams. "Damn it." He looked over the edge of the building, scanning for options. "Maybe I can climb down to the triage room, go in through the window?"

"Yeah, that'd work," Arthur sneered. "Get real. Maybe if you had rappelling gear. If you fell, it'd be all over. We're three stories up."

"Well we have to do something soon. Not just for Jennifer, but for us. We have *nothing* up here. We need food, water and of course, something for her fever."

"Fine," Arthur said emphatically. "We have to do something, I agree. But not scaling the wall of a building, in the dark, without climbing gear. That's stupid. Sleep on it. Besides, you've got a bad ankle."

Max knew Arthur was right, he just couldn't abide inaction. He ground his teeth. "Okay, okay. You're right, I know. I'm just frustrated. Thanks for the reality check." He sighed. "You want to catch some Z's? I'll take watch."

Arthur shook his head. "I can't sleep. I was always a night owl anyway."

"Then I'm going to. Wake me if anything changes." He wished Arthur would get some sleep, as he could become a liability if he were too tired and they needed to be fresh. Nevertheless, from his time in war he understood better than most how stress could keep one from sleeping. He couldn't *make* Arthur sleep.

Max checked on Jennifer again, feeling the furnace that was her forehead. She was dozing peacefully – or passed out; Max couldn't tell which and didn't want to wake her anyway. "I'm worried about that fever."

"Cooties?" Arthur inquired with a wry grin.

Maybe it's just how he copes. "Can it, Arthur," Max scolded. "It's not funny. Just shut the hell up." He sat with his knees pulled to his chin and put his head down. Exhausted, he drifted to sleep again.

†

Max was standing amidst the horror in the aftermath of the massacre at the Bate building. Lifeless, accusing eyes stared back at him from the many victims. He searched among the bodies for something, but couldn't remember what. At every step, he trod upon the corpse of someone he felt he knew, but couldn't quite identify.

He saw movement beyond the barricade. A woman was gliding past, in the hallway beyond. Her long blonde hair covered her face. Max called out to her, and she slowly turned her head towards him. Her sparkling blue eyes met his, and she smiled.

"Aimee!" he called again, remembering that it was not what, but for whom he was looking.

Still smiling, she looked away, and vanished down the hall.

Movement behind Max cause him to turn. Curtis sat on the floor, his back propped against the wall. In his hands, he held his own entrails, and was clumsily trying to stuff them back inside a cavernous pit in his midsection. He looked balefully up at Max, his terrified eyes pleading for help.

"I'm sorry, brother," Max said helplessly. "I'm so sorry. I don't know what to do."

Curtis' expression pinched with pain. He looked back at his hands and continued trying to reassemble his innards.

Max turned and saw the Professor's torso, one arm and head still attached, wriggle snakelike across the floor to Max's feet. He looked up, trying to rise on the stump of his missing arm, reaching his one great paw towards Max. He opened his mouth as if to speak, but uttered no sound.

"I... I'm sorry Professor!" Max cried. "I had no choice but to leave!"

Life drained from the Professor's eyes. He sunk slowly back to the floor and lay still.

Bodies all around Max stood in unison, pointing accusingly at him.

"I'm so sorry," he whimpered. "All of you; I'm sorry! I failed you!"

They closed around him, reaching with grubby hands as he shrank in fear.

The rattle of automatic weapons fire exploded around Max, laying waste to his tormentors as they reached for him. Screaming in fear from the suddenness of the attack, Max wrapped his arms around his head until the shooting stopped. When silence reigned again, Max cracked open one eye and, turning his head, peeked back at the barricade.

On the top of the structure stood Riggins in desert camouflage – a bold, heroic figure clutching an assault rifle with a trail of smoke issuing forth from the barrel.

"Your new friends kinda suck, Combat," Riggins said, his distinctive smile gleaming. "I mean, you failed me too, but I'm not going to harsh on you over it." Hopping down from the barricade, Riggins strode purposefully across the gore spattered floor and pushed the rifle roughly into Max's chest. "Here, Combat. You've grown soft. You'd better get used to killing again."

†

"Max! Get up!" Arthur shook him awake.

"Yeah yeah, I'm up," Max grunted, relieved his nightmare had come to an end.

"You said to get you up if anything changed. Well, it did."

"What is it?" Max said, blinking the sleep out of his eyes. The golden fingers of dawn were just beginning to creep over the horizon, exposing the open wounds of a dying city. Smoke plumes rose from where the fires had raged through the night, but Max's attention was focused on more immediate concerns. "Is Jennifer okay?" He looked for her and saw her laying on her side, sleeping.

"'Okay' being relative, yeah," Arthur said. "It's our friends below."

Max staggered over and looked down the ladder. "I don't see anything."

"What do you hear?"

Max listened intently. "Nothing."

"Exactly!" Arthur exclaimed, lightly slapping Max's shoulder. "They've been going ape shit whenever they see us, but not now. Maybe they're gone!"

Max squinted into the darkness below, but could only discern the vaguest of shapes and shadows. He wished he'd had the foresight to flip the light switch on his way in, but given their predicament at the time, couldn't kick himself too hard. "I can't see anything down there. Give me your phone."

"Why?"

"Because I lost mine in the fight. Just give it to me."

Arthur cautiously handed over his cell phone.

"Cool dog," Max commented upon seeing the wallpaper on Arthur's phone. "Yours?"

"Yeah, that's my golden retriever, Jasper," Arthur smiled warmly.

"Well, he's beautiful." Max flipped through screens of applications. "Wait, where's…" Max's voice trailed off.

"What are you looking for?"

"The flashlight app," Max said.

"I don't have that one."

"You've got to be shitting me! You've got the goddamn periodic table on here, but no flashlight? I thought everyone had that."

"I never needed it before," Arthur sniffed defensively. "Give it back, I'll download it." Arthur navigated to the store and started the download. "Well, emergency services may be out of action, but the app store still works," Arthur said, smiling. "All is right with the world after all."

Max cocked an eyebrow.

"Here you go," Arthur said as he again surrendered his phone. "My battery is at twenty percent. Don't go wasting it."

"Wasting it? You were playing games all day."

"It's my phone."

"So it is," Max conceded.

"And I haven't played any games since we left the classroom."

"I'd hope not," Max said, activating the application. The camera's flash flicked to life, slashing dimly through the gloom below. Bodies were strewn about, twisted in unnatural ways Max had seen before, in Iraq. Among them was Waldo.

"Crap. Are they asleep or something?" Arthur whispered, peering over Max's shoulder.

"I think they're dead." Max glanced back to where Jennifer lay sleeping, her breath coming in shallow, ragged gasps. He had to try and help her, if there was even the slightest chance of success. "Wait here."

Max gingerly stepped onto the ladder, keeping weight off his injured ankle as he descended, phone in hand. Stepping off the ladder, he picked his way through a grisly maze of upthrust arms topped with claw-like fingers. Rigor mortis had set in, locking their bodies in a grotesque, twisted mass.

"Well?" Arthur whispered from above.

"Yeah, they're dead," Max said aloud. "All dead." His stomach felt queasy. He realized that just yesterday at the same time of day, these people were showering, getting dressed and eating breakfast, for the last time in their lives. Max thought of Arthur and Jennifer's theory that it was some variety of rabies. If so, it burned through an enormous number of people very quickly, driving them mad, making them kill, and finally, killing them. He took a moment to study Waldo. His shirt had Jennifer's dried blood on it, and his own from several bite wounds including a deep, nasty one on his neck. The blood loss must have been extreme. How Waldo could have kept moving and attacking, even with some rabies-like madness coursing through his veins, was astounding. Max sniffed. "Man it smells like piss down here."

"You don't say," Arthur whispered from above.

Max made his way down the hall to the triage room, trying not to look at the bodies of his classmates. Their blood was pooled on the floor or dried and spattered, dripping down the walls, a grisly testament to Max's failure. Some of the victims had been ripped apart. Max held his breath, trying not to breathe in the stink of urine, feces and who knows what that permeated the building. He pushed open the door to the triage room and froze.

Standing with her back to him was the little redheaded spitfire he'd seen leading the stairwell barricade. A wave of relief swept over him, and he sighed heavily. "Thank God, someone else made it!"

The girl slowly turned, and the hairs on the back of Max's neck pricked up. *This feels wrong*, he thought, tensing. Then he noticed the bites. The spitfire was bloodied and shredded, strips of flesh and sinew dangling from her arms and legs.

She turned to face Max, surveying him with a blank stare from her one remaining eye.

"No," Max whispered. "God, please – no. Stay back."

She started towards him, but her movements were wrong, as if she had no coordination. She took a couple of stiff, shuffling steps and fell, smashing into a table and spinning stiffly to the floor in a very unnatural fall. She uttered a long, low, rattling groan.

Max wanted to run, back to the rooftop and away from the nightmare. But Jennifer needed his help, and the drugs were so close. *I can't back out now.* His injured ankle screamed in protest as he carefully and quickly stepped past the fallen spitfire. She made a slow, awkward grab at him as he passed and her fingers brushed his pants leg, but he avoided her grasp. He went to the shelf where they had stockpiled what little medicine they scrounged up before the battle. He found the bottle of acetaminophen he had used earlier for his ankle, and several bottles of water, while keeping a watchful eye on the redhead thrashing about, gasping like a fish out of water.

In a world so radically changed, where nothing was right, some things were less right than others, and something about the redhead was especially not right. Max crept back to the door as the redhead flopped towards him, groaning. He wanted to help her, but she was too far gone, and Jennifer was not; at least not yet. "I'm sorry," he whispered to the spitfire as he quietly closed the door behind him. He didn't even know her name.

Something moved further down the hall. He heard shuffling steps, groaning and the thick whack of a body falling, just like the redhead. Shadows moved, and something rustled in a classroom to the side. Max's heart pounded as he hurried, as quickly as his ankle would allow, back into the utility room and up the ladder. Arthur was kneeling next to Jennifer, brushing her hair from her forehead.

"I'm glad you're back. She doesn't look good," Arthur said quietly.

"Got some pills. And water," Max said. He handed Arthur his

phone and a bottle of water, then cracked open the acetaminophen. "Is she awake?"

"Y-yes, she is," Jennifer mumbled weakly.

"Take these," Max said, slipping a couple of pills through her dry, cracked lips. He opened a bottle of water and helped her take a sip. She got the pills down before sputtering and coughing, spitting up a mouthful of water.

"S-sorry," she mumbled.

"That's fine. You just rest. You'll feel better soon, and we'll be able to get you out of here in a few hours," Max said.

"Hours?" Arthur inquired.

"Hours?" Jennifer echoed in a whisper. "M-Max…" she stammered, her eyes filling with tears. "I don't think–"

"Shhh. You rest. That will have your fever down in no time, and you'll start feeling better." Jennifer's head rolled to the side. "Look at me. Jennifer, look at me."

She looked up at him with tear-filled, bloodshot eyes.

"I'm not going to let you down. You're going to beat this."

She nodded and tightly shut her eyes, trying to fight back her tears.

He motioned Arthur to the side. Once away from Jennifer, who looked as though she were sleeping already, he spoke in a hushed tone. "It's still dangerous. They're not all dead, but they're dying. At least I think so. But it's weird. They're like… I don't know. Slowing down. Stiff-legged."

Arthur blinked. "Like what? A nerve agent or something? Maybe the government gassed them with something. Affects them, but not us? I saw a big plane fly over the city earlier."

"I don't know. I doubt it was that. It was just… wrong. I can't describe it any better."

"Okay, this is good. We give them a little time to finish keeling over, then we leave. I like that plan," Arthur said. "Can you take watch? I'm getting pretty tired now. Been up all night. A little nap will do me some good."

"Sure, Arthur."

Arthur took a seat next to where Jennifer lay and nodded off.

Max sat next to the hatchway. He picked at the tape on his ankle until he could peel it off slowly. The tape gave support, but he felt it needed some circulation. He quietly removed it, enjoying the slowly growing warmth of solar radiation on his skin as the sun rose, and contemplated his failure in defending the building.

Was it the lack of weaponry? The failure to build adequate barricades? A bad plan? All of these thoughts drifted through his consciousness. Always his thoughts boiled down to one factor: lack of information. He didn't know what could have driven so many, so mad, so fast. Some form of rabies was the best theory they had come up with, and they had no real evidence one way or the other; it was pure speculation. The wounds suffered by the crazed students bothered him. He felt the injuries they sustained were far too severe to allow their speed and ferocity. They were seemingly unfazed by any amount of damage they took. And their faces… good Lord, the empty expressions on their faces….

A rustling sound and movement alerted Max. Looking over his shoulder, he saw Jennifer rising shakily to her feet, outlined in the golden glow of the morning sun. Arthur slept peacefully beside her with his elbow cocked over his face, blocking the sun.

"Feeling better?" Max inquired. "That aspirin must have done the trick. It's good to see you up and moving around ag…"

Jennifer turned towards Max, opened her eyes and growled. Her eyes were empty, brown orbs of madness, void of any semblance of reason.

"…ain. Oh, shit."

She burst towards Max, lips curled in a primal snarl. He tried to rise to his feet, to meet her charge, but found his ankle too weak, legs too stiff from sitting and she crashed into him. He managed to roll over to his side just in time to catch her throat with his left hand, but his right arm was pinned behind him with her weight on top.

"Arthur!" Max shouted. "Get up! It's Jennifer!"

Jennifer's claw-like nails on one hand dug deep into his shoulder while the other scrabbled and scratched at his face. He whipped his head back and forth, trying to keep her fingers out of his eyes.

Damn, she's strong, he thought. "Arthur! Get up *now!*" Max's thrashing allowed him to wrestle his right arm free and he rolled more fully on his back, allowing him to better ward off her eye gouging attempts.

Suddenly, she was off him. Arthur was dragging her away by her ponytail. She reached back, and grabbing Arthur's slender wrist, pulled him on top of her. The two rolled around in a heap for a moment, before Jennifer ended up on top, snarling.

"Dude, get her off me!" Arthur shrieked as it was his turn to try and ward off her bite.

Max bounced to his feet, ignoring the screaming pain in his ankle, and hopped quickly to where the two were tussling. Arthur had saved him, and it was Max's turn. He grabbed Jennifer under both arms, and with a grunt, lifted her off of Arthur. She may have found super strength in insanity, but she still weighed very little, something for which Max was grateful.

Jennifer's thrashing, combined with Max's bad ankle made him stumble towards the edge of the roof. Arthur shouted in alarm, but Max saw the problem developing and sat down hard, right at the edge of the roof. He jammed his tailbone and pain blasted like a cannon shot through his lower back. Jennifer's back was to him as he held her tightly in a bear hug, desperate not to let go and give her another shot at him. She was out of control, and there was nothing he could think of to help her. Tie her up? With what? Beat her unconscious? Extreme, and he wasn't sure he could, given her state of mind. His mind raced.

Suddenly, Jennifer's weight shifted and she rolled backwards. Max saw that Arthur had grabbed her legs and was rolling her back over the edge.

"Arthur! No!" he shouted. It was too late. Jennifer slipped from his grasp and over the side of the building, plunging three stories.

"*God damn it Arthur!*" Max yelled scrambling to his feet.

"What?" Arthur said defensively, looking perplexed. "Dude, she was kicking our asses!"

"That doesn't mean you kill her!" Max shouted, enraged, emphasizing it with a rude shove to Arthur's chest that sent him falling backwards to the ground, hands flailing wildly. "You don't fucking kill her! You don't! You… you…" Max's voice trailed off.

"You what? *What do you do, Max?*" Arthur shouted, picking himself up. "Your whole defensive plan involved killing the psychos, and now you say don't? Then what do we do? Tell me! 'Cause I couldn't see any other option!"

Max glowered accusingly at Arthur, but said nothing.

"Lots of people died here, and *I'm not going to be one of them!*" Arthur raged, emphasizing his words by thumping his own chest.

"Arthur, just calm—"

"What? What!?! You want me to call nine-one-one again?" Arthur waved his cell phone wildly. "It's useless, Max!" Arthur screamed hysterically, and hurled his cell phone over the edge. "*Useless!*"

He paused. A small pop and tinkling of glass and plastic followed clearly from the still, silent campus.

"Oh, shit dude. I just tossed my phone." Arthur peered after it. "Do you think it… oh, fuck me running."

"What is it?" Max asked, peering over the edge as well.

Three stories below them, Jennifer flailed about on the ground. Her torso bent and twisted unnaturally; her back clearly broken, but still her upper body dragged her inexorably towards the street.

"Oh my God," Max gasped in shock.

"I bet she's pissed," Arthur said. He continued to babble, "So… what do we do? Put her out of her misery? Or leave her alone? I mean, we can't leave her like that. Can we leave her like that?"

She wasn't dead, but Max knew she soon would be. The disease would kill her as it had most everyone else in the building, and in her raving madness she could deal with pain.

"Leave her be. I'm not a killer," Max said, grinding his teeth in rage. Memories from Iraq came roaring back into focus, making him queasy. "At least, not anymore. Look, she's dead. From the rabies or whatever. There's nothing we can do for her. God knows I wish there were. The world's gone to hell."

Max ground his teeth, his fists shaking with rage. He gazed over the Mall and beyond. Signs of destruction were visible as far as he could see, evidenced in hazy smoke forming over the city, overturned vehicles on nearby streets, and the ever present reminder of torn, mutilated bodies scattered everywhere he looked. For several minutes, Max surveyed the scene, measuring his breathing, trying to regain his self-control.

"Let's go," he said, unclenching his fists. "There's no more reason to stay here."

"Go where?" Arthur asked.

"Go wherever you want, Arthur. I'm going to the medical building to find my girlfriend, if she's still there." *If she's still alive,* he thought, but couldn't make himself vocalize it. The fear of it stuck in his throat, an evil notion he couldn't allow to manifest in words.

"Oh, okay," Arthur mumbled dejectedly. "You know, I could help you look, but I want to check on my Mom, too. My Dad doesn't live anywhere near here, since they're divorced, and he's up in…."

Max looked at him tiredly.

"Medical school first, of course," Arthur stated quickly, as if he realized he was being unnecessarily verbose. "Besides, they should have something for your shoulder."

Max looked at the angry red marks he bore from Jennifer's nails. "It's nothing," he said glumly. Scratches meant nothing to him. Death was everywhere, and he couldn't help anyone, not even Arthur. The nerd had saved himself, whether through cowardice, smarts or just an overwhelming sense of self-preservation.

Arthur gazed hesitantly down the ladder. "You're sure they're all dead, or at least gone down there," he said, more hopeful statement than question.

"Well, some were moving earlier, but they were all messed up. I think they were on their last legs. They're probably all dead by now," Max responded grimly. "It isn't pretty. You'll see a lot of blood. A lot of bodies. And you'll recognize some of them. I just want you to be prepared."

Arthur took a deep, nervous breath. "Okay."

"Just stay focused on moving past them. Head for the stairs, and we'll be out in no time at all," Max cautioned. Having seen the horrifying carnage in the hallways and from curious, ill-conceived glances into classrooms, he didn't want Arthur to freeze up at the scene. But he dreaded the stairwell most of all, where so many must have died in such a confined area. Nevertheless, they had to traverse the carnage to escape from the building that had become a tomb for so many.

"Dude, I'm good, let's just go," Arthur said curtly, but his trepidation was palpable.

Max headed down the ladder first, stepping gingerly on his injured ankle as he slowly climbed down. Arthur scrambled down after. Upon seeing the bodies twisted with rigor, he inhaled sharply, staring.

"You okay?" Max inquired.

"Mm-hmm," Arthur nodded. The two picked their way over the bodies, past Max's collapsed barricade of last resort, and into the hall. Arthur exhaled. His eyes were wide, his face pale as he gazed upon the dead. Arthur was not taking it well.

"Still good?" Max asked, unsure what to do if the answer came back negative.

"Sure," Arthur squeaked. His earlier bravado on the roof, cursing and threatening to urinate on the mob, had fled. In its place was a frightened child, who had probably never seen anything dead that was larger than a dog, and here he found himself surrounded by the bodies of human beings. Hundreds of them.

"We should grab some more water before heading out," Max said softly. Arthur simply nodded in response. "And I need to get my other shoe."

The pair quietly made their way to the triage room to pick up a few more water bottles. The tough little redhead lay still on the floor, and Max muttered a heartfelt apology as he stepped over her rigid, lifeless body. He snatched his shoe from the table, pulled it on and grabbed the water.

A blood trail led inside from the hallway; the spitfire had apparently dragged herself to the room from the stairwell. Max hadn't noticed it before, but of course, she was still moving then – sort of. He'd been too preoccupied with avoiding her and getting the pills to notice little details at the time. It bothered him, at a deep, instinctual level. Something didn't add up in his shock-addled mind. He brushed it off to focus on getting both he and Arthur out of the building.

"Here," Max said, handing Arthur a water bottle. "Let's get out of this place."

They retraced the redhead's path, following her blood trail to the stairs. Morbid though it was, it was effective to keep their attention away from the lifeless, accusing stares from the dead, partially consumed and twisted with rigor.

But the aftermath of the battle at the stairs was a different degree of horror. The smell hit them first. Many victims here had been torn apart. Not just limbs, but entrails and various organs ripped from torsos. Max had to look away quickly. He had seen bloodshed in war, but this was for more visceral than anything he had encountered, including the explosive demise of Riggins. He didn't see Roberto's body, and held out some small hope that he had escaped.

"Oh my G–" Arthur wretched. Little came up, as he'd had nothing to eat since lunch the day before, having been stuck in lockdown and then a rooftop. "Nasty. That is just foul," he spat to clear his mouth of vomitus.

Max patted him on the back. "Just a little further," he said, trying to be encouraging, although his stomach felt queasy as well. "We're almost out. Then we'll have fresh air."

"Then let's fucking get there," Arthur mumbled softly.

Picking their way down the stairs, they tried not to step on any of the dead or their pieces, and made it down the stairs to the first floor.

"Let's go out the back," Arthur said quietly. The remnants of the first barricade, where the Professor and Curtis were killed, loomed ahead.

"I hear you, Arthur," Max said. "But I've got to try and find my phone. This is where I lost it. Since you tossed yours, it's our only potential link to what's going on elsewhere, and Aimee might call. I've got to look."

Arthur was visibly disappointed in the decision, but Max was adamant.

They stepped over the ruined barricade by the main entrance. Curtis' remains were spread all around the floor, with very little identifiable but a shredded and bloodied pair of fatigues. Max looked over at the Professor's mangled body in the corner, and sighed. *It should have been me*, he thought. The Professor had sacrificed himself to save Max, and Max had been left with no choice but to abandon him. Knowing that didn't help Max shake the feeling that he'd failed the Professor. *Failed everyone*, he thought bitterly. *The Professor, Jennifer, Curtis, the spitfire and hundreds of others whose names I'll never know. They trusted me, and I failed them all.*

Max kicked aside some books, general debris and more body parts than he wanted to think about, but didn't see his phone. There were a few others he found, either from victims at his building or the attackers who killed them. With a sneer of disgust, he scraped dried blood from one of them and tried it. The lock screen came up. Max let the phone slip through his fingers and clatter to the floor. "Let's go. If it's here, I don't think I want it. We'll find something else."

Arthur breathed a deep sigh of relief. Together they stepped out through the window shattered by the mob, and into a dead world.

4

"Fresh air my ass," Arthur mumbled as his feet crunched on tiny shards of broken glass outside the Bate building. The dogwood trees were in bloom, and while beautiful, they gave off a musky stink that permeated the campus.

"This smells like perfume compared to what this place will be like in a few days," replied Max, observing the hundreds of corpses strewn about the campus. "It's going to be rank."

"I still can't believe I tossed my phone."

"Me neither," Max concurred. "That was stupid. You want to go look for it?"

Arthur shook his head. "That was three stories, dude. I heard it shatter. Besides, it's near where…" he swallowed hard. "Well, where Jennifer fell."

Max's blood boiled. Not only had Arthur pushed her from the roof, but he was describing it as though she fell. He wanted to forcibly drag Arthur to Jennifer's body, to graphically illustrate what he had done, but decided against it. There would be no point. A murder could easily go undetected when thousands were dead in riots, and if believing she fell helped Arthur cope with what he'd done, then perhaps it was best to let him believe it. While it *was* arguably in self-defense, Max felt that there had to have been an option besides killing her. "I understand," he replied coldly.

"So, we're off to find your girlfriend?" Arthur chirped, trying to change the subject.

"Yeah," Max motioned to the west. "Over in the Medical

District."

"You know there were riots there, too, right?"

"Yeah," Max muttered. "I know."

Trees cast long shadows across the Mall in the morning sun, still low on the horizon, as Max and Arthur headed across campus to the student parking lot. Picking their way past hundreds of faculty and students victimized by the raging insanity that had engulfed the university, they gave a wide berth to each body they encountered. It just seemed a necessary show of respect.

Max's eyes fell across one body in particular, a large one he recognized despite the mass of mangled flesh where his cheek used to be. "Shit, they killed Roberto." He knelt beside Roberto's rigor-stiffened corpse, slick with blood. "I'm sorry hombre."

"Damn," Arthur whispered. "Didn't anyone else make it?"

"I hope so, Arthur," Max shook his head in disbelief. From the Professor to Roberto, everyone who saved Max's life paid for it with their own. "Let's get moving." They continued towards the student parking lot.

"Um, listen. My mom's house is kind of near the Medical District. I can check on her in like five minutes. Looking for your girlfriend... what's her name?"

"Aimee."

"Looking for Aimee could take hours. And I'll help you find her, but um..." his voice trailed off.

"You want to check on your mom first," Max finished.

"Yeah, I do. It won't take long, I swear. It's more effective use of our time."

Max sighed, grinding his teeth. He tried to tell himself it was only a difference of five or ten minutes, that such a small amount of time added wouldn't matter in locating Aimee. Arthur had his concerns as well, and until Max had a better grip on the situation, it was best that they stick together. And Arthur was right; he could search one house faster than the two of them could search the medical school. *Best get the low hanging fruit first*, he thought. "Sure,

Arthur. But promise me you'll be quick about it."

"I promise."

Upon reaching Max's old battered brown pick-up truck, they hopped in the cab.

Arthur kicked some empty fast food bags and papers from the floor, clearing a spot for his feet.

"Sorry about that," Max apologized. "I've been meaning to clean it out."

"Breakfast!" Arthur squealed, reaching into a plastic bag retrieved from the floor. He withdrew a skinny, processed beef treat which he waved proudly in front of Max.

"Oh, so that's where that went. I wondered about that," Max said. "I picked it up just the other day. Rip it open, I'm hungry."

Arthur peeled the plastic wrap off as one might a banana peel and tore the snack in half, giving Max one part. Max wolfed down his share, while Arthur sniffed his close under his nostrils as if it were a fine cigar, relishing the spicy scent. "Breakfast of champions. I love these things."

Max cranked the truck's engine, which sputtered to life with a cough and a roar. Dark, sooty smoke enveloped them until Max put the truck in gear and rumbled forward from the cloud.

"You actually drive this thing?" Arthur asked, entranced by the thick gray cloud of fumes. "You're braver than I thought."

"Nice," Max muttered. The truck bumped over a curb and out of the lot, as Max scanned through the radio settings looking for news or emergency instructions. He found a station that was playing a looped recording:

"This is an emergency broadcast message. There is widespread rioting ongoing in numerous cities within our listening area, including but not limited to: Charlotte, Raleigh, Greensboro, Durham, Winston-Salem, Fayetteville, High Point, and Greenville. Similar reports of rioting are coming out of most metropolitan areas in the country. The President has declared a national emergency, and a state of martial law is in effect for the duration of the crisis."

"Wow," Arthur said. "Did he just say—"

"Can it!" Max hissed, turning up the radio's volume.

A recording of the President's address to the nation followed:

"My fellow Americans. This is your president speaking. It is with a heavy heart that I must inform you that today's crisis has forced me to authorize martial law over the entirety of our great nation. All citizens are to follow instructions from military personnel, and all local law enforcement and other emergency first responders are to assist our troops in restoring order while they endeavor to protect lives and property.

"We do not know what has caused the widespread and violent civil unrest, but rest assured, we will put an end to it and bring the perpetrators to justice. There can be no excuse for the type of violence we have seen erupting across the face of our country.

"As a result of this violence, our brave soldiers have been authorized to use deadly force to restore order. Law abiding citizens are to shelter in place until further instructions from the military. Stay in your homes or places of business, and off the streets. Let our military do their job unimpeded. Evacuation centers will be set up near you. Soldiers will locate you in your homes and businesses, and escort you safely to these centers. Comply with their instructions and we will weather this storm, as we have so many crises before. God bless you all. God bless America."

The message repeated, and Max turned the radio volume down.

"Can you believe that?" Arthur asked, incredulous. "Martial law. In America. This is unprecedented. But after yesterday, I can totally dig it."

"Keep your eyes peeled for soldiers," Max cautioned. "Or anyone else, for that matter." Greenville was quiet and still as they drove, but for bits of trash blown aimlessly by the breeze and the occasional cry of a burglar alarm drifting from neighborhoods they passed. He maneuvered the truck through streets strewn with car wrecks, bodies and other debris, until they reached Arthur's neighborhood. It was quiet with small, wooded lots. The houses were mostly from the 1950's, simple but charming.

The truck's brakes complained with a metallic screech as it rolled to a stop in front of Arthur's house. They climbed out of the cab.

"Wait here," Arthur said. "I'll just be a few minutes."

"You sure you don't want me to come with you?" Max asked.

"Yeah, I'm sure," Arthur responded, and strode purposefully to his front door.

†

Arthur slipped his key into the lock, glancing over his shoulder to see Max leaning on his truck, arms crossed. He didn't know if Max understood his need to do this alone. This was a family matter. He had braced himself mentally for the worst, but if he weakened in front of Max –

He turned the key and felt the deadbolt slide clear, and quietly pushed open the door.

Yes, it was fear. Fear that he would lose his mind if he found his mother dead, fear of looking weak in front of his new friend who had shown such courage and resilience through the nightmare of the previous day.

"Mom?" Arthur croaked, stepping into the entryway. His mouth was dry, but he worked up a little saliva and swallowed hard. "Mom?" he repeated softly as he closed the door behind him. "Are you here? Are you okay?"

Only the quiet ticking of a clock greeted him. Arthur padded softly into the kitchen, glancing at the clock over the breakfast table. It was a kitty clock, a curious memento his mother had picked up at a garage sale years ago. The eyes and hanging tail flicked to and fro in time with the seconds. His mother loved it.

The kitchen was neat and orderly as always. He opened the refrigerator and grabbed a soft drink, as much out of habit as to moisten his parched throat, but also to grasp at a moment of normalcy before continuing the dreaded search for his mother. The can gave a brief hiss as Arthur popped the top. He took several big gulps that made his eyes water and cleared his throat.

"Mom?" he said more forcefully, and walked into the living room. It was decorated simply, with clean, modern furniture. The bookshelves were loaded with the romance novels and murder mysteries that she loved to read, as well as an abundance of family photos of staged "happy times" replete with fake smiles plastered on the subjects' faces. Arthur always thought the pictures seemed empty, remembrances of what might have been, rather than what was. Pictures of cousins he barely knew, of vacations he barely remembered with a father he'd rather forget.

Perhaps having photographs that gave the impression of a normal, happy family life was more valuable than having one, but only in Loretta Poole's own pill-popping, alcohol-hazed world. She had her artificial reality; Arthur had his. He would crawl inside video games for hours on end, where he could be a hero feared by his enemies and beloved by all others. It was an escape that gave him a sense of power and control that was otherwise lacking in his life. Only after the new, horrifying reality overwhelmed his fantasy world was he beginning to realize how much of his real life he had missed, sinking his time – his life – into files that could be deleted with a simple keystroke. And, fearing for his mother's safety, he realized how much he would like to have that time back.

As Arthur surveyed the room, he turned and saw through the picture window, to the backyard with its blooming flower garden. His mother was seated on the ground, next to the doghouse, with her back turned.

Arthur dropped his canned drink, spilling its contents across the rug, and bolted for the kitchen which led to the yard. "*Mom!*" he shouted, flinging open the screen door. It slammed noisily against the doorframe with its slightly peeling white paint.

She sat motionless. Arthur instinctively sensed that his worst fears had come true.

"Mom?" Arthur approached her, knobby knees trembling.

As he came near, he saw the shredded golden fur on the bloodstained grass around her, saw the ribs and cracked bones of his beloved dog Jasper torn into little meaty pieces.

Arthur turned away, sinking to his knees as bile and Mountain Dew boiled up his throat and burst forth from his trembling lips.

"Oh, God!" Arthur gasped through tears and heaved again. He took a deep breath and turned once more to the grisly scene, and reaching a trembling hand to his mother, touched her shoulder. It felt wrong. Artificial. Stiff like a mannequin. Arthur's world spun as he tried to digest the facts of a new reality. He forced himself to gently brush back her dark hair and gaze at her face, while kneeling over Jasper's shredded remains.

Loretta Poole had a blank, yet eerily peaceful expression, despite Jasper's dried blood and fur that caked her lips. Her throat had been largely ripped out, and her own blood dried streaming over her cornflower blue shirt and worn, tan overalls. She was still wearing her gardening gloves.

"I... I'm sorry, Mom," he choked, tears flowing freely. He added with a whisper, "I'm sorry Jasper. I'm sorry I wasn't here for you guys." He sat next to her for several minutes, wiping tears from his eyes as he stared at her garden, focusing his thoughts. The whole series of events, from the report of a shooter, to the assault on the building, to the night on the roof – none of it had struck Arthur in a truly meaningful fashion. It was surreal. Logically, he knew this was a likely outcome, but at a deep, instinctual level, he had somehow expected things to be normal when he got home. Seeing his mother and dog both dead drove home the harsh reality to Arthur: he was now alone in a devastated city.

Not quite alone, he thought. *Max is still around. Max can help me.*

"I'm sorry," he whispered again, and slowly climbed to his feet. He made his way back through the kitchen, past the kitty clock, and out the front door, to Max waiting at his truck.

†

Arthur's ashen, downcast face told Max all he needed to know. Without a word, he opened the passenger door for Arthur, who climbed quietly into the cab and stared despondently at his red canvas high tops. They drove together in silence through the sun-dappled streets of his neighborhood. As Max made the turn onto Arlington Boulevard, choked with wreckage, Arthur lifted his head and spoke.

"I don't…" he paused, collecting his thoughts. "I don't suppose a traditional funeral can be arranged for some time," he muttered, biting his lip. Arthur's voice quivered with emotion. "After we find Aimee, I want to go back and bury Mom in her garden. She'd like that."

"You got it." *After we find Aimee.* Until Arthur spoke those words, Max had felt alone in his quest to find her. Hoping but not believing, operating on autopilot. He found it amazing that such a simple phrase could change his outlook entirely. *After we find Aimee.*

Max continued driving towards the Medical District, in awe of the devastation around them, carefully weaving the truck around bodies and wrecked vehicles in the street. Max took heart in seeing that the further they got from Arthur's house, the more the cloud of despair lifted from his companion's countenance.

In front of them, Max saw a military Humvee turn off Dickinson Avenue, carelessly bumping over the legs of a body that lay in the street. It was in an open-air troop carrying configuration Max was familiar with from the war. Two soldiers with rifles sat in the back, looking out over the cab. The Hummer flashed its lights.

"Damn it," Max grumbled. "They spotted us."

"Isn't that a good thing?" Arthur inquired.

"They might not let us go to search for Aimee, or bury your Mom after," Max said.

"Shit. You're right. Maybe we can talk our way out of it, convince them that—"

"Hang on!" Max veered hard to the right, banging his truck over a curb and into the parking lot of a small apartment complex. *I'll be damned if weekend warriors are going to keep me from finding Aimee.*

"Or we can make a run for it! Your call!" Arthur screamed, white-knuckling the handhold above his door.

Max floored the gas pedal and flew through the parking lot. In his rearview mirror, he saw the Humvee bounce over the curb. He slammed on his brakes and turned left, into a grassy area between two buildings, and narrowly missed a tree between them. He hit the gas again as the troops gave chase, but had to brake hard before hitting a wooden fence. There was a narrow strip of grass to the left, with a walkway between the fence and the apartment complex's fenced patios. Max looked back over his shoulder as he turned, and saw the Hummer in hot pursuit, squeezing past the tree. He maneuvered his truck into the strip of grass, scraping a fence with his fender.

"No way they'll fit down here," Max said through gritted teeth. Having made it around the building, he could see Arlington Boulevard before them. He gunned the engine again, cursing as he pinballed off the fence in the narrow space and took out a couple of boards on each side.

"I don't wanna die!" Arthur screamed.

"Just relax man, I'm insured." The truck roared from the walkway, over the curb and onto the street. In his rearview mirror, he could just make out the Humvee stuck in the tight area, making what Max guessed would be about a twenty point turn to get out. He cut the wheel hard to the right, barely avoiding a wrecked car.

"It'll take them a few minutes to get out of there," he said. "We'll be long gone by then."

Avoiding bodies and abandoned vehicles, Max turned right again on Dickenson, then left on a side street. There were fewer obstacles to avoid on the smaller street, and he sped towards the Medical District.

They pulled into the parking lot of the medical school, a modern, six story tan and white building with an enormous glass façade, that dominated its immediate environs. Max's heart sank when he saw that the doors had been smashed off their hinges and several bodies lay outside. The truck brakes squealed and it shuddered to a stop by the front entrance.

"Well, this is it," Max sighed in resignation, climbing out of the cab. He was fearful, but determined to discover Aimee's fate.

They stepped quietly inside. The hallways were well-lit and mostly empty, with only about a half dozen bodies on the first floor. *They must not have made a stand, like we did,* Max thought, *or there would be more bodies in the hallways.* The doors to the classrooms were smashed open.

"Which room would she be in?" Arthur asked softly.

"Hell, man, at this point I'm hoping she's not in any of them." The prospect of finding Aimee dead sent shivers through Max. He wanted to find her *alive.* "But I don't know which would be her classroom. We'll have to check them all."

"Great," Arthur moaned.

As they made their way down the first floor hall, they diligently checked each room they passed. All had been hit hard. Bodies were strewn about, and in each room there was a small pile of shredded bodies in a corner, as if the victims had clustered together for herd-like protection before being overwhelmed. Some windows had been smashed open, and Max hoped that meant some students were able to escape. As with the Bate building and the campus in general, all of the bodies they encountered were stiff with rigor mortis, in various conditions ranging from single bite wounds to evisceration to complete dismemberment. Whenever Max saw a corpse with blonde hair, his breath caught until he saw it wasn't Aimee. Someone's loved one was dead though, and he couldn't help but feel a pang of guilt over his selfishness in being relieved that it wasn't Aimee.

"We should check all the bathrooms, too," Arthur said.

"Okay," Max responded. "Let's check the bathrooms."

"I mean, if I hadn't been able to get to the roof of our building, the bathroom would have been my second option. You can hide in the stalls, you have access to water – gross, but it's water – and you even have a chance for graffiti or the odd newspaper or magazine for reading material. The downside being, you're trapped. But it beats jumping into a classroom with the other food items."

"Reading material? You really thought that through," Max said as he pushed open a bathroom door. "Anyone alive in here?" He was greeted with his own voice echoing off cold tile. Max grunted, then proceeded to check every stall. "Empty."

They checked the remainder of the rooms on the first floor to no avail, then made their way up to the second floor.

"Teacher's lounge!" Arthur exclaimed, rushing for a nearby break room. "There might be food here, and I'm hungry. Half a beef treat and a soda pop for breakfast just doesn't cut it."

"When did you get a soda?" Max asked.

"At my house. Sorry I didn't bring you one. I got distracted."

Max waved his hand dismissively. "Understandable, don't worry about it. Let's check the break room."

They entered the teacher's lounge to find the remains of a balding, overweight middle-aged man who'd had his belly ripped open, sprawled across a table. His entrails spilled onto the floor, where his apparent killer, a male student with a bloody stump for a leg, had been feeding. The student had left his meal and crawled to a closet door. His bloody handprints were low on the door, as if he'd been slapping at it from his position on the floor, trying to get in.

Max gagged at the sight, and the stink of death. He couldn't see the student's missing leg, but assumed the fact it was gone kept him from having the leverage to get into the door. "Still hungry, Arthur?"

"Uh, no. No I am not," he said, transfixed. "Dude, that's just nasty!"

"I wonder what he was trying to…" a faint rustling sound in the closet answered his question. He snapped his fingers to get Arthur's attention, and pointed to the closet door. He pressed his finger to his lips, telling Arthur to stay quiet. Arthur slunk back to the doorway while Max grabbed the student with the missing leg by his blood-soaked, purple sweatshirt and dragged the corpse away from the door as slowly and quietly as possible.

The rustling sound from the closet came again, with a faint metallic knocking as if a person hiding inside bumped into something while trying to stay quiet.

Max stepped silently to the door and slowly, quietly turned the doorknob. He found it unlocked. As the bolt slid free, Max prepared himself to throw open the door.

It suddenly flew open, striking Max square in the nose, knocking him to the floor. He tried to fight through the pain and scramble to his feet, only to stumble backwards, knocking the man's body from the table. Max groaned in pain. His vision blurred with tears from the impact on his nose, but he could hear high-pitched squeals of pain and terror. "Hang on, Arthur!" Max yelled as he wiped tears from his eyes with the back of his hand, trying to focus his vision. He staggered to his feet.

Arthur was wrestling in the hallway with his attacker, a wild mane of black hair attached to an athletic-looking girl. Max stumbled over, and wrapping his arms about the girl's waist, hoisted her off his friend. He grunted with effort as he hurled her back into the break room where she crashed to the floor.

Max turned to help Arthur up, but was struck in the back by a chair thrown from the room. He dropped his still-screaming friend to the floor and spun just in time to painfully block the next chair with his arm.

"Stop! Stop! Just *stop* it! We're not going to hurt you!" Max yelled.

The girl faced them wielding a third chair, her wild mane of black hair partially covering her brown eyes which shone with intense fear and determination.

"Seriously, man! What is it with chicks kicking our asses lately?" Arthur added, clambering to his feet. "Nice Xena Warrior Princess thing, though. I about wet my pants."

"Are you finished?" Max asked in a tone that was more of a

demand. The girl didn't answer. "I said *are you finished?* As in, can we have a conversation or do we go for round two?"

The girl quickly nodded, but held the chair at the ready.

"We're looking for someone. This is Arthur, and my name's Max."

The girl eyed him warily, breathing hard, and lowered the chair. "Eva. Eva Hernandez."

"¡Hola!" Arthur said, smiling broadly at her.

"Uh, yeah. Hola," she replied cautiously.

"Just try and ignore him," Max mumbled, pulling painfully on his nose to see if it was broken. "It's what I do. It doesn't work, but I keep trying."

"I'm… sorry about that. I was just scared. A bunch of psychos stormed the building. They were killing everyone, and no one would help," Eva said, her face scrunching up as the pain of the past day hit home. Tears flowed. "No one helped! The emergency line was busy every time I called, and the police never came! I hid in the closet. I didn't know what else to do!"

"I know," Max said. "We spent the night on a rooftop for safety, never did get through on the phone. Listen, Eva. It's not just this building. It's not just the Medical District. It's all over the place. The university, the neighborhoods, even other cities."

She desperately searched his face for any hint of a lie, and found none. "Oh my God."

"The president has declared martial law. There are troops searching for people and evacuating them," Max explained. "We're looking for my girlfriend, then taking care of some, uh," he nodded towards Arthur, "other business. Then we're going to try and find the evacuation center."

"Look around!" Eva said, exasperated. "Your girlfriend's dead! Everyone's dead!"

"You aren't," Arthur said. "You found a hiding place. You survived."

"He's right," Max nodded. "She could be hiding, like you. Maybe other people are, as well. We have to look."

"So look!" Eva shouted. "Do whatever you need to do! I'm going to find the evacuation center."

Max nodded. "Okay. Okay," he sighed in disappointment. He would have loved to have another pair of eyes looking, familiar with the building, but Eva was in a state of panic and had her own affairs to deal with. He couldn't make her stay. "Good luck to you. Maybe we'll see you there."

Eva stalked down the hall, car keys already in hand.

Arthur turned to Max, smiling. "Well, that was invigorating. It's a shame she's leaving, I found her rather pulchritudinous. What's the plan now?"

"Pulchriwhat?" Max asked.

"Pulchritudinous. Look it up."

"I don't have a dictionary handy. Don't be a dork, just tell me," Max demanded.

"Good looking," Arthur whispered.

"You've been saving that one for a long time, haven't you?" Max observed. Arthur grinned. Max continued, "the plan now is to check closets. All the nooks and crannies. Call out. Maybe there's a PA system we can use."

"Damn it!" Eva's voice echoed down the hall. She turned and stormed back to Max and Arthur. "Fine. I'll help. Let's look for her and get the hell out of here. Quickly."

"Awesome," Arthur smiled.

"And it's not because you used a big word to call me pretty, so don't get any ideas."

"Wait! You know what it means?" Arthur asked, shocked.

"It's got a Latin root, idiot. I'm in medical school."

"Oh, dude. Shamed," Arthur groaned. "Hey Eva, do you have a cell phone?"

"I'm not giving you my number."

"I know, I know," he turned to Max. "Believe me, I know. But I was thinking. If Aimee is in this building, we can call her phone, Max.

Even if she… if she can't answer, for any reason, we might hear it ringing while we search."

"Well, we could," Max said doubtfully, "If I knew her number off the top of my head."

"You don't know your own girlfriend's number?" Eva asked, incredulous.

"It was programmed into my phone!" Max cried. "I never had to *dial* it."

"Damn technology," Arthur mumbled. "It's awesome, until it's not. We get so dependent that we're stupid without it."

"Speak for yourselves," Eva replied. "Let's just focus on the task at hand, okay?"

The three searched each room of the building, checking lecture halls, closets and bathrooms. They came across a well-stocked medical supply closet, and Eva took the opportunity to clean Max's shoulder wound. They continued the search, even making their way to the roof, but found no sign of Aimee or any other survivors.

"Okay," Max admitted. "She's not here." He looked at his companions. "Maybe that's a good thing. There's still hope. I'm not giving up."

"It's about time," Arthur said, exasperated. "We've been looking for almost two hours! Maybe she's already at the evacuation center and we'll find her there. Can we *please* go bury my Mom now?"

"Arthur, you lost your mother?" Eva asked.

"Yeah. Max promised me he'd help bury her," Arthur sniffed.

"I'm sorry for your loss. I guess I'll help, too," Eva consoled. "I'm not jazzed about it, but I can understand loyalty to family. I just want to find the evacuation center before nightfall."

"We will," Max said. "I promise."

They reached the first floor and headed outside to Max's waiting truck.

"Should I take my car and follow you?"

"What kind is it?"

"A little coup."

"The streets are a mess, Eva," Max said doubtfully. "Lots of wrecks and too many bodies. It's probably best if you come with me in my truck. Best to stay together in any case."

"Shotgun!" Arthur cried, sprinting ahead to the truck.

"You ride in the back," Max yelled after him. Civilization may have fallen apart, but he'd be damned if he wasn't going to try and remain a gentleman by allowing Eva ride in the cab. He grimaced instinctively, remembering the trash Arthur had kicked aside. Then he felt foolish, realizing a messy cab was the least of his worries that day.

Arthur vaulted into the bed of the truck and froze. "Allow me to rephrase that. *Shotgun!*" Arthur raised his hands in the air in a gesture of surrender.

The unmistakable double-pump click of a shotgun chambering shells sounded in the quiet of the street, and a large black soldier stood up from behind Max's truck, his shotgun trained on Arthur. Two more soldiers armed with rifles popped up from behind vehicles flanking the first, and a fourth approached from Max's left, also with a rifle.

"Nice try, son, but there aren't nearly enough streets in this town for you to avoid me!" the first soldier yelled at Max. "Get out of the truck and join your friends," he told Arthur. "Do it slowly, and keep your hands where I can see them."

Arthur climbed out of the truck bed. His eyes were wide with fear as he walked to Max, hands still held over his head.

"Now all of you, on your knees. Hands behind your heads," the big man said. Max noticed sergeant's insignia on his uniform.

Arthur collapsed to his knees with a barely audible whimper. Max and Eva also knelt as instructed.

Two of the soldiers shouldered their rifles and patted down the trio, looking for weapons while the shotgun-toting soldier and apparent leader questioned them.

He addressed Max. "Why did you run from us?"

"To get away," Max retorted.

"Don't get cute with me! Answer my question!" barked the Sergeant.

"I don't mean to be a smartass, Sarge, but why the hell else would I run? To get away." He hoped his identification of the Sergeant's rank would identify him as a veteran and buy some goodwill with the soldiers.

Arthur spoke up. "I think the properly phrased question would have been, why did you feel the *need* to get away. I totally got that as the intended question."

"Thanks, Arthur. And the answer to that," Max continued, "is that I needed to come here to find my girlfriend. I didn't think you would have allowed that, so I ran."

The Sergeant grunted. "Fair enough; I wouldn't have. You found her?" he nodded towards Eva.

"I'm not his girlfriend," Eva said quickly. "In fact, I barely even know these men. We just met."

"We found her inside," Max explained. He understood why Eva wanted to distance herself from them; merely being with them already had her at the business end of several guns.

"You searched the whole building?" the Sergeant asked.

"Yes sir," Max responded. "Lots of bodies, but she's the only one we found alive."

"We even checked the bathrooms!" Arthur proudly chimed in.

"They're clean, sir," one of the soldiers searching them said.

"Well, no, they weren't as clean as you might—"

"That is, they have no weapons, sir," the soldier quickly added, cutting Arthur off.

"Okay then. Let's load 'em up," the Sergeant ordered, shouldering his shotgun. Soldiers helped the trio to their feet. "We'll take you to a staging area where we're collecting survivors. From there you'll be taken to the evacuation center at the airport, where you'll be protected. You'll also receive food, water and medical care. You'll be briefed there."

"Where are we being evacuated to?" Max asked. "Where is it

safe?"

"Right now, the airport," he responded. "It's secure. You'll be safe there while we assess the situation in the rest of the city."

"Can't I follow you in my truck?"

"Negative," the Sergeant responded. "We'll take you to the staging area. Once you're transferred to the airport, you'll be briefed on the situation."

"Can't you tell us anything?" Eva asked nervously. "I mean, what the hell happened?"

"You'll be briefed at the airport."

Eva sighed with frustration.

"You'll have to forgive him, Eva. He's just a weekend warrior," Max said disparagingly. "He doesn't know anything."

The Sergeant chuckled. "Active duty, son. Ft. Bragg. Airlifted in last night."

"Hey, I think I saw you guys land–" Arthur volunteered.

"Then stop with the bullshit and level with me, Sarge," Max begged, interrupting. "You must know *something!*"

The big man rolled his eyes and sighed. "As I'm sure you know, a bunch of people went nuts. Started killing each other, and it spread from there. It pretty much hit every city in the country simultaneously. Scuttlebutt says it's global, too. I'm Sergeant Collins. And I don't have time to get into more detail, but you're right – I don't know anything. I like it that way. Keeps things simple. Like right now, all I need to do is get you folks back to the staging area and continue my search for other survivors – simple. We've burned enough time because of your little stunt, running from us. Now pretty please, with sugar on top," he motioned to the Humvee, "get in the back. See? I even asked nicely."

"Fine," Max grumbled as he and Eva climbed into the open air back of the Humvee.

"But what about my m–" Arthur protested.

"Can it!" Max hissed.

"No, man, that's bullshit! You told me we were–"

Sergeant Collins gripped Arthur roughly by the collar, snapping his head around like a ragdoll. "I do *not* have the patience for this crap! Get in the fucking truck!"

"I just w-wanted to bury my mom. She's dead," Arthur stammered.

The sergeant's face softened. The big man let go of Arthur's collar and instead clapped his oversized paw on his shoulder. "I understand, son. We've all lost loved ones. You have to trust me when I say that we'll take care of her. It will take some time, but she will be buried. You have my word on that. Now, get in and we'll take you to the staging area. From there you'll be taken to the airport, where you'll be safe. Your mother would have wanted you safe, right?"

Arthur nodded dejectedly.

"Of course she would. So your job right now is to trust us, and let us help you."

"Yes, sir."

Arthur reluctantly joined Max and Eva in the back of the Humvee, followed by two of the soldiers, while Sergeant Collins and the driver got in the cab. They sat quietly as the vehicle wound its way around corpses and wrecked vehicles back the way they came, towards Dickenson.

"I'm sorry, Arthur. We'll find a way to get it done," Max said.

Arthur sniffed and nodded sullenly.

Max looked at Eva. "Not that the good sergeant is likely to cooperate with this idea, but do you have anyone we need to try and track down when we can? A husband or boyfriend... family?"

Eva shook her head.

"No one?"

"I don't want to get into it, Max," she stated curtly. "I barely know you."

Max bit his lip.

"It's sweet of you to ask; it's just not necessary."

They drove in awkward silence for several more minutes. Max

wracked his brain trying to imagine where Aimee could have gone, if she escaped the insanity that had engulfed the city. *Maybe she got in her car and made it into the countryside*, he thought. *It's bound to be safer there.* He swallowed hard, knowing that fleeing trouble wasn't in Aimee's nature. She would have fought to help the injured and the sick until the last possible moment. *There's still a chance. There has to be.*

The Humvee arrived at the staging area, which turned out to be a supermarket that had been repurposed by a group of soldiers. Several had formed a security perimeter around the parking lot. Max looked to the roof of the market and saw two more soldiers with binoculars and scoped rifles. Sergeant Collins' Humvee turned into the lot and stopped, its brakes squeaking slightly.

"Looks like we're here," Max said, hopping out of the vehicle. "Time to see what Uncle Sam has in store for us."

Max surveyed the setup at the supermarket as Sergeant Collins and his team drove off again in search of more survivors.

The market itself looked as if it were open for business. Several cars were parked neatly in their slots, owners unlikely to return. The lights inside were on. Ominously, there was a large blue tarp nearby with multiple lumps beneath it that could only have been bodies. The corners were weighted with chunks of broken concrete.

The market's automated doors slid open and two more soldiers walked out. One was carrying a jug of water in each hand; the other, several boxes of canned goods. They set them down with a pile of similar requisitioned food items that they had collected by a troop transport truck in the parking lot, and headed back inside. Max saw their rifles leaning on the wall by the entrance, with a third soldier nearby, standing guard at the entrance to the store. Five more soldiers had taken up various positions around the lot, standing watch, while two more handled the civilians.

A fit, middle aged man with short salt and pepper hair and captain's bars on his collar approached them. "Welcome. I'm Captain Jenkins," he said, introducing himself. "This is a temporary stopover for you people. We'll be transporting you to the airport for processing. Should be no more than about twenty or thirty more minutes, and we'll take you over there. You're safe here for now, but you'll be fed, receive any needed medical attention, and be better protected there. You three wait with them," Captain Jenkins motioned to a group of five civilians sitting on several blankets that had been spread on the ground.

The trio did as instructed.

The other survivors waiting included an elderly gentleman with a balding head and his wife, and an exhausted mother with her two precious little girls of about four and six snuggled up close to her, regarding everyone around them with wide-eyed suspicion.

"What are your names?" Eva asked them in a friendly tone. The little girls responded by burying their faces into their mother's arms and clutching her even more tightly.

"Sarah and Becca," their exhausted mother said. She had shoulder length blonde hair that was misbehaving, and brown eyes that nearly disappeared into the dark circles under them. "They saw their father killed yesterday."

"I... I'm sorry," Eva apologized.

"You had no way to know. I'm Sharon," she said.

"Eva. And this is Arthur, and Max," Eva said, gesturing to her companions. "They rescued me from the medical school. I hid in a closet when it all went down. So how long have you been here?"

Max listened as Eva gently coaxed information from Sharon, while he watched the two soldiers make several trips for foodstuffs from the store. Sharon and the girls fled to a tree house after a crazed homeless man killed her husband in the yard below them. They spent the night trapped by the madman, with Sharon trying to keep the girls from seeing their father's body being 'defiled', which Max took as a euphemism for being fed upon. When morning came, the homeless man was dead and her husband's body was nowhere to be seen. She and the girls were rescued when they heard the military driving down the street. They had been taken to the market at about seven o'clock in the morning for safety while the military continued to search for survivors.

An hour after their own arrival, they had been joined by the elderly Reverend Miller and his wife Donna, who had been rescued from their home by the military. They had seen neighbors they knew for years viciously attack one another, and survived by staying in their house, out of sight until rescued in the morning.

"Does anyone have the time?" Max asked.

Eva looked at her watch. "About a quarter past noon."

"So you've been here for a little more than five hours," Max concluded, "and including us, only eight people have been rescued?"

Sharon nodded.

"Wow. That's not very many," Max observed. "Not for that much time searching."

"Well, that's at *this* staging area," interjected Reverend Miller. "I think they have several more around Green–"

One of the soldiers appropriating foodstuffs came running out and snatched up his rifle. "Davis! On me." he yelled to his fellow soldier who was standing watch near the entrance. Both ran back inside the store, guns at the ready.

"Everyone stay here, remain calm," cautioned Captain Jenkins, drawing his sidearm. The other troops on the perimeter of the parking lot looked around uneasily. "Stay at your posts!" the captain commanded. "Eyes up! Watch the perimeter!" The soldiers did as ordered and maintained the perimeter, but cast wary glances at the store behind them.

Moments later, the sound of yelling wafted from the store, followed by a barrage of gunfire, then about a minute of total silence. To Max, it seemed like time stood still. At length, there came a clatter of cans being knocked over inside.

"Coming out! Need a medic!" came a voice from within. Two of the soldiers came out, team carrying the third who was bleeding profusely and looked to be unconscious.

"Nearest medic is at the airport!" yelled the captain.

"Then we need to *find* one, sir! Now!"

"Medical student here!" Eva yelled, jumping to her feet. "I can help!"

The captain looked at her briefly, sizing her up, then motioned her to where the soldiers lay their fallen comrade on the pavement. She ran to assist. Eva crouched over the wounded soldier, assessing his wounds and taking his pulse. Davis ran to the truck and returned with a first aid kit, which Eva tore into, rapidly donning protective gloves before grabbing scissors and cutting open the wounded soldier's shirt.

All of the other survivors were on their feet, watching the drama unfold. Sarah and Becca hid their faces and cried into their mother's side as she tried fruitlessly to console them.

Satisfied that Eva knew what she was doing, Captain Jenkins turned his attention to the other soldier from the requisitioning team. "Rodriguez! Report!"

"One of them dropped out of a ceiling vent and attacked me, sir," said Rodriguez.

"That building was supposed to be cleared!" the captain yelled.

"It was, sir!" said Rodriguez defensively, gesturing to the bodies covered in the blue tarp. "But we didn't know to check the air vents! Why would they be in the air vents?"

"Because the head cases can't climb," Arthur whispered aside to Max. "I bet they were bitten, climbed into the air duct for safety and went crazy up there. Same way Jennifer got up on the roof."

Max grunted and nodded.

"Damn it," the captain grumbled. "Go on. What happened next?"

"Peterson managed to pull him off of me, but then he grabbed a hold of Peterson. I couldn't get him off. I tried, sir, but he was just too strong! I had to come out and get a weapon and backup."

"Sounded like you took down an elephant. How many shots did it take?"

"I don't know, sir. A lot. We couldn't get a clear shot with him wrapped around Peterson, but between me and Davis, we got him off and shot him. But he kept on coming. We shot him a bunch, sir, but it didn't even slow him down. I killed him myself with a shot to his head. He was crazed, sir, out of control, like he was on PCP or something."

Captain Jenkins nodded. "Good work, son. Now go tend to that wound," he said, touching his own cheek.

Rodriguez aped him, wiping his cheek, and examined the blood on his fingers. Cursing, he walked over to the pile of supplies he and Peterson had collected and tore into a roll of paper towels, ripping off a few to stanch the bleeding.

The captain turned his attention to Eva, who was tending to Peterson. "How's he doing?"

She looked up at him and whispered something, shaking her head.

"Son of a…" the captain's face flushed red with rage, and only his pursed lips held back a string of expletives, likely for the benefit of the civilians, particularly Sarah and Becca. He whispered to Eva, and Max could barely make out the words. "You're sure? There's nothing you can do?"

Eva nodded. The captain kicked a stray can of peas in response, sending it skittering across the parking lot.

"Guess he's not happy about the extra paperwork," Arthur muttered.

"Can it," Max warned.

"Right right, I was being sarcastic," Arthur said. "Hey Max – why didn't they take their rifles? Or pistols or something?" Arthur asked.

"They were grocery shopping," Max explained. "I guess they didn't see a need to shoot a can of peas. Having a rifle would just limit how much they could carry each trip. As for not having pistols, most grunts only carry a rifle. More weapons mean more weight, and more types of ammo that ideally, you won't need. The rifle will kill before the enemy gets into range of a pistol."

"Only if they've got them," mumbled Arthur.

Max grunted in agreement as he eyed Rodriguez, noting the crimson stained paper towels he clutched to his face. As Rodriguez lowered the sheet to flip to a fresh, unbloodied piece, Max saw a roughly circular wound on his cheek. "Bit."

"Huh?" Arthur asked.

"He's been bitten," Max said, nodding gravely towards Rodriguez. "Remember what it did to Jennifer?"

"Duh, of course I remember," Arthur yawned. He had dark circles under his eyes. "You think they know he's screwed?"

"He's treating it with a paper towel, so I'm guessing that's a negatory."

"Well, uh… you gonna tell them? Someone should tell them, right?"

"Someone has to. If Sergeant Collins told them about my running, they're probably not too fond of me right now."

"So, seeing as how they probably don't like you anyway, you might as well be the one to give them the bad news that their boy is gonna wig out and die."

"Seeing as how it can be said with greater sensitivity, I agree," Max responded. "But in a little while. That other soldier. Peterson I think they said his name was. He's dying. Now's the time for us to shut up and be respectful."

"Sorry. I'm feeling a little punchy. Didn't sleep much last night, don'tcha know."

Eva covered Peterson's face with his own shirt that she had cut off, and checked her watch. Captain Jenkins removed one of Peterson's dog tags, pocketing it, and thanked Eva for her efforts. He then whispered something to her and motioned to Rodriguez.

"You there… Rodriguez? Let me take a look at you." She led Rodriguez over to the truck. Pulling on a new pair of latex gloves, she began cleaning his wound. Rodriguez let loose with a string of expletives when she rinsed the wound with alcohol from the first aid kit.

"She's lucky she's got a valuable skill set," Arthur murmured.

"Or not. They could press her into service. Well, I guess they *could* do that to both of us, too. But I did my time. I did my duty. I'm not theirs to command anymore. There are other things I need to be doing."

"Like finding Aimee," Arthur surmised.

Max nodded. "Eva's got some warm fuzzies to spend with them, though, since she's helping out. She might be the best choice to tell them that this thing transmits with bites."

Eva finished dressing Rodriguez's wound with gauze. When she finished, she walked slowly back to sit with Max and Arthur, whose eyes were slipping closed. Every few minutes, his drooping head would jerk upright, only to start nodding off again and repeat the process.

"It was good of you to try and help," Max said to Eva. "That's a tough break."

Eva wiped away a tear rolling down her cheek.

"You've never seen a man die before, have you?" Max asked.

"I have," Eva bit her lip, emotional pain clear on her face. "Once before. But he was very sick, and it was expected. Never someone young and healthy. I mean, I've worked on cadavers, but he died right there, while I was working on him. He was there and then just… gone. Maybe if I'd had the proper equipment, I could have saved him. He needed a blood transfusion. The bites were deep. One of them may have nicked an artery."

"It's never easy, seeing someone die," Max said softly, "but it gets easier."

"How would you know?" Eva asked.

"In my case, I wasn't trying to save a life. I was… on the other side of the equation. It was war," Max grimaced, grinding his teeth as he distractedly picked at his shoelace. "No. No, that's a cop out. I knew what I was doing, I just…" he swallowed hard and glanced nervously at Eva. "A story for another time. At least you were trying to save a life, not take it. Maybe you're a better person than me."

Eva just smiled sadly and shook her head, as if to say that she wished she could help. They each had their demons with which to wrestle.

Max caught movement from the corner of his eye. Peterson was sitting upright, and pulled the shirt from his face. Captain Jenkins stood nearby with his back turned. Peterson struggled to his feet and turned toward him.

"Captain! Behind you!" Max shouted in alarm. Captain Jenkins spun around just in time to meet Peterson's charge. The impact sent them both hard into the collection of requisitioned food and supplies, crushing boxes and sending cans clattering across the concrete. Max was on his feet, his ankle screaming as he hobbled to Jenkins' aid, when several shots rang out amid the grunting and swearing. One final gunshot sounded. Jenkins rolled Peterson's lifeless body to the side. "Clear!" he yelled as he got up, sputtering and swearing. He glared hatefully at Max, standing a few feet away.

"Your little girlfriend fucked up! I just had to kill my own man!"

Max was taken aback by Jenkins' hostility towards him, and felt his face flush with anger. "Sounded like you took down an elephant," he taunted. "How many shots did it take?" He knew the captain was reacting to the shock, surprise and pain of the attack, and was likely training his anger on Max simply as a target of opportunity. That didn't mean Max would let it slide; it wasn't in his nature. He didn't owe any particular respect to the captain until it was earned.

Captain Jenkins scowled at Max, fingering his weapon before abruptly holstering it. Max could see the rage burning in his eyes, but looked past him to Peterson's body. A gaping hole had been blown out of the top of his head.

Eva skidded to a halt beside Max, staring in shock at Peterson's limp body. "I don't understand. He had no pulse. He was dead!"

"Well halle-fuckin-lujia!" Captain Jenkins mocked. "God must have miracled him back from the dead to take a chunk out of me!" he held up his forearm, a visible red stain spreading beneath the sleeve.

Eva rushed over to check his wound. "Let me take a look."

"Get your incompetent ass away from me!" he shouted, roughly shoving her away. Max instinctively took an aggressive step towards Jenkins, but the captain turned away, shouting over his shoulder, "Civilians! Sit down! Shut up! Soldiers! Let's load this goddamn truck and get the hell out of here! I've *had* it with this shit!"

The soldiers quickly set about loading the pile of supplies into the troop transport, followed by Peterson's limp and bloodied body, which they carefully and respectfully wrapped in a large plastic sheet from the store. Captain Jenkins broadcast from a radio in the truck, calling back his search and rescue teams.

"I don't understand," Eva said, sitting down again with the other survivors. "He was dead. I'm sure he was dead!"

"So much for the warm fuzzies," Arthur mumbled.

"Arthur?" said Max.

"Hmm?"

"I know you're slap-happy and all? But can it."

"I just don't understand how I could have been so wrong!" Eva said, exasperated. "I know he was dead. And yet, here we are."

"Here we are. Eva, this... cooties thing–" Max started.

"Cooties?" Eva scoffed.

"It's a technical term!" Arthur interjected proudly.

"Until such time as it has an actual scientific name, we're calling it cooties. It pleases the nerd, so just roll with it. Whatever this is, bites can transmit it. Now, the good captain and Rodriguez over there, have been bitten. That is likely to become a problem."

"You're sure?" Eva asked.

"We're sure. Our friend Jennifer was bitten. Now, she..." Max nodded to Arthur, "...wigged out and died. Or would have once the cooties ran its course."

"But it didn't run its full course?"

"N-no, not exactly. Her death was, uh..."

"Gravitationally encouraged," Arthur explained.

"After she wigged out and kicked our asses, yeah. And I'm still mad at you, Arthur," Max said pointedly.

"Acknowledged. But I still saved your life."

"I beg to differ; I had her under control."

"No you didn't."

"Did so."

"No–"

Eva dramatically cleared her throat.

"Sorry, Eva," Max apologized. "What I was trying to say is, just look at all the bodies under the tarp there, or those laying around the streets. This thing kills its victims. We were with Jennifer the whole time, and it took ten, maybe twelve hours."

"From a bite?"

"Yes, from a bite. I was with her. I saw it happen," Max ground his teeth, remembering with regret his failure to protect Jennifer when they fled to the roof.

"But Peterson only took…" she looked at her watch, "…seventeen minutes."

"Yep."

"So, what does that mean?"

"Haven't got a clue," Max replied. "But my gut tells me that's too big a time difference not to be important. Maybe the location or severity of the bite somehow makes a difference. I saw a critically injured police officer suddenly jump up and take down a colleague. One thing I know for sure," Max gestured at the soldiers, "Rodriguez and the good captain are going to become serious threats to anyone near them in a matter of hours, if not sooner."

Eva intently watched the soldiers loading supplies, concern clouding her face.

"And another thing I know," Max continued, "is that when Rodriguez and Peterson were attacked, Rodriguez said it took a headshot to stop their attacker. And the captain just stopped Peterson with?"

"A headshot," Arthur finished.

"Give the man a gold star. On campus, I saw these psychos get shot, and it didn't even slow them down. It looks like only headshots work. Now that's weird in and of itself, but also they're generally tougher to get on a moving target than firing center mass. I think it's important to keep that in mind."

Eva bit her lip, deep in thought. "Maybe I missed something. I… I must have. But even if he wasn't dead, you don't go from undetectably low blood pressure to pouncing like Peterson and your police officer did, beating the hell out of armed men. Men who are trained to fight. It doesn't make sense."

"But hey, if they *were* dead, and still attacked, then they'd have to be zombies," Arthur blathered, fatigue slurring his words. "I mean, that *is* kind of the definition."

"Don't be stupid, Arthur. Zombies?" Max scolded. He watched as a Humvee pulled into the parking lot and four soldiers got out, with two new survivors that were instructed to sit with Max and the others. They were a young couple in their twenties, and like everyone, were badly shaken by their experience. A search and rescue dog was with the soldiers, wearing an orange reflective vest and being tended to by a young soldier that reminded Max of Riggins. "No, there's another answer. An incubation period that feigns death, or something."

"Sorry, dude. Like I said, I'm punchy. Haven't slept."

"And whose fault is that? You wouldn't take a shift sleeping, Mr. I'm-A-Night-Owl."

"But it's dayti–" Arthur protested, but was cut off.

"You two quarrel like an old married couple," Eva observed. "Maybe if I could examine Peterson's body, I could figure something out."

"They think you're incompetent now," Max replied. "They aren't going to let you anywhere near his body."

"Not that you could do much more damage at this point," Arthur commented.

"Can it," Max warned.

"You're right. It's just frustrating," Eva emoted, ignoring Arthur. "I know I was right. I know it. He hardly had any blood left in his body. That's what killed him. That he then got up and was killed *again* by a bullet to the head just doesn't make sense."

"Unless he was a zombie," Arthur interjected. "Then it fits the–"

"*Can it!* Damn! Just go to sleep or something and shut up!" Max turned to Eva. "So you had to be wrong about him being dead. I saw plenty of them back at the university, looked to have life-threatening injuries. I'm talking missing arms, or being partially disemboweled. Should have bled out. But they kept on coming, and enthusiastically. They were alive, and dangerous. It had to be something that feigned death."

"Feigning death or no, you don't get up without a pulse and attack people. The body just doesn't work that way. It's not possible. Peterson had no pulse. Not a weak pulse, *no* pulse."

"That you could detect," Arthur interjected. "But whatever, they've been dropping like flies, and I'm happier for it. We just have to ride this storm out, like we did on the roof. Most are done already."

"For now, we'll do as we're told, and try to keep a safe distance from Rodriguez, the captain or anyone else who's bitten. We'll warn whoever will listen. I sure as hell don't want to be the one who has to put them down when they go berserk. I'd likely get killed by the soldiers for my trouble."

Another Humvee rolled into the parking lot. Sergeant Collins and his team dismounted. Collins nodded noncommittally at Max. They brought back one more survivor, a pot-bellied middle aged man, bringing the total survivors rescued to eleven.

"Maybe we can convince them to be quarantined for a day or two," Eva said thoughtfully. "We'll have to get the lay of the land once we get to the airport and see what our options are."

"Civilians! On the truck! Now!" barked Captain Jenkins. "We're going to the airport!"

"And speak of the devil," Max muttered.

5

The small convoy rumbled down Memorial Drive. From the covered back of the transport truck, Max could see wrecked or abandoned vehicles had been pushed to the side of the road, creating a clear path. The scattered bodies so disturbingly prevalent around the rest of Greenville were notably absent, even on the side of the road. A pickup, its bed loaded with workmen, pulled in behind them. It was followed by a large flatbed truck with a heavy tarp strapped over its cargo, corners flapping in the breeze on the roadway.

Arthur leaned lightly against Max, sleeping with his head back and mouth agape. Max watched as a bit of drool slowly wound its way down his companion's chin, but determined its track would roll down his neck rather than dripping onto Max. Keeping tabs on its progress was more interesting than the conversation among the exhausted group, which was nonexistent save for Sharon cooing softly to her children in a vain effort to console them over the loss of their father.

Eva tried to engage the other survivors in conversation, but no one wanted to talk about their recent experiences. They were too exhausted, emotions still too raw, so Eva didn't press the matter and instead sat quietly for the ride to the airport.

After about ten minutes, Max spotted a runway on the other side of a chain link fence. The convoy passed a car rental business and made the left turn towards the tiny Pitt-Greenville Airport. They turned, but the flatbed truck following them continued straight. As it passed, the tarp that loosely covered the bed flapped in the breeze, revealing the truck's grisly cargo.

Max pointed. "Eva, are those…" Max's voice trailed off.

"Bodies. Yes," she replied. "The streets in this area have been cleared. They're not wasting any time gathering them for mass burial. That's good; they're on the ball. Try not to think about it, Max. It has to be done."

The convoy rolled to a stop in the parking lot of the National Guard armory just before the airport. It was nothing fancy, just a one story brick building built around a two story high assembly hall roughly the size of a gymnasium. Soldiers lowered the tailgate of the big transport, and helped Max and the other civilians out of the truck.

Standing in the glare of the midday sun, Max surveyed his surroundings.

Several tents had been erected in the parking lot. An open air shelter, little more than a tarp atop poles, covered several small tables and an assortment of coolers and boxes. Next to it was a full sized tent with side flaps concealing its interior. To the side there was a dark, smoky plume rising from a small fire fed with scraps of burning clothes. Looking to the west, Max could see the terminal with its distinctive metallic red roof punctuated by decorative tower-like structures. In the terminal parking lot, smaller emergency shelters were being set up in long rows by a team of weary soldiers. Pallets loaded with boxes were set around the lot and a small forklift was parked off to the side. Over a hundred more people in civilian clothing milled about the bivouac area or sat cross-legged on the ground.

Across the street from the armory, a fenced-in dirt parking lot was set up with a half dozen large tents with the distinctive red cross that denoted their use as a medical facility.

"This way, please." A squat woman in a hazmat suit motioned the new arrivals to a table where she had set up a laptop computer. She had thick round glasses and dark hair in a bobbed cut that Max thought made her resemble Marcy from the "Peanuts" comic strip, all grown up. A large emergency response vehicle, similar to an RV, was behind her. On its side was a logo with blue lettering on the side that read, "Central Outbreak Response."

Max and the other survivors shuffled over to the table as two soldiers pulled Peterson's body, wrapped in the plastic sheet, from the truck. They grunted with effort as they lugged their fallen comrade to the armory.

"I'm Doctor Eleanor Brookings," the woman in the hazmat suit began. "I'm with Central Outbreak Response; Central for short or COR for shorter," she chuckled briefly at her own joke. "We're here, working with the military and civilian authorities during this crisis, as the CDC and FEMA are focusing their resources on larger population centers. I don't mind saying that everyone's resources are stretched to the breaking point, and we need your cooperation and help, when required."

Max leaned close to Eva and whispered, "I've never heard of these guys. Do you know anything about them?"

She nodded, and pressed her finger to her lips, listening attentively as Dr. Brookings continued.

"First things first. I'm sure you've all noticed many of us wearing hazmat suits. Do not be alarmed. This is a precaution for select personnel with potentially risky responsibilities. We do not yet know what has caused this outbreak of violence, but we are trained and equipped for this, and we are going to help you all through this crisis.

"Second, we will begin processing you. This entails taking your names, a little personal information about you, then scrubbing you down in the decontamination tent and giving you new clothes," she motioned dramatically to the long, full sized tent nearby. "Again, that's just a precaution, and should not alarm you. Then we will give you a physical, and provide you with any medical care you require.

"Thirdly, you will be moved to the airport grounds proper, where you'll be assigned a tent to sleep in, and be provided with food. Now, understand that this is not a free ticket. You will be expected to work, if you are able. We have a great deal to do and not nearly enough people to do it."

"What if we don't want to work?" Arthur asked. "It's not like we were given a choice in coming here. If we say 'no', do we get to leave?"

"Saying 'no' would deprive you of food, medicine and protection, so no one has been stupid enough to do it," Dr. Brookings said, frowning. "Are you? We need everyone to work together until the situation is stabilized. But as we are operating under martial law, I suppose it would be up to the military to decide what to do with you. Maybe they'll set up a brig for those who rock the boat. I would also like to remind you that they have authority to shoot you, so I don't recommend pressing the point, dear." She smiled condescendingly at Arthur, who rolled his eyes. "If there are no more questions, let us begin."

Max and the other survivors stood in line, each waiting their turn to be processed. His eyes drifted to the evacuees already on airport grounds, and his heart raced at the prospect that Aimee could be among them. Another transport truck arrived and dropped off a dozen more refugees from the madness that had enveloped Greenville. They waited their turn as Max's group finished. Eva stepped to the table.

"Name," Dr. Brookings pointedly asked.

"Eva Hernandez."

"Hometown?"

"Atlanta."

"Any skills you believe may prove useful?"

"Medical. I'm a third year medical student at the university," she replied.

"Wonderful! We'll put you to work right away, I'm sure," Dr. Brookings said excitedly. "There are plenty of people who will need your help."

Dr. Brookings directed Eva to the decontamination tent.

Eva proceeded into the tent, looking back at Max as she pulled the flap closed behind her. She was calm, but Max thought he saw concern flash in her eyes.

"Name," Dr. Brookings asked Max, pulling his attention back from Eva.

"Max Newsome, Birmingham, Alabama."

"Skills?" Dr. Brookings asked while she typed his previous answers.

"Can you tell me if someone has been processed through here already? I'm looking for someone."

Dr. Brookings' brow furrowed and she sighed deeply. "Everyone is." She paused a moment. "I'd love to help, but I can't search for your whole family. If I do that for one, I'll have to do it for all, and there's a line behind you."

"No, I understand," Max begged. "It's just one name."

"Go ahead," she grumbled, angrily punching some keys on the computer.

"Aimee Wilson, from Memphis, Tennessee," Max spelled out her name so there would be no mistake. His stomach twisted into a knot as he waited for Dr. Brookings to run the query.

"I'm sorry. She's not here. Maybe she'll be brought in later, but in all honesty you shouldn't get your hopes up. Her chances aren't good." She punched some more keys on the computer. "Skills?" she repeated in a too-friendly tone that belied her annoyance.

Max's heart sank. He had put a lot of hope in finding Aimee among the airport survivors, only to find disappointment again. "Combat veteran, but I'm majoring in English at the university," Max answered.

Dr. Brookings' pencil-thin lips twisted with disappointment. "Even basket weaving would be more useful here."

"Sorry I'm not a doctor, but give me a gun and I'm a good shot," Max replied. "Of course, that's only a critical skill when one's life is in danger. And how often does *that* happen?"

"Oh, I didn't mean to offend. I'm sure we can find a use for you." Dr. Brookings waved him on to the tent for decontamination.

As the flap closed behind Max, he heard Arthur getting the same treatment from Dr. Brookings. He smiled, confident that Arthur would be at least as much of an irritant to Brookings as she would be to him.

Once inside the tent, another worker in a hazmat suit bearing Central's logo instructed Max to remove his clothes and place them in a bag.

"You're burning them?" Max asked, pulling his tee shirt over his head.

"Yes sir," came the response. "It's a precaution against disease. You'll be given new, clean clothes. Please note your sizes on this," the man said, setting a clipboard on a folding chair, "or your new clothes may not fit well."

"Fine, I suppose I could use a bath anyway," Max grumbled. "I'm stinking like my gym." He placed his clothes in a small plastic bag and filled out the required paperwork before being ushered naked into the next chamber of the tent. Two more COR personnel waited within.

"Step into the tub and raise your arms above your head, please," one said, his voice muffled by a respirator.

Max stepped into an inflated ring on the ground, and the two workers passed an octagon-shaped hoop that sprayed water from eight nozzles, over his body.

"Geez! That's cold!" Max exclaimed. "Are you sure this is necessary?"

"Sorry, sir," the man responded. "Hot water is a luxury. It won't take long, and it's a necessary precaution."

"Seems like everything is a precaution," Max grumbled, shivering.

The workers scrubbed Max with sponges on long poles for about a minute, then rinsed him clean with the decontamination hoop and handed him a towel. "Dry off and step into the next chamber please, you'll find your clothes there."

"Hey, I think you missed a spot," Max said, pointing to his elbow.

The workers just stared at him.

"Never mind," Max said as he stepped into the last chamber and was given clean, plain white socks, underwear, white tee shirt, jeans and a cheap pair of sneakers.

He dressed quickly, then stepped out of the tent. Eva and the other survivors who went before were waiting in a group, dressed in similar cheap clothing. They were each waiting their turn for a medical screening from two men in lab coats embroidered with the Central logo.

Eva smiled when she saw Max. "Now we know what a car wash feels like, from the car's point of view."

"Sort of a dehumanizing experience," Max concurred. "We look like extras from 'Grease'."

"Dude! Careful with my dongle!" came Arthur's complaint from the tent. A couple of minutes later he emerged in full bitch mode, and joined the group. "Cold water, disturbingly friendly customer service and damn it, that was my favorite shirt they burned. You can't just find those anywhere. These guys owe me big."

One of Central's doctors identified himself to Max as Dr. Banerjee, and asked him standard boilerplate about allergies, medications and preexisting conditions. A blood sample was taken, and as always, everything was quaintly explained as a "precaution." Banerjee identified Max's ankle as a simple sprain, painful but not incapacitating. He gave Max some medicine for the pain and a brace for support, instructions to keep it elevated when he could, and told him it wasn't bad enough to keep him from being assigned a work detail. Max muttered a noncommittal agreement.

When the medical examinations were finished, the group was escorted to the airport grounds by a stocky woman in a Greenville police uniform, who identified herself as Delores. A bivouac was set up in the parking lot, where rows of emergency shelters awaited occupants.

"These are your sleeping quarters," Delores explained. "Two to a tent. Those of you who are able, will have assigned duties starting in the morning. In a few days, we'll move everyone into the terminal, where we're going to build out better accommodations. We're all in this together, and everyone has to do their share."

"What exactly is 'this'?" Max inquired. "We still don't have any real explanation of what has happened."

"People went crazy and attacked their neighbors—"

Max interrupted her. "Yeah, that's what I keep hearing. Nothing more specific?"

"I'm told it's probably a virus," Delores sighed, "but we're not sure and we're not taking any chances. That's why we are going through all of these elaborate procedures."

"Because you don't even know what you're looking for," Eva interjected.

"That's correct," Delores admitted. "We don't know what we're looking for. Whatever it is, it hit without warning, is widespread and appears to be one hundred percent fatal in a matter of hours. Therefore, it has been determined to use stringent screening procedures. That is the wisest course of action, wouldn't you agree?"

"No I wouldn't. I mean, the screening procedures are fine, but *this* is wrong," Eva said, gesturing to the campsite and challenging Delores. "You quarantine the sick, not the healthy. If you've got a suspected virus, then tightly packing people together in a camp is the exact wrong thing to do. You're endangering everyone."

"She's got a lot of spunk," Max whispered to Arthur, who nodded in reply.

Delores scowled. "In a normal outbreak, you would be correct. You quarantine the sick to keep them away from a larger, healthy population. But here, the dead and dying outnumber the healthy population. The roles are reversed. So yes, in effect we're quarantining the healthy."

"I hadn't thought of it like that. The role reversal, I mean," Eva conceded.

"It's far from ideal, but it's not just the virus. It's also the threat of violence from the sick, or…" Delores licked her lips nervously, "…opportunistic criminals. We've been forced to marshal our resources here, with military protection, and procedures to guard against the virus."

"But the violence has subsided," Max observed.

"For now," Delores stated.

Max's eyebrows shot up in alarm. "What do you mean by that? Are you expecting even *more* trouble?"

"Listen, young man. Knowledgeable, experienced people have determined this as the best course of action at this time," Delores said, her face clouding with frustration. "The military is calling the shots now. If you have further complaints, I'd suggest you take it up with them, or Central. I'm basically a public relations officer now."

Delores' irritation with the questioning from Max and Eva was apparent. Max had learned enough for the time being. The military was in charge, they were expecting more violence, and they weren't forthcoming in sharing their intelligence.

"Which brings me to all of *your* duties," Delores continued. "On your cots, you will find a card with the tasks that have been assigned to you. Treat them as real jobs. You will all be awakened at six o'clock in the morning for breakfast before being directed to your respective tasks, which will begin at seven.

"Now, you have the rest of the afternoon to rest and get acclimated. Dinner will be served in about three hours. I wish you all the best of luck as we weather this storm together. If you have any problems, you can find myself or another peace officer."

Shelter assignments kept the group from the supermarket near each other rather than splitting them up. Reverend Miller and his wife were assigned a tent next to Max and Arthur. Across the aisle, Eva had her own tent, pending assignment of a tent mate. Next to her, Sharon and her two daughters were to be placed in a larger tent that was being set up for them by a pair of soldiers. Everyone else immediately ducked into their tents to find their assignments.

Max and Arthur found theirs on the two small cots within.

"IT support," Arthur read off his card. "Well, at least they know talent when they see it. What'd you get?"

"Damn it," Max cursed, and stepped out of the tent, as if he could find someone to whom he could complain. Arthur followed.

"What'd you get?" he repeated.

"Burial detail," Max grumbled. He thought of the flatbed loaded with bodies and winced. "That's just great. They're trucking them in for mass graves. Like I haven't seen enough bodies for one lifetime."

"Hey, don't feel too bad," Arthur consoled him. "It's got to be done. There's a lot of bodies out there, and they've got to get them in the ground before disease spreads."

"Yeah, no shit."

A cloud came across Arthur's face. "Wait a minute. When that sergeant promised my Mom would be buried...."

"Arthur–"

"*That's bullshit!*" Arthur exploded. "Mom is going to buried in her garden like we said! Not dumped into a pit with a bunch of strangers!"

"Problem out here?" Eva asked, poking her head from her tent.

"Hell yeah there's a problem!" Arthur stamped his feet in a full-blown rage.

"Arthur! Can it!" Max snapped. "We aren't in a position to–"

"Don't tell me to 'can it', Max!"

"You don't like your assignment, Arthur?" Eva asked innocently.

"*My* assignment is peachy. Max's bothers me."

"Burial detail," Max explained.

"It has to be done, Arthur," Eva explained. "Otherwise we get dis–"

"Diseases, yeah yeah I know," Arthur interrupted. "But not *my* mom. She'd already *be* buried if the military didn't get in the way." He looked pleadingly at Max. "You promised to help me bury her in her garden. You *promised*. We could've buried her back at my house if we didn't have go on a wild goose chase looking for your *girlfriend!*"

"I know, Arthur. I'm sorry," Max said. "At least we found Eva!"

Arthur pointed a bony finger at Max's chest, as if he were somehow responsible. "This is bullshit, Max. This isn't over."

Muttering, he turned and tore open the flap to the tent and ducked inside, still grumbling as he pulled it closed behind him. "It's not over."

"He'll be himself again after he gets some sleep," Eva said.

"I doubt that will be an improvement. So what's your assignment?"

"Medical, of course," she gestured to the cluster of tents away from the bivouac, adorned with red crosses. "People who are sick or injured when they're brought in are kept separate. That's where they want me; helping take care of people. I don't mind helping people – heck, I *want* to, that's why I went to medical school – but I'm a little nervous about this unknown virus."

"Be careful Eva," Max said. "Don't take any chances if you can help it. And now that we're getting settled in and can talk, tell me what you know about this Central group."

"Central Outbreak Response. I only know a little, from an article I read about them," Eva said. "They're a private organization, somewhat controversial. If you privatized the Centers for Disease Control, crossed it with Doctors Without Borders and gave it enormous financial resources – you'd have Central. Their focus is response to disease outbreaks. Not talking about the seasonal flu, but the nasty stuff like Ebola or SARS."

"That doesn't sound like a bad thing. Why do they give me the creeps?"

"Because we've met a few arrogant jerks," Eva squinted as she tried to recall something. "Although, the article mentioned that there were some concerns about transparency. And they've got a private security force, which is unusual for a medical outfit. Being private, they could hide a lot of things, and that made some very powerful people nervous. They're supposed to be global in scope, but I wasn't aware they were even operational yet."

Reverend Miller emerged from his tent, frowning and rubbing his balding head as he stared, mouth agape, at his assignment card.

"Hello, Reverend!" Eva chirped, trying to lighten the mood.

"What assignment did you get?"

Reverend Miller regarded her with a deer-in-the-headlights expression that Max couldn't ignore. The man was petrified.

"Reverend?" Max asked.

The reverend sighed, closing his eyes and tilting his head upwards, as if he were sending a small prayer heavenward. He then opened his eyes and gazed over the encampment, taking in the mass of humanity buzzing in a state of barely controlled chaos. "Lord have mercy," he whispered under his breath, shoulders drooping as if under the weight of a tremendous burden. "They want me to be a counselor."

"You'll be a great counselor," Eva said, trying to bolster his flagging confidence.

"Counseling all these people. They expect me to do that and I don't even know where to begin," he complained. The assignment card rattled in his trembling hands. "How can I help others make sense of this when I don't understand it myself?"

"Practice," Max stated without thinking. "Practice on us, and never let your new flock see you sweat. As a man of faith, they have confidence in you. They trust in you from the get-go. That's your edge. So practice on us until you believe in yourself."

"Yeah," Eva said. "No one understands *anything* about all of this. Not yet. We haven't had time to process it. At this point, they're probably just expecting you to comfort people. Practice on me and Max, sort of role play it. Then you'll have more confidence in what to expect when you're on the clock, so to speak. We'll ask you questions we want to ask, or what we think others will."

Several soldiers passed by carrying large folding tables, preparing the dinner service station. Max dragged over some nearby folding chairs and the three of them pulled into a close huddle and spoke softly.

"Assuming God exists, then how could He let this happen? I mean, I get that bad things happen to good people sometimes. But this is over the top."

Reverend Miller raised an eyebrow and regarded Max in silence for a moment. He blinked slowly once, then took a deep breath. "It's only natural that an event like this shakes our faith. It's easy to have faith in good times. But when they get difficult, like now, our faith is tested."

"Is that what you think this is, Reverend? A test?" Max prodded.

"Shit hits the fan," Eva interjected.

"What?" inquired Max.

"Don't say 'when times get difficult', Reverend," she clarified. "Max is right, this is over the top. Say, 'when the shit hits the fan.' Being a reverend may give you an edge in credibility to begin the discussion, but it can be a barrier once it's begun. Use colloquial speech to break down that barrier and speak to people on their own level. No one will expect it from a reverend, so it shatters expectations and lets you deliver the goods – spiritually speaking – on their own terms."

The reverend nodded and turned to Max. "When the shit hits the fan, our faith is tested. Those trials can help us grow closer to God. We can't make sense of everything. We're not meant to. Our lives are the whole of reality to us," the Reverend continued. "But there is a deeper, more meaningful reality in Jesus. In our minds, we see death as a permanent state, but to God it is a transient thing. Through Christ, it is also transient for us. But we are creatures of limited comprehension, and still have an innate understanding of it as final. We judge people, events, even God, according to our own standards. This is naïve. Christ defeated sin and death. We must trust that God knows what he is doing, that it will unfold according to His plan."

Max pounced. "So you're basically saying we should suck it up and accept this because mass casualties of an admittedly biblical scale are somehow *good* for us?"

Reverend Miller licked his lips nervously. "I guess I need to hone my explanation."

"That's fine. You'll know when you're on track," Eva said. "Just keep going."

"I'm sorry," Max said. "To me it sounded like you punted. To a Christian, what you said might make perfect sense, but here, your audience could be of any denomination, any faith, or no faith at all. Your job here is to calm frayed nerves and focus the individual on survival, without the benefit of knowing what their religious status is."

"We're operating on different wavelengths, Max. I'm a man of faith," Reverend Miller defended. "My job isn't necessarily to calm frayed nerves. Sometimes it is to expose them and rub them raw."

"Go on," Eva prompted. "You may be onto something."

"My job, first and foremost, is to spread the Gospel. To let people know that salvation and everlasting life are available. Jesus isn't the touchy-feely hippie most people imagine from popular media. He's a radical, a revolutionary."

"Nice," Eva commented, urging him on.

"In the book of Luke, Jesus states, 'Do you think I came to bring peace on earth? No, I tell you, but division.' He *makes* us make hard choices. There is no middle ground. Accept Him or reject Him, choose life or death, salvation or sin. *Nothing* will assuage the anguish you are feeling right now. You have to fight through it, and through the fight, grow stronger. Soothing nerves isn't Jesus' purpose; nor is it mine."

"Not to burst your bubble, Reverend, but Central didn't assign you as pastor," Max argued. "They assigned you to be a counselor. They need you in that capacity, helping save sanity now, rather than souls."

"No. No! You accused me of punting, after my initial explanation," Reverend Miller challenged, his eyes aflame with passion. "If I'm not true to my calling as a servant of Christ; if I merely act as a counselor, now *that* would be punting. Our hosts have their mission, but I have my purpose. Faith without action is hollow, meaningless. My service to Christ comes before my service to the military, or Central, or whomever it is that thinks they are running this show.

"To answer your question more succinctly, we don't know the reason this happened. Is it a natural occurrence? Is it fair to blame God? Or is it that He allowed us free will, and we're reaping what we've sown? We don't have enough information to know the ultimate cause. Without knowing that, we cannot reasonably affix blame.

Max rubbed his chin doubtfully. "Still a punt."

"You're looking for an absolute, Max. I don't have one for you. So here's a shorter version still," Reverend Miller stated. "God can let it happen because He doesn't answer to us. We answer to Him."

"That's not very satisfying, Reverend," Max said.

"It isn't meant to be. It's meant to make you think."

"So is God punishing us for our sins, then?" Eva asked.

"That's a conclusion that I bet many people will find reasonable, because it helps them affix blame. But it is incorrect. I don't know the cause of this mess, but I am certain that God is *not* punishing us for our sins. Christ paid the wages of our sin on the cross, for all time. Through Him, we are redeemed. Period. We must endure, and with God's help, we will triumph."

"I think you're on a roll!" Eva exclaimed.

Reverend Miller smiled, stood and pulled his shirt straight. "Thank you. Both of you. This has been more helpful than I thought it would be. It's helped me focus. I have some tall thinking and praying to do. If you'll excuse me." He ambled off among the tents, smiling and nodding at the other refugees, a confident, peaceful aspect to his stride.

"Well, that wasn't quite what I expected," Max said.

"I doubt either of us is qualified to tell him what to say, or how to say it," Eva replied. "He'll figure it out. We got him to thinking, though, put him over the hump. That's all we could have hoped for."

The smell of soup cooking wafted over them, and refugees began to drift over in anticipation of dinner. Max's stomach growled.

"Dinner will be ready soon," he said.

"Good, I'm starving," said Eva, rubbing her hands together.

"Yeah, I guess you had about as much to eat, trapped in that closet, as Arthur and I had trapped on that roof."

"And not a bite since," added Eva. "Of course, for a lot of that time, our appetites were gone."

Max grunted in agreement. He watched Sarah and Becca race each other for dinner, dodging through the crowd to the front of the line as Sharon tried to corral them. *Kids are resilient*, Max smiled, *they'll be fine.*

"I don't have any family," Eva said quietly, staring at her hands.

"What?"

"Earlier, you asked me if there was any family I wanted to look for, and I shut you down. I'm sorry. It's just that I don't have a family anymore. They're all dead."

"From this—"

"No, no. Not from this... crisis. Event. Whatever you want to call it. In high school, I watched my father die of cancer. It was awful. I wanted to be a doctor, to fight that monster so others wouldn't have to go through that pain. I went to college, graduated with honors. I got accepted to medical school and even got some scholarships and loans to help out. But it just wasn't enough."

"Not enough money?"

She shook her head. "I needed forty thousand dollars more. I was crushed as the deadline for registration approached. My dreams were falling apart before my eyes."

"So what happened?"

Eva smiled sadly. "My little brother, Miguel. He walked in the room one day, kissed my cheek and handed me an envelope with the money." She looked up at Max, her eyes glistening with emotion. "He dropped out of college and joined the military. His college savings, plus the enlistment bonus covered the difference. He sacrificed his future for mine, because he believed in me so much. He's my hero."

Max nodded.

"Miguel was sent to Afghanistan. The vehicle he was riding in was hit by a roadside bomb."

"I'm sorry, Eva."

"Mom took his death hard. So did I, but he was always her baby. She couldn't get over it and died nine months later, I think of a broken heart. I buried her, then buried myself in my studies. Becoming a doctor and curing people became my sole focus. I think it was my way to honor his sacrifice, and now…" Eva looked over the camp and sighed. "I don't know what will become of me. Of all of us."

"I never knew my parents. As a kid, I bounced around foster homes, so I never really had a family to count on. To care for. But now I have Aimee, if… if I ever find her in all this madness. If she's even alive. That's why I have to find her. She's all I have left."

A soldier on the food preparation team vigorously banged a spoon on a pot, signaling that dinner was served.

Eva eyed Max thoughtfully for a moment before they got up to get in line. "You're a good man, Max. I hope you find your girlfriend."

6

After mumbling and swatting at phantoms in his sleep for what seemed to Arthur an eternity, Max was sleeping quietly in his cot, snuggled under his blanket. It was the moment for which Arthur had been waiting.

He slipped quietly from his cot, hoping the slight rustle of the blanket and creaking of the cheap metal frame wouldn't wake Max. Arthur picked up the sneakers he had been issued by Central and slipped them on his feet. They were half a size too big and he wriggled his toes in dismay before lacing the shoes tightly. A folding chair by his cot held a paper plate with a peanut butter and jelly sandwich. He smiled, and silently thanked Max for the thought as he scooped up half of the sandwich and wolfed it down for the energy he would need. He whispered a curse as a glob of grape jelly dropped onto his white tee shirt. Arthur stretched his shirt with one hand, and flicked the offending jelly with the other. He heard it splat somewhere in the darkness of the tent, then examined the small stain left behind, barely but definitely visible even in the darkness of the tent. He shook his head, then shrugged. *Not really my shirt anyway*, he thought. Arthur cautiously peeled back the flap to the tent and peeked outside.

The moon had slipped below the horizon. Judging by how quiet and still the camp was, Arthur figured it to be three or four o'clock in the morning. He could hear Sharon comforting one of her girls, who was crying softly for her father in their nearby tent. No one was setting out breakfast yet, but he could see a few soldiers moving on the perimeter under the light of streetlamps by the armory, medical tents and the military's own bivouac area, which they had set up apart from the refugees. Stepping from the tent, Arthur avoided Sharon's and picked his way through the camp, making his way to the edge of the parking area. The lights were on the edge of the lot, so the center was dark enough for his comfort, but he knew he'd have to cross a brightly lit area to get out. He'd have to go the long way around the terminal for any chance to avoid the soldiers, but felt confident he could slip away undetected. *After all, they're guarding against attack, not escape*, he thought. *I have the advantage.*

Arthur reached the edge of the camp and sprinted across the passenger pickup lane. He skidded through some gravel, coming to a halt by a fence. He could see the runway beyond. The fence was topped with barbed wire, and Arthur cursed under his breath. He followed it a short way until he found a gate, and was pleased to see it unlocked. Opening it a crack, he slipped onto the tarmac. He winced as his foot kicked a chain on the ground, sending it clanging several feet away. He stopped to examine it, and found the padlock, still hanging on it, had been cut. *Why bother with keys when you've got bolt cutters?* Arthur smiled and silently thanked the military for their direct approach to problem solving.

So far so good. He turned and scanned the camp for any sign of pursuit. Satisfied there was none, he continued, hugging the terminal building to avoid being seen by anyone who might be looking from the windows. He made his way under the two jetways, past baggage carts and fuel trucks. As he neared the far end, the smell of cigarette smoke hung in the air and he heard soldiers talking.

"You're lucky," said one with a southern drawl. "You know your family's safe. I don't know where mine is, how my folks are doing, if they're even alive."

"I've got my concerns, too," said the second soldier. "I heard a rumor earlier."

"What was that? What'd you hear?"

"It's just a rumor. I don't know if it's true and probably

shouldn't spread gossip–"

"Hey, you brought it up. Just tell me."

"Well, okay, but remember this is just hearsay." He paused nervously. "They say... well, I *heard* that we've lost contact with Fort Bragg."

"You're shitting me!" said the first soldier.

"You didn't hear it from me. Remember, it's just a rumor, but I don't think I can sleep until I know my family's safe. I mean, they *should* be safe on base, right?"

"Of course they are. Hey man, you know... it could just be our equipment here. Or maybe it's not true at all," the first soldier drawled, trying to make his friend feel better.

"I hope you're right. The not knowing is the hardest. I can't just up and ask the captain. He'd throw a line to me about duty this and duty that and suck it up, cupcake. But I'm scared man," said the second soldier. "I mean, even if my wife and kids are okay, odds are most of our extended families are... well, you know."

Arthur waited patiently as the two soldiers talked, expecting them stick their heads around the corner at any moment, and see him. One flicked a burning cigarette butt through the air and onto the tarmac, where it exploded in a burst of red hot embers before dying. He waited for the soldiers to move off, but they stayed and gossiped.

Arthur quietly withdrew the way he came. He would have to find another way. *What would Captain Kirk do*, he mused.

Arthur's shoulder smacked into a box protruding from the wall, and he hissed in pain. His eyes fell upon the offending box, marked "vehicle keys." The cover was bent back. Someone had taken a crowbar to it, preventing it from closing all the way. Arthur grinned and again thanked the military. *A diversion. That's what Kirk would do!*

Arthur looked over the vehicles under the jetway, selecting an electric baggage tractor; vehicle number seven. He opened the key box. Squinting to see in the darkness, his fingers fumbled through the keys until he found the one he was looking for. *Lucky number seven*, he thought, kissing the key. He located a large pair of airplane wheel chocks under the jetway. Groaning slightly as their unexpected weight pulled at his muscles, he managed to loop them over his shoulder and lugged them to the baggage tractor. He put it in neutral before turning the key in the ignition, then jammed the baggage tractor pedal down with the chocks. Arthur put the tractor in gear. It lurched forward and he hopped off, smiling with satisfaction as it rolled across the tarmac towards a line of single engine planes. He crept back along the terminal building where the soldiers stood guard.

The tractor zipped quietly into the darkness of the runway, lit intermittently by soft flashes of light from the strobes of the approach lighting system. Arthur's breath caught in nervous anticipation, fearful it would be too quiet or too distant to draw their attention.

"What the hell is… *stop!*" yelled the first soldier as both ran after the tractor, flashlights dancing across the runway in the darkness.

Arthur exhaled and smiled. "Fetch, boys," he whispered as he darted past their abandoned post. He kept his eyes on them. If they turned around they would see him, but the plucky baggage tractor kept their attention as it sped away. Arthur cringed when it slammed into a private plane and stopped, but it had served its purpose. He had reached cover at the private hangars and was making his way to the far end of the runway. *That was awesome! Just like Captain Kirk!* Arthur was unable to stifle a snorting chortle in his excitement. His heart was pounding in his chest as he made his way to the far end of the private hangars and into a cluster of trees that ran next to the perimeter security fence.

Arthur kept low, hoping to avoid standing out in the darkness with his white tee shirt, and made his way along the fence that guarded the runway. Barbed wire across the top discouraged him from climbing over, but he held out hope there would be a place where he could dig under, perhaps by widening a drainage channel. At the end of the runway, he found what he was looking for; a small field of fist-sized gray rocks for erosion prevention that ran right under the fence. He picked a spot next to a small tree growing on the other side, which he hoped would provide cover if a military convoy should happen down Memorial Drive, which ran parallel to the airfield. He spent a few minutes removing rocks until he had built a small chute under the fence. He then slipped underneath, groaning as the rocks dug into his flesh and scraped his back.

With one final push, Arthur was free. He stumbled down the grassy bank and splashed face-first into a retention pond filled with foul, mucky water. He flailed about, sputtering and cursing, until he found his footing on the spongy bottom. The water was only waist deep, so he slogged across it towards the road, about thirty yards away. The viscous mud sucked hungrily at his feet with every step. He was far away from the camp, and feeling more secure about his escape. Halfway across the retention pond, the mud claimed a shoe. Arthur spent several minutes groping about, desperately trying to locate it, but the water and the chill of night left him shivering. As speed was essential and the eastern horizon was brightening, Arthur abandoned the search and continued working his way to the street and out of the water.

He frowned when he saw that even under starlight, his white tee shirt shone brightly in the pre-dawn darkness. Arthur scooped up a handful of smelly muck from the pond bottom and rubbed it all over his tee shirt, hoping to camouflage himself. Satisfied, he kicked off his second shoe and scrambled up the grassy embankment to Memorial.

He kept alert for any vehicles traveling on the road. As it was still fairly dark, he figured he would see them first, gambling that he could hide before he was spotted.

Arthur walked for about thirty minutes in the slowly brightening dawn. He cursed the loss of his shoes as his feet throbbed from the relentless pounding on the pavement. He wagered it was better than if he had tried to cut through the nature preserve to his right, filled with bugs and snakes and who-knew-what-else, especially without shoes. He crossed the bridge over the Tar River and into Greenville proper as the sun peeked over the horizon.

Arthur passed by several small houses off Memorial and decided to search them for anything useful. He walked up to a one-story brick house, the door of which had an 'X' spray painted in neon orange with numbers scrawled around it. Arthur remembered seeing similar symbols in news reports after Hurricane Katrina hit the Gulf Coast. Arthur didn't know what the numbers meant; to him it was simply an indicator the house had been searched and cleared. The door had already been broken open by the search team, so Arthur pushed it open and stepped inside.

The interior was dimly lit by the rising sun. Arthur left the lights off to avoid drawing attention to his presence. He quietly toured the house, not fully trusting his theory that the search marker meant he was alone. When he was satisfied there would be no surprises, he breathed a sigh of relief, then wandered into the kitchen and wolfed down some plain bread and milk. He ransacked drawers in a bedroom, locating some fresh, dry clothes. The best he could find that even came close to fitting were a flannel shirt, gray sweat pants and work boots several sizes too big. He cinched up the pants as tightly as he could to keep them from falling down, clopped around awkwardly in the boots and hoped he wouldn't have to do any running.

Satisfied he had done all he needed, he checked the garage, where he found an old bicycle. "Great. A girl's bike," he sighed. "Well, at least I have another reason to avoid being seen."

Arthur pedaled out into the brightening day and took to the side streets, hoping to avoid contact with anyone before he got home.

†

Max awakened with a start. Someone was walking down the aisle between the tents, banging a spoon around in a pot to rouse the sleeping survivors. *Typical of the military*, he thought. *Goddamn reveille*.

He'd been dreaming about something he couldn't quite recall, but it was pleasant, and a welcome change from his usual nightmares. He felt invigorated with the change, and smiled as he stretched, warm and content under his blanket. The tent flaps glowed a soft white from the morning sun.

"Arthur," Max called out groggily. "Time to get up, in case you missed the asshole banging on the pot." He wiped the sleep from his eyes. The cot beside him was quiet. "Arthur?" Max looked over and saw that the cot was empty and half of the sandwich he'd left was gone. He quickly got dressed and stepped outside into the crisp morning air. The other survivors were emerging from their tents as well. Across the aisle, Eva yawned in mid-stretch, her breasts straining against the thin fabric of her tee shirt. She caught Max looking and pulled her arms down. He quickly looked away.

"Good morning, Max," she said with a wry grin. "Sleep well?"

He forced himself to meet her gaze, as if he could boldly deny checking her out, but flushed with embarrassment. He told himself it was only natural to notice, and wasn't a betrayal of his love for Aimee. "Yeah," he answered sheepishly. "Best sleep I've had in a while."

"Is Arthur sleeping in?"

"He's not here," Max responded. "He went to bed early, so I guess he got up early, too. Maybe he's checking out the camp." *Dammit, don't say 'checking out'!* Max winced. "He ate half his sandwich, though."

"Are you going to tell him it was my idea, or steal the credit?" Eva asked. She gave no outward indication that she caught Max's slip up, but he knew she must have.

Max smiled. "Steal the credit, of course." A line of survivors formed at a table where breakfast was being served. The smell of scrambled eggs and toast filled the air, and his stomach growled. "Buy you breakfast?" he smiled at Eva.

"I've got this. It fits my budget," she replied. "You can pay when it actually costs something."

They chatted idly while waiting to get food. It was pleasant for Max to spend a few minutes talking with Eva; almost enough to make him forget why they were there; that the world had gone to hell and they were refugees.

"Good morning," Sharon smiled as she handed them each a paper plate with eggs and toast. "I'm told the powdered eggs are particularly good today."

"Sharon! You're on kitchen duty?" Max asked.

"That and watching the children," she said, shrugging. "It's what I would have chosen if it were up to me, so I don't mind." Becca came scurrying up behind her, bringing a fistful of napkins. She smiled shyly at Eva and hid behind her mother.

Max and Eva carried their plates to tables set up nearby and ate. As they finished, soldiers came by to get their teams for the day, standing on chairs for a view over the crowd of refugees and calling out names. The survivors slowly filtered out of the bivouac, led by their team leaders to perform various tasks. Some groups headed into the airport terminal, others went to the National Guard center and still others filtered out among the camp.

Eva's name was called. As she brushed past Max to leave, he grabbed her by the arm and pulled her close, whispering in her ear.

"Remember how Delores was evasive on the threat of further violence? See what you can find out about it. Someone knows more than they're telling us, and if you're working with Central you might be able to find out."

Eva nodded, then joined a small group of refugees called by a COR representative. She smiled and waved to Max as the group headed for the makeshift medical center across from the armory.

"Max Newsome!" barked a soldier wearing a hazmat suit.

"Here sir," he responded.

"Come with me," he said. He joined five other men and they gathered around the soldier, who passed out white hazmat suits, rubber boots and respirators. "Put these on. My name's Connor, and you're all on my team today. Lucky you."

"I'm not comfortable with this. Can we volunteer for a different task?" asked a big, muscle bound fellow with long, greasy blond hair.

"No chance, Thomas. Recovery teams bring in bodies, we dig and dump. It's not fun, but we don't need cholera or something on top of the disaster we've already had." Connor winced, making a short sucking sound.

And it keeps us busy, Max thought, stepping into his white hazmat suit and pulling on his rubber boots. *Smart. It keeps us from thinking too much about the past couple of days.*

After gearing up and testing the air filters, the group threaded their way through the other refugees waiting for their assignments.

"Poole! Arthur Poole! Who's his tent mate?" yelled a young man in glasses, khakis and a short-sleeved shirt with a Central logo, who was animatedly sorting through index cards. "Newsome? Max Newsome!"

Max called out, "Over here!"

The young man stalked over in a self-important huff. "Where's your tent mate, Arthur Poole?"

"I have no idea, I haven't seen him this morning," Max responded. "He went to bed earlier than I did. I just assumed he got up early. Figured he'd be around, though."

"That's great. Just great. If you see him, you send him over to the National Guard center. Tell him to ask for David. David Wright. That's me. David Wright. I'll need to straighten him out on some things. This is unacceptable."

"Good luck. He's pretty crooked," Max chuckled. He thought the guy was high on the authority granted him by the crisis, and was making sure everyone knew – *he was important.*

"Crooked," Arthur's supervisor cocked his head quizzically at Max. "Please elaborate."

"It's a joke, David Wright," Max explained.

David Wright blinked once, his insect-like eyes never leaving Max's.

"Never mind. It wasn't that funny."

Arthur's disappearance was only mildly disconcerting. Max wondered if his hostile attitude the night before regarding his mother meant he headed off on his own, personal mission for the day. If that were the case, Max could respect and even admire him for that, and would say nothing to ruin it. Maybe he had guts after all. Arthur had potential.

"Are you done questioning my man?" Connor sniped at David Wright. "We've got our own work to do."

Arthur's supervisor waved his clipboard at them and, grumbling, took the two other members of his team to the terminal.

Max turned and smiled appreciatively at Connor. "Thanks for the save. What the hell do they need an IT team for, anyway?"

"Hell if I know," Connor said as he led Max and the rest of the team out onto the runway. "Doesn't seem like it would be a priority to me. But they're moving computer gear to the armory."

Connor steered the group to a small pickup truck with the Pitt-Greenville Airport logo.

"Requisitioned truck?" Max asked as they approached.

"Of course," Connor said, shrugging. "So's the backhoe. And your breakfast. And most of the crap we're using in camp. Odds are, the original owners are dead. They don't need it, we do. Requisitioning rocks."

"They called it 'stealing' when I did it," laughed Thomas. He quickly looked at the ground to avoid Connor's icy glare, his long, greasy hair hiding a mischievous grin.

"Where are we burying them?" asked one of Max's other teammates.

Connor motioned to the backhoe, parked by a runway. "For now, over there. Lots of open ground by the runways," he explained. "There's a back gate off Belvoir Highway. The recovery trucks can go through there and keep the other civilians from seeing thousands of bodies being trucked in."

"Thousands?" echoed Thomas. "Shit."

Connor winced, producing the odd sucking sound. To Max, it

sounded like someone spitting tobacco juice. "The dead are easier to find than the living these days," Connor said. "As teams move deeper into Greenville, they'll find places closer to where they find the bodies. Probably parks and shit. These bodies were found in this part of town."

He hopped into the cab of the truck and cranked the engine. Max and the others climbed into the back. The truck raced over the runways to the backhoe. Max could see where they had already excavated some ground and filled it in, and could only guess as to how many bodies were already buried. More bodies awaited burial, in gruesome heaps where the recovery trucks had dumped them.

"I'm sorry you men have to see this," Connor said. "Hell, I'm sorry *I* have to see this. Try and think of them as cordwood, if it helps. But don't expect it to."

"Who buried them yesterday?" asked Thomas.

"Myself and some other soldiers," Connor replied. "Now they're out as another recovery team, which probably sucks only a little less than this."

Connor hopped on the backhoe and cranked the engine. "Alright, pair up into three lift teams."

The other four workers paired up with one another, and Max was stuck with Thomas. While Connor dug a new trench with the backhoe, the teams began the grim work of moving rigor-stiffened bodies from pile to pit.

†

"What can you tell us about the bites?" Eva asked her team leader, Dr. Brookings. They had assembled in a small tent for a question and answer session prior to beginning their rounds, and she wanted to grill Brookings for information.

"Most of you will be working with survivors with broken bones and lacerations, or our handful of diabetics and asthmatics. We only have three bite victims."

"But regarding the disease transmission, the bite victims should demand more of our attention, and new cases may come in. What do we know about it?" Eva inquired.

"We know that most of the deceased we've encountered suffered bites. When they occurred – whether before death or postmortem – is still a matter of conjecture. In some cases, it appears to be both," she sagely offered. "The virus appears to be a fast acting, rabies-like virus."

Eva nodded. "What are we doing with the victims?"

"They're being kept under observation in the armory to keep them separate from other patients. We've taken samples and are keeping them hydrated. There's little else we can do at this juncture. We're studying the samples we took."

"But you're restraining them. Right?"

"We will if they become aggressive, but so far none of our charges have done so."

"Have we had any fatalities from the disease?"

Dr. Brookings frowned. "No, but we expect to. Their conditions are rapidly deteriorating."

"I've heard that it takes ten to twelve hours to drive the victim insane, and that they die in another ten to twelve hours."

"Our two sickest patients were bitten nearly twenty hours ago. What you heard was either inaccurate, or our treatment is delaying progression. Neither has gone insane, or died. You already know them."

"Captain Jenkins and Private Rodriguez," Eva concluded.

"Yes," Dr. Brookings said. "We also have a civilian brought in late yesterday, Jonathan Winthrop. You'll assist me in working with all three as you're the closest we have to another doctor among the recruits. Dr. Banerjee is in charge of the other patients. The captain and Rodriguez are the most advanced cases you and I have to deal with."

Eva nodded. Caring for diabetics, or people with lacerations or broken bones would be easier and still noble, but the key to the entire crisis was coursing through the veins of the bite victims. Eva wanted to be part of that fight.

"Are there any other questions?" Dr. Brookings prompted her gathered staff.

"Yes, I have another," Eva said.

Dr. Brookings' sigh belied her irritation, but she allowed Eva to continue.

"When did Central come online? I mean, I read about it, but didn't know you were operational."

"You are a curious one, Eva. Technically, we're not operational. This crisis caught us somewhat unprepared, or we'd have more resources at our disposal. We had planned to go live about six months from now, but…" she shrugged and her voice trailed off.

"Mother nature had other plans," Eva finished.

Dr. Brookings gave a grim smile. "The incident is so widespread that CDC and FEMA are stretched too thin over the major metropolitan areas. Central was asked to cover some of the smaller communities, such as Greenville, but the CDC is still calling the shots. Technically, at least," Dr. Brookings looked expectantly at her staff. "Any more questions?"

Dr. Brookings' use of the word 'technically' made Eva uneasy, but she decided against pressing the issue. She had pushed Dr. Brookings as far as she was comfortable.

After a few procedural questions from other team members, who had backgrounds as either nurses, paramedics or military medics, they all donned medical smocks and masks, and set about their rounds. The other medical staff members were to handle tasks such as taking blood pressure, running blood work of new arrivals, and drawing blood from healthy donors to build a small blood bank for any further emergencies.

Eva followed Dr. Brookings across the road towards the armory, stopping by Central's emergency response vehicle. She opened the door and waved Eva inside.

It was essentially a recreational vehicle, cramped but not

uncomfortable, with several workstations of viral analytics suites, including an array of microscopes, centrifuges, gas chromatography-mass spectrometry instruments and more that Eva couldn't identify.

"Welcome to Central's RV," Dr. Brookings said.

"You research the virus here?" Eva asked.

"Oh, heavens no!" Dr. Brookings laughed. "We have everything we need here, but this is used for basic blood work and communications with Central headquarters in Kansas. They're doing the heavy lifting in a BSL-4 lab. But this thing hit so hard, so fast, that by the time they solve this bug there may be no one left to cure."

"And the CDC? They're researching this also, right?"

"They share data with us through Central HQ." Dr. Brookings snatched up a remote control and activated a monitor mounted to a wall. After a few seconds, the screen warmed up and the squiggly image of a virus as viewed through an electron microscope came into view.

"This is our bug. Some call it the Rage virus, for the effect it has on its victims, some the E-virus – 'e' for 'extinction' as they fear that is what could happen. Others call it the Terra virus, as it appears to have emerged all over the earth nearly simultaneously. This fact alone leads us to believe it is an engineered virus. We believe this was an attack."

"Who would do such a thing? Who *could?* " In her mind, Eva could almost hear Arthur blame aliens, but dismissed the notion.

Dr. Brookings ignored Eva's musings and continued. "That's not for public consumption, Eva. Not yet, anyway. We don't want panic on top of panic. Whatever it's called is of no importance; it has no formal designation as yet. We simply call it the Bug," she stated with a lilt to her voice that betrayed a genuine admiration for the virus.

Eva could understand; one could both hate and admire the efficiency with which the virus spread and killed.

Dr. Brookings turned to face Eva. "Have you much experience working with viruses, Eva?"

"Now, this could be good news," Eva mused. "If it's engineered, then whoever engineered it probably designed a cure before—"

Dr. Brookings cleared her throat. "Have you experience working with viruses?" she repeated, smiling as she stepped behind Eva, giving her an unobstructed view of the monitor.

"Some," Eva responded as she turned to face Dr. Brookings. "But it was fairly basic. I was part of a research team engineering retroviruses to attack cancer cells. A very junior member. My job wasn't very hands-on; I was more like an intern."

Dr. Brookings nodded, then gestured to the monitor. Eva's gaze drifted back to the virus. "Well you'll be getting hands-on experience soon. We'll be learning a great deal about this bug in the coming days. And you'll be doing it with us, from the ground floor. Real field experience." Dr. Brookings laid a pale hand on Eva's shoulder.

"Central has a lot of pull. Do your work to our satisfaction, and I'm sure you'll receive credit for that last year of medical school, regardless of the interruption this crisis has caused. And the medical community was hit hard in this; we'll need good doctors."

The door to the vehicle opened. Dr. Brookings quickly withdrew her hand from Eva's shoulder.

A tall, dark-haired and athletically built man in his late twenties or early thirties stepped inside. He wore a black military-style jumpsuit with a Central logo. He had a shoulder holstered pistol and a utility belt jangling with keys that slapped softly against a small flashlight when he moved. "I'm not late, am I, Dr. Brookings?" he said in a strong, deep voice.

"No, of course not," Dr. Brookings replied curtly. "Jake, this is Eva. She'll be working with the bite patients."

Jake's deep brown eyes met Eva's. A broad smile crossed his chiseled features and he extended a warm handshake. "Jake Billings. Pleased to meet you." She shook his hand firmly and professionally, but the touch of his skin on hers was electric.

"Jake is head of security for Central in Greenville," Dr. Brookings explained.

"Wow," Eva cooed demurely, not impressed but unable to resist giving him the impression she was. *You sound like an airhead! Stop it!*

Jake rolled his eyes in embarrassment, still smiling. "Head of a team of three. It's not that big of a deal. We're drafting help from the military because we're understaffed."

"Why does Central need security?" Eva asked. She was attracted to him, but not so much that she couldn't remember to prod some information from him. Ever since reading the article about Central, she was curious why an outfit like theirs would need private security.

"Mostly for out-of-country operations," Jake readily explained. "Central's role is to go anywhere there's an outbreak of disease. That can be a situation where people are desperate, and desperate people are unpredictable. Security is needed to protect personnel, equipment and patients."

"If you'll pardon the interruption," Dr. Brookings said curtly. "We have work to which we must attend, do we not Mister Billings?"

"Of course, Doctor. This way," he motioned for them to follow.

They stepped from Central's RV and walked to the armory.

"We'll gear up in the hazmat suits for protection," Jake announced.

"I thought the virus transmitted through bites," Eva commented.

"By blood and saliva, so I'm told – but 'bites' is close enough," Jake said. "But some of these guys are vomiting blood."

"Best to err on the side of caution, Eva," Dr. Brookings added.

"Use a raincoat," Jake whispered with a mischievous grin, winking at Eva.

Eva blushed, but figured two could play the game of innuendo. "You're coming, then?"

Jake chuckled and was about to respond, but Dr. Brookings answered for him. "The patients have the potential for violence. Keeping a former Navy SEAL nearby is prudent."

"You're a SEAL?" Eva asked him, genuinely impressed.

"Was, yeah. COR pays better," he laughed. "That's only part of it, though. I'm proud of the work I did in the Navy, but this gives me a chance to help people in a different way. Central is special, you know? And I'm in on the ground floor, at the start of it all. That's exciting."

They geared up and walked quietly down a hallway, passing through a set of plastic sheets that served as an ad hoc airlock. At the end, a man in a hazmat suit and armed with a rifle sat in a chair. He stood at attention upon seeing the three of them. Jake flicked his fingers, motioning for the man to sit back down.

Dr. Brookings gestured to the end of the hall. "We have four rooms reserved for bite patients. We'll double or triple occupancy if needed, but right now each patient can have their own room. We're keeping them hydrated and monitoring their conditions. Security is on duty at all times to assist with any problems." Dr. Brookings lowered her voice conspiratorially and leaned towards Eva. "We do not expect any of them to recover, but we have to keep them comfortable and monitor progression of the disease. They are unaware that they are going to die, though they may suspect it. Keep them calm. Give them hope.

"Chart their temperature every hour, make sure they're getting enough fluids, clean up any vomitus and draw blood every four hours. You're a smart girl, I'm sure you can handle all that. I'll be working in here if you need me," she motioned to a room next to her. Dr. Brookings threw open the door and stalked inside. Jake paused, smiling briefly at Eva, then followed.

Eva checked the chart for the first room, hanging on a nail driven into the door, and read the name. She steeled herself and stepped inside.

"Good morning, captain, are you feeling any better today?"

Captain Jenkins was awake and frowned when Eva entered, recognizing her through the clear helmet of her hazmat suit. He was sweating profusely, with dark circles under his bloodshot eyes.

"They put you on medical duty, eh?" he rasped through labored breathing. "I guess they're desperate."

"Perhaps so," Eva responded. "I need to take your temperature."

Captain Jenkins coughed up some bloody phlegm, and Eva wiped it from his chin with a tissue.

"I may die because of your mistake. Just don't misdiagnose me as dead before I am," he growled.

Eva bristled at the barb, and stabbed a thermometer in his mouth. "Don't talk with your mouth full." *Be more professional,* she scolded herself, flushing with embarrassment. *Don't let him under your skin.* The man was dying, and there was no point arguing with him.

She gave the captain some acetaminophen for his fever, drew some blood and made notations on his chart.

"It looks like your fever's dropping," she lied. "Can I get you anything else?"

"No. You've done enough."

Her lips pursed tightly, Eva slipped from the room and crossed the hall to check on Rodriguez.

Upon entering, she could not stifle a gasp and froze in place. The private lay unconscious, connected to a patient monitor. His breathing was shallow and raspy, his face sunken with a waxen appearance that bespoke of imminent death, a look that Eva had seen before when her father was on his death bed. The bite wound on Rodriguez's cheek was badly swollen and moist with pus. Small rivulets of blood streamed from his nose and mouth. Eva blinked hard and forced herself to shuffle further into the room. She noted the private's weak vitals on the chart, grateful for his sake that he was unconscious at the end.

†

Dodging the military patrols had proven easier than Arthur expected. He had no problem remaining undetected as he worked his way past the one large flatbed he saw being loaded by a recovery team, and never saw Sergeant Collins or any other search team. He passed them far from his neighborhood, and guessed they hadn't been there, either, judging from the number of bodies in front of a house one block away. The burglar alarm was wailing in the otherwise quiet morning. The door and windows were smashed open and dozens of bodies were piled alongside the house, as if drawn by the alarm. Arthur didn't waste time contemplating the scene; he was concerned with getting his mother buried quickly, before the recovery teams reached his neighborhood and lumped her in with the rest of their load.

Arthur sped through the neighborhood to his house, coasting the bike up the driveway and around his mother's parked car. He skidded to a halt before the open garage, cluttered as it was with piles of dusty boxes and an array of gardening tools. He unceremoniously dumped the stolen bicycle on the pavement. Arthur quickly decided that he should bury his mother before getting a change of clothes, even as he hitched up the sweatpants that had again slipped low on his narrow hips.

Arthur stepped inside the garage. He paused a few moments to let his eyes adjust from the brightness outside, then wound his way around a pile of boxes to where his mother kept the shovel and other gardening utensils. He suddenly stopped, rooted where he stood, clamping both hands over his mouth.

Laying on the floor at the back of the garage was the body of Mr. Mullins, an older man who lived only three doors down. Mr. Mullins was a kind soul. He always gave Arthur extra candy at Halloween, when he was young enough for that sort of thing.

Arthur swallowed hard, and knelt for a closer look.

Mr. Mullins could have been asleep, save for the gore trailing from his mouth, and the large garden shears rammed upwards through his jaw.

Arthur could see events unfold in his mind's eye. Mr. Mullins attacking his mother as she worked in her garden. Being a friend, he would have been able to get close before she knew anything was wrong. He imagined his terrified mother ripping away from him, bleeding as she fled into the garage to grab a weapon, Mr. Mullins quick on her heels. *She must have killed him, then collapsed trying to get back in the house*, he thought. *Then went crazy and killed Jasper.*

Tears welled up in Arthur's eyes as he looked upon the body of Mr. Mullins, at once his friend and his mother's killer. He blinked the tears away and wiped them on his sleeve before grabbing the shovel from the gardening rack. Confused, Arthur leaned on it and wept. He took a deep breath, trying to sort through tempestuous and conflicting emotions that threatened to overwhelm him. He felt sadness for the brutal deaths of two people he loved most in the world, pride in his mother for admirably defending herself, disgust that they'd killed one another, betrayed to be left so alone in a cruelly savage new world.

He was uncertain whether it would be proper to bury Mr. Mullins as well. It seemed wrong to bury them together, but he didn't feel physically or emotionally capable of dragging Mr. Mullins' body to the yard anyway. Sighing, he leaned the shovel against a wall and rummaged around the garage, eventually locating a drop cloth which he spread over his neighbor's grisly remains.

Arthur stared at the drop cloth for several minutes, remembering. It was Mr. Mullins who gave Arthur his first beer when he was fifteen, since Arthur's father wasn't in his life much. It was their little secret; Arthur had never told his mother. He smiled at the thought, and decided to try and remember his neighbor as he was then. It was a hot day. Arthur had helped him plant a new sapling. They were sweaty, covered in dirt. Mr. Mullins, dressed in denim overalls, brought out two ice cold bottles of beer. He told Arthur that he'd done a man's work that day and deserved a man's drink. Arthur recalled that it didn't taste very good, but didn't think that was the point – it was a cold, wet and oddly refreshing treat, shared between two friends on a hot summer day.

"Goodbye, Mr. Mullins. Thanks for all you did for me." Arthur wiped at his eyes without bothering to remove his glasses.

He steeled himself for another day of hard work digging,

dreading the thought of tossing dirt on top of his mother. No one, and nothing could have prepared him for such a task. He grabbed the shovel again and trudged to his backyard, resolute, determined to finish what he started and bury his mother. Arthur walked through the open gate to the backyard, then saw the doghouse and froze, numb with shock.

Her body was gone.

7

"What did you say?" Thomas asked.

"I didn't say anything," Max replied, voice muffled by his breathing apparatus.

"Thought you did," Thomas mumbled.

The entire seven man team – three "lift teams" of two men each, plus Connor, the supervisor – were outfitted in their hazmat suits with breathing apparatuses to guard against the potential spread of disease from handling so many corpses. Max was thankful for the protection, although it made the work hot in the late morning sun. One at a time, they pulled rigor-stiffened bodies from the piles brought in by the recovery trucks, and tossed them into the trench Connor had dug with the backhoe. The team was respectfully quiet as they set about their grim task, but were starting to chat more as the day wore on. They were becoming emotionally numb to the horror of the work they were doing.

At first, the lift teams were laying bodies in the trench, but as the hours wore on they resorted to unceremoniously tossing them into the hole. Max winced as the bodies crashed into the mud, but found it was faster, and there were still a lot of bodies to bury. Speed was important. He took Connor's advice, telling himself they were just cordwood. It didn't work. The meager supply of body bags had been used up the first day, but they had some plastic sheeting to lay over the bodies once they'd laid several in. Soon, they would run out of that as well.

Max tried not to look at the faces of the dead, but found it almost impossible. They stared back at him with accusing eyes. Every time he saw a girl with blonde hair, his breath would catch until he saw she wasn't Aimee. The fear of finding her body in one of the recovery piles gnawed at him, sapping his strength for the task.

"This has got to be the shittiest job they give," Thomas complained to Max in a low voice. "I don't think I'll ever be able to get this out of my mind. I'll probably have nightmares the rest of my days."

"Welcome to my world," Max mumbled as they tossed another corpse into the trench and turned back for another. His back and shoulders ached, and he stretched in hopes of alleviating the pain. "Hey Connor, how many have we buried?"

True to his job as supervisor, Connor sat his ass on the backhoe. He also had the unenviable task of counting the bodies his team buried, and he referred to his clipboard. "My count is four hundred and seventy four. Today. Yesterday we buried one thousand three hundred and twenty two." He looked up at the sun climbing higher in the sky. "I'm thinking we're going to fall short of that number today. We need to work faster," he gestured to the growing number of piles the recovery teams were bringing in by the truckload. They had dug several long trenches and after loading them with bodies, filled them in. The work was brutal, thankless and inhuman – the kind that would haunt a man for the rest of his life.

"When do we break for lunch?" asked Thomas.

"You can eat after this?" Max asked, incredulous.

"Hell yeah man. I need energy for this bullshit."

"Let's push on through one more hour, then head back for a bite," Connor instructed, still sitting on the backhoe.

"Can I at least get a few minutes for a cigarette break?" Thomas asked.

Connor winced, making the odd sucking sound again. "Sure. Take five."

Thomas went to the pickup and retrieved his cigarettes, offering them to the rest of the crew. The smokers removed their masks. Max passed on the offer and instead used the break time to stretch his tired muscles. While the three smokers chatted, the others stepped upwind. Max wasn't feeling right, and the very thought of cigarette smoke wafting in his face made him queasy.

He frowned as he listened to the idle chatter of his coworkers as they bantered about sports or women. It struck him that they were speaking as if they were in an office, around a water cooler. He could see how they might want to ignore the obvious horror of their situation and grasp at something normal in their conversation, but couldn't bring himself to participate. Their clucking amidst thousands of corpses was making him angry. Rage pulsed in his veins like a poison and he began to hyperventilate. His vision blurred and he blinked rapidly, trying to focus.

Oh hell. Not now.

Trying not to let his fear betray him, Max walked quickly around the pickup. No one seemed to take notice of him. He ripped off his mask and dropped to his knees, gulping air. Thoughts of Riggins dying in the alley flooded his mind. He remembered the blast throwing him to the ground, remembered sliding through broken glass. *Breathe!* He saw squad mates shredded by the blast, recalled grasping for his rifle, seeing insurgents in the windows above. *Dammit, Combat, breathe!* A tall man with a beard leaned out a window above him, holding a detonator, and Max dispatched him with a single shot. His mind spun as he tried to replace the memories with positive thoughts. *Breathe... easy...* Max told himself, shaking with rage over the memory of the ambush in the alley. He slammed his fist hard into the soft earth. *Think of Aimee.* He visualized Aimee at lunch the day before and his chest tightened. *Think of Aimee.* Adrenaline coursed through his veins, threatening to push him over the edge of his PTSD. *It's not working,* he thought. *Think of... Eva....* In his mind's eye, he saw Eva smiling next to him at dinner, and his breathing became more regular. *Think of Eva....* He rhythmically pounded the soft ground with his fist in time with his breathing, and felt his chest loosen as his breath steadied. *Just breathe,* he told himself. He remembered Arthur's comment that she was 'pulchritudinous', and smiled.

"You coming, Combat?" he heard Riggins say.

Max's breath caught and his eyes shot open. "What?"

"Break time's over. It's time to get back to work," Thomas said, rounding the truck. "You coming, or do you want to keep jerking off?"

Max stood and took a deep breath to steady his nerves before replacing his mask and turning to Thomas. He was angry with himself, that his tortured mind was more at peace thinking of Eva than Aimee. He'd have to figure it out later; there was work to be done. "Let's do it."

†

Dr. Brookings silenced the beeping alarm from the patient monitor in Rodriguez's room. "Brainwave activity has now ceased as well. He's gone. What's the time?"

Eva stopped administering chest compressions and checked her watch. "Twelve thirty-six," she replied, fatigue evident in the softness of her voice. Rodriguez was deceased. Captain Jenkins was comatose across the hall, near death himself. Taken as a whole, Eva's first day working for Central was shaping up to be a disaster.

"Unhook him from the patient monitor," Dr. Brookings said. "Get him out of here quickly and quietly, so we don't disturb the other patients. Clean the room and equipment also. We may have other customers."

"Yes, doctor." Eva didn't mind acting as a nurse for Dr. Brookings. She was curt and arrogant, but efficient. Eva wasn't a doctor yet, and still had much to learn. She wondered what the crisis would do to her plans for the future, then felt guilty for being so selfish.

"Take his body to room thirteen; we're using that as a morgue for now. Appropriate, is it not?"

"Of course, doctor." She stiffened at the realization that Peterson's body would already be there, a potent reminder of her failure at the supermarket. "Any news from the rest of the country?" Eva asked, hoping to clear her mind for the grim work ahead. There had been no new information provided to the evacuees regarding the fate of other cities and indeed, other countries. She suspected the military and COR were withholding at least some information, because they said so little.

"If there is any new information, we'll tell everyone in the briefing after dinner," Dr. Brookings replied. "Until then, try and stay focused on your job. We need you here, one hundred percent, physically and mentally." She stalked into the hallway. "I'll be in the RV. I've got to call Dr. Gray in Kansas."

"Yes, doctor." *Dr. Cyrus Gray.* Eva recalled the article on Central that she had read about a year earlier. It had described him as an eccentric genius and the brains behind Central Outbreak Response.

She unhooked Rodriguez from the patient monitor and closed his eyes for the final time. She then pulled the sheet over his face and turned, leaving the room to get help with the body.

"You there," Eva called to the soldier sitting at the end of the hall with his head down, as if he were trying to sleep. His lackadaisical attitude towards his assignment, even if it was boring, rankled Eva. She felt her face flush with anger. "What's your name?"

The guard slowly lifted his head. "Toby."

"Toby, I need help in here, moving Private Rodriguez."

He grunted as he eased himself from his perch. Ambling over, he leaned into the room, taking in the view of Rodriguez's body draped in a sheet. "He's dead?"

"Yes."

"Shit. Well, I'm sorry, ma'am, but that's not exactly my job."

"What *is* your job, exactly?"

"Security."

"Security," Eva parroted back to him, letting him know it was a weak answer.

"Security," he made a gun with his fingers and flicked his thumb forward, "if they go crazy."

Eva's jaw dropped open. "I can't think of any situation where shooting patients would be a *good* idea, but it's an especially bad one when they have a virus present in their blood."

Toby nodded casually towards Rodriguez. "But he didn't go nuts, now did he? Just croaked. No blood spray. Sweet and simple. I like that."

"No, I guess he didn't," Eva admitted. *Odd. They've all gone berserk. Every one.*

Toby shrugged. "If you don't want me here, I'll go. I didn't want this shit assignment anyway. I'm just on loan to Central."

"Fine. I'll do it myself," Eva growled, shaking her head in frustration.

"There should be a cart in the morgue," Toby offered, as if the suggestion were a peace offering.

Eva gave him a mocking two-finger salute and headed down the hall. Several steps away, anger got the best of her and she spun on her heel to face him. "If security is your job, then do it. If there's such a threat of them going bonkers without warning, then restrain the patients."

"Restrain the patients? Like, tie them down?"

"Yes!"

"Is that a formal request from Central?"

"Goddammit, *yes!*" Eva cried in exasperation. She didn't know if she had the authority to speak on behalf of Central, but if it got Toby to do something constructive, she was willing to bluff it.

The door beside her opened and Jake stepped into the hall. "Problem out here?"

Eva became self-conscious over losing her cool and fought to moderate her voice. "No, no problem at all, *if* you consider the prospect of shooting patients a solution and not a problem itself."

Jake nodded grimly. "I don't like the policy either, but we don't have the staff to ensure the safety of ourselves or our other patients, should one of them go crazy. You've seen them; it would take half a dozen men to restrain one, and all of them would be at risk while they did it."

"Well I don't like it," Eva growled.

"That doesn't matter, Eva. This isn't negotiable. You'll have to get used to the idea. I'm sorry."

Toby seized upon his perceived opportunity. "There's a 'formal' request from Central's medical person here that we restrain all the patients."

"The bite patients," Eva clarified.

"Then do it," Jake said sternly.

"Seriously?"

"Goddamn it, Toby, I don't care what medical asks, you do it and stop embarrassing yourself and the military by trying to weasel out of it. If Dr. Brookings, myself or anyone working with Central asks you to stand on your head, vote Green Party or do anything equally useless, you fucking do it," he punched a thumb toward Eva, "and right now, she speaks for medical."

Toby's shoulders slouched in defeat. "Yes sir."

Jake turned to Eva. "I'll come with you."

They turned and strolled down the hall together. "My hero," Eva whispered.

"Sorry about that," Jake apologized. "Toby's on loan from the military because Central is short on manpower. I think they gave him to us so they didn't have to deal with him. Completely unprofessional."

"Shit rolls downhill, huh?"

"Exactly."

"When's your shift on guard?"

"I don't do that detail. Rob, though – an actual Central guy – is more agreeable than Toby."

"Mmm-hmm."

"Dr. Brookings doesn't want me taking an assignment like that, anyway. I've got more important things to do, like planning security matters."

"Yeah."

They walked a few steps more in silence.

"Damn, you're making me feel bad," Jake said with a chuckle. "Fine, I'll take a shift on watch over the bite patients tonight. Just for a few hours, to spell Rob."

Eva smiled, grateful it was hidden from Jake by the construction of her suit helmet. She may not have dated much since entering medical school, but she could still coax a man into doing what she wanted. And what she wanted was to spend time with Jake. He would be easy to pump for information about Central, but she also wanted him there because his presence made her feel safe in the midst of the hell that had enveloped the world. "Keeping a former Navy SEAL nearby is prudent," Dr. Brookings had said. *And it doesn't hurt to have him be a damn good looking one*, Eva thought.

They rounded a corner and Jake pushed open the door to room thirteen, serving as the morgue. He flipped the light switch and ushered Eva within. Several long folding tables were lined up against the wall, and an occupied body bag rested atop one.

"Is that Peterson?" Eva asked softly.

Jake strode over and looked at a tag attached to it. "Private James Peterson, yeah. You know him?"

"I worked on him before he… died. He was attacked when we were at the staging area."

Jake nodded. "I know they brought him in yesterday and put him in a body bag for transport. The military will take their casualties to Bragg for burial."

"Speaking of the military, they *are* calling the shots here, right?"

"The President declared martial law, so yes."

"And Central is in agreement with the way the military is handling this?"

Jake pursed his lips. "Mostly, but not entirely. That's something you should ask Dr. Brookings."

"I'm asking you, Jake."

He hesitated, shifting his weight from one foot to the other. "Well, we wanted to take the bite victims to our own facility, away from here, for treatment and study. And we wanted to burn recovered bodies in pyres instead of burying them. The military overruled us on both counts."

"A COR facility?"

"We bought one of the old Voice of America sites nearby. Site A was mothballed until we picked it up. They thought about turning it into a nature preserve, but..." he shrugged dramatically, "the disposition was handled by politicians, and money speaks to them like an old lover."

"What about the other sites?"

"Site B is still functional, broadcasting shows mostly to Africa, and I think the Caribbean. Site C went to the university a few years ago. ROTC uses it for training, and there's some other stuff there."

"Bio research," Eva added. "I'm familiar with that one. Has the military said anything about expecting further violence? I heard some rumors."

Jake smiled grimly. "Oh, that. They sent a team to secure the county jail and didn't like what they found. Or rather, what they *didn't* find."

The thunder of gunshots rolled down the hall of the armory. Jake cursed and darted from the morgue, pulling his sidearm, and sprinted down the hall. Eva followed close after.

"Stay back, Eva!" Jake commanded as they approached the corner.

The gunshots stopped, replaced by high-pitched screaming that almost didn't sound human. Jake glided to the corner and peered around as the screaming morphed into a wet gurgle.

Eva skidded to a halt behind Jake, slamming clumsily into him.

"Wait here," he ordered, ignoring the impact as a bull elephant might a fly, and stepped around the corner, weapon at the ready in a two-handed grip.

Another high-pitched shriek ensued, slightly muffled. Eva

chanced a look around the corner.

Jake was moving fast down the hall, cautious and controlled, in an almost flowing motion, methodically checking and clearing the side rooms as he went. At the end of the hall, Toby lay slumped against the wall, a crimson cascade of blood flowing down his chest, pooling around him. Jake reached the doorway of the room with Jonathan Winthrop, the civilian, with his gun pointed at a target within.

A flash from the room lit the front of Jake's hazmat suit as a single loud pop echoed down the empty hallway. The high-pitched screaming continued unabated.

"Clear!" Jake shouted. "Eva! Get down here!"

Eva's pulse pounded as she ran down the corridor, through the makeshift airlock and toward Winthrop's room. She winced when she glanced at Toby's twitching body in the hallway next to the door. His throat had been ripped out through his hazmat suit. Cries of terror and pain from the room prompted Eva to abandon him and focus on the injured civilian. From what she saw of Toby, he was already lost.

Entering the room, Eva saw Rodriguez's body on the floor before a large spatter of blood and brains trailing down the wall. Winthrop lay writhing and hissing in agony, covered in his own blood. Several large bites had been taken out of his arm. As Eva assessed the damage, guilt boiled up when she saw the straps on his wrists and legs. *He was helpless,* she realized. *Helpless because of me.*

"Oh my God. He's all torn up," Eva gasped. "Jake, get Dr. Brookings. Hurry!"

†

Arthur rode the stolen bike down Dickenson, towards the supermarket that had served as a staging area the day before. He would have taken his mother's car, but couldn't find her keys. He assumed they were still on her body. A Humvee rumbled in the distance, turning onto Dickenson. Arthur quickly hopped off the bike and rolled it into a bush, uncertain if he would get in trouble for stealing it. He looked down to check his clothing.

Even with the horror of finding Mr. Mullins' body, but not his mother's, the saggy sweatpants had persistently reminded him that he needed to change into his own clothes. He had selected a beat up old pair of his preferred red canvas high tops, jeans and his second favorite tee shirt, which sported a spiral galaxy with an arrow pointing to one of the arms from text that read, 'you are here'. He patted his pocket to make sure he still had a photograph of his mother he had taken from a picture frame. He hoped Max would remember her face if he had buried her, but he took it mostly as a keepsake for himself. Maybe she wasn't the greatest mother in the world, but damn it, she was *his* mother, and through all of their fights, all of their problems, he loved her.

Satisfied he had everything he needed, he broke into a light jog towards the Humvee and waved to get their attention. The vehicle steered towards him, flashing its lights. As they pulled alongside, he forced a smile and stuck his thumb out. He was tired, and wanted a ride back to the airport. He didn't care if they were angry with him. Sergeant Collins and two other soldiers climbed out of the Humvee.

"Didn't we rescue you yesterday?" Sergeant Collins said, incredulous.

"Yeah, I had some unfinished business to take care of."

Collins cursed and looked back at his men, then back at Arthur, then back to his men. "What the hell kind of operation are we running here?"

"Government, what else?" Arthur shrugged. "I could use a ride, if you're still rescuing today."

Collins' irritation boiled over, manifesting in short, jerky movements that Arthur found almost comical. "What the hell were you doing, kid? What unfinished business?"

"Burying my mom, of course," he stated flatly. "I told you I needed to do that."

Collins furrowed his brow. "I recall telling you we'd take care of that."

"You left out the part about it being a mass grave."

"Well, I wouldn't—"

"Not *my* mom, you stupid jerk," Arthur interrupted, pointing angrily. "Screw that! I broke out of the airport last night and snuck home."

Sergeant Collins glared at him for a moment, and Arthur wondered if he'd gone too far with the "stupid jerk" statement, but suddenly the big man broke out into a loud guffaw.

"That was *you?* The guards got chewed out until they 'admitted' they were joyriding on the damn baggage tractor and crashed it. You're saying they really did let someone sneak past?"

Arthur smiled. "They didn't have much say in the matter. The tractor was a diversion and when they ran after it, I snuck out behind them."

Collins roared with laughter. "I admire that, kid. You've got brass in your sack. So you got home and buried your mother after all?"

Arthur's brow furrowed and he looked at the ground. "No. You guys already took her body."

Collins' smile faded. "I'm sorry, son."

"Why didn't you guys clear the other bodies on the street?" Arthur asked. "There was a whole pile of them at one house, and you left them. Just took my mom. Why?"

The sergeant shrugged. "I'm on rescue detail, you'd have to ask the recovery guys; maybe that's where they collected them. But I'm glad we found you all the same. We're on our way back. Things are getting weird."

"Well now *that's* saying something, considering the past few days." Arthur commented, climbing into the open air back of the Humvee. Collins climbed in behind him, followed by a second soldier. "Weird how?"

"We're seeing a bunch of sick people walking around, where I know we already searched for survivors. They don't respond to commands and are hostile. Some crazy son of a bitch got close and we had to blow him away. But he bit one of my men."

"So that's why I'm graced with your company here in the back of the truck?"

"I'm a military man, not an asshole. There's a difference. Private Nguyen has a big chunk taken out of his forearm, and I can give up my seat for that."

"Sarge, about the bites," Arthur said. "Your boy's gonna wig out and–"

"I know," Collins bluntly interrupted. "So does he. He's a damn fine soldier. I hope those Central pricks are as good as they say. Even if they are, I know the odds are against him."

"I'm sorry, Sarge."

"Me too. My job is to rescue civilians, not blow them away. I need to know what they want me to do with these whack jobs. And get my injured man cared for as best we can."

The Humvee lurched forward, and wound its way back through the streets of Greenville.

†

"Can we break for lunch now?" Thomas whined. "Something longer than a cigarette break? I need to clear my nerves. I'm getting seriously creeped out here. And I'm hungry."

"Sure, we can break for about thirty minutes," Connor affirmed. "Then it's back at it, so don't run off or anything."

The crew, including Max, whooped in relief and climbed into the back of the pickup truck. Connor drove them back down the runway to the camp. The thought of food made Max's stomach grumble in anticipation, gruesome work of the day be damned.

"That was some seriously creepy shit, Max," Thomas said. "I swear a couple of those bodies were looking at us. Their eyes moved."

One of the other workers cackled dismissively.

"It was your imagination, Thomas," Max said, trying to reassure him. "It's grim work. A man's mind starts to see things." Max could have used some reassurance himself; he also thought he saw the eyes of some corpses move, and that wasn't the worst of it. Several times, he thought it was Riggins he threw into the pit. Knowing it was an hallucination, he ignored his dead friend's protestations and kept working, imagining himself a body-burying machine. If the military, Central, Arthur or Eva caught wind of his emerging problem with hallucinations, he could become a liability. He was still in control. He knew he was hallucinating, and wasn't acting on what he thought he saw. *Best to keep it to myself for now, but I'm going to have to seek professional help when all this is done.* He smiled grimly at the thought. *Then again, who isn't? Crazy might be normal after this.*

"Yeah, I know it was my imagination," Thomas conceded, "but it was still creepy. That's all I'm saying."

The truck rolled to a stop by the terminal outside the camp and the crew hopped out. Following Connor's instructions, they hosed each other off and scrubbed their suits clean, as many bodies they had handled were slick with blood from whatever violent end they met. They unzipped their suits and stepped out of them, folding them around their boots so they could easily step back in and suit up again. They left their gear in a neat line and walked through the gate and into the camp, winding their way to the dining area.

"Max!" Eva called out from the lunch crowd. She motioned him over.

"Hold my spot," Max told Thomas. He stepped out of line and walked over to Eva. Seeing her lightened his mood, but he saw concern in her eyes. "What is it?"

"Sit, we need to talk."

He pulled out one of the rickety folding chairs they had set up in the makeshift eating area and took a seat. "What's up?"

"I found out a little about the violence they're expecting. It has something to do with the county jail. I couldn't get the whole story, though. There was an... interruption. Maybe I can get more later."

"I bet some inmates escaped in the chaos. Keep working on it, though. It could be important to know. Anything else?"

"Central and the military aren't in full agreement on the course of action, but the military's still in charge. Something about how to dispose of bodies and where to treat bite patients. Didn't sound like a big deal to me, but it was to Central. And better yet, they have a facility nearby. I think that's where they wanted to take the patients."

"Damn, Eva, you're just a font of information. No idea where this facility they're talking about is located?"

Eva shook her head. "Not exactly, but it's an old VOA facility, so it has to be pretty big. Also… Rodriguez is dead."

"And that's a surprise?"

"No," Eva sighed. She leaned forward and lowered her voice to a whisper. "I'm not supposed to tell anyone this, but he jumped up a few minutes later. He took down an armed guard, then attacked another patient. He kept going until Central's security chief put a round in his head."

Max winced. *More casualties. Does it ever stop?* "And the guard he attacked? He got back up, didn't he?"

Eva bit her lip and nodded. "About fifteen minutes later, while I was working with the patient he bit."

"So the whole feigned death thing—"

"Feigned my ass. The patient monitor showed Rodriguez was dead, and Dr. Brookings confirmed that the guard was dead before he got back up and was… killed again."

"With a shot to the head no doubt. Eva, I'm just playing Devil's advocate here. You know they'll say it was a malfunction. You'll have to prove it wasn't. How else do you square it with apparently dead people getting back up?" Max leaned back in his chair, crossing his arms. "Are you going to pull an Arthur and call them zombies? To a bunch of doctors?"

Eva wrinkled her nose. "And scientists. No, of course not. Well… not yet. But a malfunction seems unlikely. I unhooked Rodriguez from the monitor minutes before he jumped up and attacked. Thank God I wasn't there. I was getting a cart to transport his body, or else he could have bitten *me*. But it justifies my take on Peterson being dead back at the supermarket if even the monitor was fooled."

"Congratulations."

Eva's face fell.

"I'm sorry. I know it's been bothering you, and it's great that you didn't make a mistake, at least not one that other doctors and a machine didn't also make," he explained, "but it doesn't change our situation. What does it change about how we're handling things?"

"We're restraining all bite patients now," Eva whispered, grabbing Max's arm and leaning over to whisper, her warm breath tickling his ear. "Captain Jenkins is near death. We're going to leave the monitor attached for a while. I'm going to pull a double shift so I can be there."

"Interesting," Max said. "Let me know what happens?"

Eva nodded and winked at him. "You'd better get back in line or you'll miss lunch."

Max stepped back into line with Thomas.

"Who's the fox?" leered Thomas, looking past Max as Eva walked away.

"Back off, Thomas," Max growled protectively, bumping Thomas roughly with his elbow. He was taken aback by his own response, unsure if he was trying to run Thomas off because he didn't like him, or because he did like Eva. Again, Max felt as if he were betraying Aimee. He realized he wasn't just acknowledging a beautiful woman; he was actively pushing away competitors. It wasn't his place to protect Eva in such a manner. "Sorry, man. I'll introduce you later if you like. Right now I've just got a lot on my mind." *And I'll beat your ass stupid if you bug her after she says 'no'.*

†

Under the watchful eye of Rob, Jake's only remaining

subordinate, Eva watched as the last moments of Captain Jenkins' life played out on the patient monitor, but her mind was elsewhere. She kept information from Max when she spoke to him at lunchtime. As she waited for Captain Jenkins to expire, Eva recalled the events after Rodriguez's attack.

Jake had brought Dr. Brookings, who briefly examined Toby and pronounced him dead. She was helping Eva clean and bandage Jonathan Winthrop's bite wounds when there was a low groan followed by a single thunderous gunshot.

As soon as Toby stirred, Jake executed him without hesitation. It was not lost on Eva that Jake had also fired only once to stop Rodriguez. He knew to shoot them in the head. Dr. Brookings expressed no surprise or alarm when he shot Toby, either, just kept dressing Winthrop's wounds. Eva intuitively felt Central knew more than they were letting on, but had decided against telling Max because she didn't want him to worry. There was no real proof, and once a rumor began circulating, there would be no stopping it. She had to figure things out first, to make sure she wasn't imagining or misinterpreting events. She needed more information, and was right where she needed to be to get it.

Captain Jenkins gasped a few times, then inhaled deeply, and his breath rattled out in a long, rasping sigh. He did not breathe again. The patient monitor next to him beeped an alarm. Eva reached over and muted the alert.

"Get Jake and Dr. Brookings," Eva told Rob as she made a note of the time of death. "Tell them it's time." She double checked the restraints on Jenkins' wrists and ankles, tightening them to satisfy her concerns, as Rob darted from the room.

He returned a minute later with Dr. Brookings and Jake, who had been resting in a side room nearby.

"The captain has died?" Dr. Brookings asked.

Eva nodded. "Just a minute ago. All vitals are flatlined."

The trio watched and waited. Each minute was agony for Eva, waiting to see if her theory held up, if the captain's vital signs would become active again. Five minutes passed. Ten. Fifteen minutes.

The monitor beeped.

"EEG is active!" cried Eva. "There's brain activity! It's weak though. Erratic. A very odd signal."

"How are the other vitals?" asked Dr. Brookings, leaning over the captain.

"ECG is flatlined. No heartbeat," Eva replied.

Captain Jenkins' eyes fluttered open. He snarled and snapped at Dr. Brookings face, inches away from his own, staring at her with cold, empty eyes. He screamed like a wild animal stuck in a trap, struggling against his bindings with such ferocity that Eva took a step back towards Jake, fearful the straps wouldn't hold.

"Interesting," Brookings said amid the cacophony of Jenkins' bizarre rebirth, and coolly stepped away.

"Is he alive?" asked Jake. "I mean, he *was* dead. There's no argument; we can all agree on that point. But is he alive *now*? Did I murder Rodriguez and Toby?"

"No. Your actions saved lives, Mr. Billings. The captain has no heartbeat, which would indicate he's dead. There is brain activity, even if it's minimal – which would indicate he's alive," Dr. Brookings said, brow furrowed. "I've seen people placed on life support for less. But those people generally weren't dead for fifteen minutes beforehand. With no heartbeat, there's no blood flow and the brain dies quickly. Normally." She gestured to Captain Jenkins, raging against his bonds. "Clearly, this isn't normal."

"A friend suggested the virus causes a feigned death before… *this*. What is your professional opinion, doctor? Is he dead or is he alive?" Eva asked.

"If I had to pick one, I'd say both." She chuckled nervously. "I don't even know if that's a valid answer; we're in uncharted territory." She frowned at Captain Jenkins as he growled and raged at her. "Can we sedate him? His carrying on is distracting."

"There's no pulse, doctor," Eva responded. "No pulse means no blood flow. No blood flow, no delivery of medication to the brain.

So no, I don't think we can sedate him."

"You're right, of course." Brookings stood silent for a moment, tapping a pen against her pursed lips, deep in thought. Captain Jenkins continued to rage against his restraints. "I want to keep him as he is, then. Give me an update every hour. As for all the noise he's making, I don't want him upsetting other patients with his carrying on." She turned to Rob. "Gag him."

Rob picked up a pillow and removed the pillowcase. He crumpled it up and tried to stuff it in the captain's mouth, but Jenkins' head was whipping about as he snapped his jaws in fury. "Screw that! A bite put him there, and I'm not going to risk him biting *me*."

"Oh, hell, give it here," Eva said, snatching the pillowcase from Rob. She twisted it into a tight rope of material. Leaning over the captain, she waited for him to focus on her. His head bobbed forward as he snapped his jaws. Holding the pillowcase on each end, she quickly pushed forward as he hungrily opened his maw, and slipped the pillowcase into his mouth. Leveraging her position above him, she pushed his head back into the pillow and gained control of his thrashing head. "I've got him. Now someone go get some duct tape or something and tape his mouth shut. And don't report me to the medical board for this. It's not like I'm duct taping a kindergartner to the wall or something."

Rob darted from the room. Returning a few minutes later with the tape, he peeled off several strips and placed them over the captain's mouth, muffling his groans and screams.

"Well done, Eva," Dr. Brookings said, smiling. "You've got guts."

†

"Damn, you talk too much!" the soldier growled at Arthur as the Humvee drove down Memorial Drive towards the airport. "Do you ever shut up? It's not important!"

"Come on, dude, just answer the question!" Arthur needled.

"Just answer the question," Collins parroted, unable to stifle a wicked grin.

The soldier sighed in resignation. "Fine, whatever. Kirk."

"Damn right Kirk would kick Picard's ass. Team Kirk, one hundred percent!" Arthur held up his fist for a fist bump, but the soldier just sighed again and shook his head.

"I'll take some of that," Collins said, and lightly punched Arthur's outstretched fist. "Kirk's got style."

"Right on," Arthur said. "So what are the best and worst things you guys have seen on your search and rescue so far?"

Collins took the question. "Best? Just after we first hit the streets, we rescued a kid, maybe ten or eleven years old. He climbed into a dumpster to avoid a couple of those freaks. It was on wheels, and they'd been pushing it around a big parking lot like it was some sort of game. He was terrified. The gratitude from that kid was pure gold, you know? Lucky it didn't tip over."

"And the worst?" Arthur asked.

"Dog," Collins stated flatly.

The soldier thought for a moment, sucking on his lip. "Yeah, had to be with the rescue dog. We sent her into a building to locate survivors. Problem is, the dogs couldn't tell the difference between a normal person and one of those head cases," the soldier frowned. "She got all torn up. We had to put her down ourselves. Yeah, that was the worst. That happened to the dogs for other teams, too. We've only got one left, and we don't even bother taking her with us now. No point."

"That sucks," Arthur conceded. He thought about Jasper, cornered in his doghouse, and fell silent the rest of the trip.

The truck turned left into the airport and Arthur hopped out. There were two other survivors waiting for processing.

"I'm Doctor Eleanor Brookings," Brookings started her speech. "I'm with Central Outbreak Response; Central for short or COR for shorter—"

"Been here, heard this before, Doc," Arthur interrupted. "Can I go on in?"

†

Max and Thomas tossed another body into the trench, and headed back to the pile for another.

"Is that... hey, this guy's got a Rolex!" Thomas whispered to Max. He surreptitiously looked over his shoulder at Connor, sitting on the backhoe, and made a grab.

Max slapped his hand away. "Leave it."

"Dude, what the hell? I've *never* had anything that nice, and he won't even miss it." He reached again, and yet again Max slapped his hand away.

"I said leave it," Max growled, stepping close to Thomas in a threatening posture. "Maybe it helps to not think of them as people, but they *were* people. They were mothers and fathers, husbands and wives, sons and daughters. They died. They're not here for you to steal from. What they have gets buried with them, understand?"

"Problem over there?" Connor yelled from the backhoe.

Thomas glanced at Connor, then back at Max, anger flashing across his face.

Max's fists were clenched and he kept his eyes riveted on Thomas as he answered. "No, no problem," he replied. "Just clearing something up."

"Then get your lazy asses back to work," Connor snapped. "Let's finish strong."

Thomas grumbled, but helped Max carry the man's body to the burial trench, and tossed him in.

†

After receiving a righteous chewing out for his stunt, Arthur and David Wright struck up a conversation on a mutual interest, debating the merits and shortcomings of various "Star Trek" captains. They reached the terminal building before coming to a consensus, and David held open the door as Arthur stepped inside.

"So what are we doing here?" Arthur asked.

"We're unhooking the computer systems," David said. "Cataloging all the parts. We're going to use them to expand the armory's network and start hacking into databases. Property tax databases should provide information on who lived where, cross reference that with census data to show how many people were in each house. That should help with search and rescue, and body recovery. We need to know who's missing, how many are missing, who we're burying, stuff like that. Data, data, data."

"We're going to hack local government databases?"

"Yep," David smiled. "Excited?"

Arthur shrugged. "Wouldn't breaking into their offices be more efficient? It's city or county government. They're right here. I doubt the databases are even encrypted. If they are, they're probably eight bit encryption at best," he sniffed derisively. "Heck, they probably keep the passwords taped somewhere on a secretary's desk. And if hack we must, can't we hack something more challenging?"

"Like what?"

"The Pentagon?"

"I doubt the military would go along with that, but what's the Pentagon got that we need anyway?" David asked.

"More population data, I should think," Arthur responded. "Probably classified information on the crisis. And if not, then locations of weapons depots, current satellite imagery and the like." He smiled greedily, rubbing his hands together, "and probably a 256 bit key to crack."

"That'd take longer than the–"

"Age of the universe, I know," Arthur finished. "But you know it can still be done. It's just a matter of processing power. And I'm keen to take a whack at it, since I don't think there's anyone left to get in trouble with."

"Maybe some other time," David said. "Let's walk before we run, and focus on simpler tasks, like disassembling the systems here in the terminal, cataloging the parts, and moving them to the armory." He handed Arthur a clipboard with a notepad and gestured to a small office. "Start there. I'll be down the hall checking with some other geeks, see how they're doing. They're "Star Wars" nerds, and I don't fully trust their expertise."

8

The red orb of the sun stood vigil in the late afternoon sky as the refugees returned to camp from their daily tasks. Back in his tent, Max rolled his aching body into his cot and let out a deep sigh. He was looking forward to a short rest before dinner, and a long one after. He hadn't been as tired since the war.

The tent flap whipped open and Arthur ducked inside.

Max stirred, propping himself up on his elbows. "Arthur! Where the hell have you been? There was some creep looking for–"

"David Wright, yeah yeah, I met him," Arthur said, "he's an idiot. He thinks Picard could take Kirk. Can you believe that?"

"I like Captain Janeway, myself."

"What the? Captain J?" Arthur stamped his feet and spun in a spastic little circle, flapping his arms like a chicken in distress before stopping and glaring at Max. "Don't get me started, dude."

Max chuckled. "Just messing with you. But you owe me a scoop. Where did you disappear to?"

"I snuck out!" Arthur beamed, and recounted his escape, telling Max about the military unwittingly opening the gate and the key box for him, the baggage cart diversion, the stolen bike – he even confessed that it was a girl's bike.

"Good for you, Arthur!" Max laughed. "I didn't know you had it in you! So, did you get her buried?"

Arthur's countenance darkened. "No. Her body was gone."

"Shit. I'm sorry, Arthur." Max felt like a jerk for laughing over Arthur's story, when the escape was over a serious matter for his friend.

Arthur pulled the photograph of his mother from his jeans pocket.

"This was my mom," he said.

"You've got her eyes," Max said, glancing at the picture.

"Do you by any chance remember burying her? Take a good look."

Max studied the photo more carefully, then shook his head. "I buried a lot of bodies today, Arthur, and to be honest I tried not to look at their faces. But she doesn't look familiar. I don't think she was one of them." He handed the photo back.

"You're sure?" Arthur asked, pushing the photograph back at Max.

"Yes Arthur, I'm sure! I could look at it another twenty minutes and my recollection won't magically improve."

"Sorry."

"Me too. I know that the bodies we buried were collected from this part of town, so it's not likely she was one of them." Max collapsed back onto his cot and sighed deeply. "I'm beat. Once dinner is ready, I'm going to grab a bite and turn in early. Eva's working the night shift in the armory, so she won't be around. You're kind of on your own."

"I'll rustle around and find something to do. Sleep tight," Arthur said glumly. He pushed open the tent's flap and stepped outside.

†

Eva gazed out the window as the setting sun touched the horizon. She was exhausted, taking a second shift with the patients, but she'd insisted and Dr. Brookings was accommodating. She was thankful Jake was there as promised, to watch over the patients; more grateful still he was spending most of it with her and not dozing in a chair like Toby. He was broad shouldered and strong, an attractive male presence that gave her a sense of normalcy in a world gone mad.

"Can I get you anything?" he asked, leaning into the room.

"Dinner? You're buying," she responded flirtatiously.

He flashed his broad, toothy smile. "I'd order lobster, but until search and rescue comes back with more chow, we're down to ham sandwiches or MREs."

"I'm not a lobster kind of gal anyway," she replied, yawning. "Ham sandwiches are fine. Or coffee. Really strong coffee."

"That guy friend of yours won't mind?"

"Who, Max? We just met yesterday. He's a big boy, I'm sure he can scrounge up dinner without me."

"That's not what I meant, and you know it," Jake mumbled. "I've seen you two together, talking in the camp. Are you saying there's nothing there?"

"No. Er, yes. I mean, no, there's nothing there. We just met!"

Jake rubbed his chin. "Yes, you said that."

"Well, we've... been through a lot in a short time." Eva sat quietly, gathering her thoughts as Jake watched her expectantly. "Max is loyal to a fault. There are worse traits a guy could have. He's convinced he'll find his girlfriend alive somewhere, somehow. I hope he's right, for his sake."

Jake's eyebrows arched with interest. "Girlfriend, huh?" Silent, tortuous seconds crept between them like an unwelcome guest. It was Jake who spoke, breaking the spell. "How's the new guy settling in?"

"Private Nguyen?" The military had brought in one of their own for treatment that afternoon, a young soldier who had been attacked and bitten while on rescue patrol. "He's as well as can be expected at this point. I can tell he's frightened. He has reason to be."

"And the captain? How's he doing? Sounds like he's calmed down at last."

"Oh, shit!" Eva cried, jumping from her seat as she realized the captain had stopped raging and was quiet. She ran down the hall to Jenkins' room with Jake on her heels. She cracked the door ajar and peeked inside the darkened room.

Captain Jenkins appeared to be resting comfortably, despite the restraints and the gag on him.

Eva pressed her finger to her lips, signaling Jake to stay quiet, and they slipped inside. The monitor was still showing the bizarre readings of weak brain activity and no heartbeat.

Jenkins' eyes were open, staring blankly into space. Eva waved her hand in front of his face. There was no reaction.

"Weird," she whispered. "Hand me your flashlight."

Jake unfastened his small flashlight from his utility belt and slipped it into her outstretched hand.

She clicked it on and shined it in each of Jenkins' eyes in turn. "There's no pupil dilation. Hit the lights."

Jake flipped the switch.

"His skin looks different, too. It's kind of mottled and gray." Eva cautiously reached over and touched his face, then quickly withdrew her hand, looking at Jake with grave concern in her eyes. She then grabbed the captain's hand and tried to move it, but it was stiff and cold. "Rigor mortis."

"How can that be?" Jake asked. "He's got brain activity."

"But no pulse. He's clinically dead already," Eva explained, peeling back the sheets. "Only normally, the lack of blood bringing oxygen to the brain causes it to die. Something else is keeping his brain just barely working, but there's no higher functions." She rolled Jenkins body slightly to view his back. Dark, ugly bruises had formed.

"Blood pooling?" Jake asked.

"Get Dr. Brookings."

†

"You sure are a pretty girl," Arthur cooed to the rescue dog as he ran his fingers through her soft golden fur. She licked his forearm in response.

It broke his heart to see her chained to a fence, largely ignored.

A water bowl and some food were left for her, but her handler was nowhere to be seen. Arthur figured that if no one stopped him from introducing himself to the dog, then no one would care if he did. It was a pleasant way for him to pass the time. Sergeant Collins had told him that the other rescue dogs were killed. She was of no further value in the search and rescue operation, as she would likely be killed as well. Chaining her to a fence, though, struck Arthur as cruel and ultimately, unnecessary. *They use dogs to cheer people up in hospitals.* He smiled at the thought. *She could do that. Maybe I should speak to someone about it.*

"Sure wish you could have met my dog Jasper. He would have liked you. Of course, he had his nuts cut, so I guess it would have been pretty platonic."

"What's your dog's name?" came a tiny voice nearby.

Startled and slightly embarrassed to be caught talking to the dog, Arthur looked up and saw Sarah and Becca. Behind them, Sharon cast a protective eye as she spoke with Mrs. Miller, her motherly radar keeping tabs on her offspring.

"She's not mine," Arthur replied. "I don't know her name."

"I think it should be Lassie," said Becca.

"You're stupid. You think every dog should be named Lassie," countered Sarah.

Becca pouted. "But I like Lassie."

"You've never even seen the show. It's not even the right kind of dog," Sarah said condescendingly. The older of the two and no doubt in her mind infinitely wiser, she took her little sister by the hand and walked closer. "She has a collar. Maybe her name's on that."

Arthur fumbled with the dog's collar and found her silvery tags. He squinted to read them in the gloom of night. "Clara. Her name's Clara."

"Clara?" Sarah wrinkled her nose and shook her head doubtfully. "That's a terrible name for a dog."

Arthur defended the dog. "That's kind of harsh, kid. Maybe

she's named for someone."

"I want to name her Lassie!" Becca insisted.

Sarah rolled her eyes. "Well it's better than Clara. Okay, we'll call her Lassie."

Arthur grumbled. "But her name's—"

"Lassie," Sarah said, glaring at Arthur.

Arthur considered the futility of arguing with two little girls over the name of a dog that wasn't even his. He shrugged. "Lassie it is."

"Can we pet her?" Becca asked.

"Sure, I guess," Arthur said. "But if the army guys tell us to stop, we have to stop, okay?"

The girls walked over and hugged Lassie, who soaked up the attention like a sponge. They spent several minutes visiting with the dog before Sharon called them over, telling them it was their bedtime. Arthur also said goodbye to the dog and strolled back to the camp. Slipping quietly into the tent, he found Max already fast asleep. He crawled under the covers of his own cot fell into a deep slumber.

†

Something clicked or snapped near Riggins, and the alley exploded in a blinding flash of light and heat. Max felt himself airborne, landing hard on concrete and sliding. He cried out as pain lanced through his shoulder, and his rifle was wrenched from his grasp. Reaching back to his shoulder, he felt something wet. Withdrawing his hand, saw thick crimson blood covering his fingers. He brushed bits of Riggins off of himself in revulsion.

Max looked around in confusion, trying to get his bearings. He saw pieces of bodies strewn about. His squad mates screamed a silent chorus, their cries overwhelmed by the ringing in his own ears. Shadowy figures of insurgents moved in the windows above him, taking potshots at the Americans. Max's hands scrabbled desperately for his rifle amid the shattered glass and concrete. His fingers found purchase, and he snatched it from the rubble.

An insurgent poked his head from a window. He was short, with a close-cropped beard, and Max saw a detonator in his hand. Max drew a bead on him and fired. A fine red mist spattered the wall behind his target, who was thrown back into the room from the round's impact, dropping the detonator into the alley below.

Bullets ricocheted angrily around Max as the din of battle penetrated the ringing in his ears. A pair of hands grabbed Max from behind and roughly pulled him into cover in a doorway, out of the line of fire. Max looked up to see Riggins, wide-eyed and splattered with blood.

"Get up, Combat!"

†

Max sat bolt upright in his cot, soaked in sweat, muscles tense. Arthur lay sleeping peacefully a few feet away on his own cot.

He drew a deep breath and slowly blew it out through teeth gritted with rage. His shoulder hurt, and he subconsciously reached back and rubbed it. Peeling back his blanket, Max pulled on his shoes and slipped out of the tent for a breath of fresh air, and to calm his rattled nerves. He looked towards the armory and saw lights in the windows. At lunch, Eva had said she would be staying there for the night, to keep an eye on Captain Jenkins and the other bite victims. He felt comfortable when she was nearby. He couldn't explain why, but he felt protective of her, and couldn't keep an eye on her when she was in the armory. Perhaps it was simply because he had rescued her from the medical school. Perhaps it was something more primal. Max knew he needed time and some space to sort out his feelings, and that her being in the armory for the night would probably be good for him. Aside from one day's work detail, they had spent a lot of time together. *Hell, I'm even beginning to see Arthur as a friend, and I didn't even like the little shit a few days ago. Things change.*

Movement caught Max's attention out of the corner of his eye. He saw, dimly lit by the moon, the form of a man in street clothes stumbling through the camp towards him. *What the hell is he doing? Sleepwalking?*

Several dozen more shambling forms approached the edge of the bivouac from the airfield, with several dozen more slowly trailing through the open gate to the runways that he could just make out under the dim reach of the parking lot lights. *From the mass grave*, his tortured mind told him. He stared in disbelief, his breath caught in his chest.

One of the strangers bumped into a tent, knocking it down. Max heard the occupant swear. The shambling figure fell forward, or lunged, followed by a high-pitched scream of terror and pain that pierced the night air, chilling Max to the bone.

"Eyes up! Alert! Everyone up!" he yelled. "We're under attack!"

Almost as one, the staggering intruders turned to face Max, and lurched towards him.

"Oh… crap." He ducked back into his tent and shook Arthur violently. "Arthur, get up! We're under attack!"

Another scream nearby brought Max quickly back out from his tent as Arthur scrambled out of his cot. Refugees were coming out of their tents, answering Max's alarm, and the intruders were falling upon them like a pack of rabid wolves. Other refugees savagely beat the attackers, to no avail, while still more fled, scattering over the camp in the night, knocking down chairs, tables and tents in their flight.

"What is it?" Arthur asked, bewildered by the pandemonium as he emerged from the tent. "What's going on?"

Max saw an intruder coming their direction stumble against the tent where Sharon and her girls were sleeping, knocking it over. He heard the girls' screams as he and Arthur sprinted to help. Max bent down and gripped the man's ankles. He hoisted the attacker's legs up, dropping him hard on his face, and dragged him away from the tent.

"Get them out of there, Arthur!" Max yelled as he dragged the man, growling and writhing, away from Sharon and the girls.

Reverend Miller and Donna stepped from their tent. Seeing

Max, the reverend ran over to help.

Arthur darted in and helped disentangle Sharon, Sarah and Becca from their collapsing shelter as Max and Reverend Miller repeatedly stomped the attacker, who flailed about trying to grab their feet.

"Where do we go?" Arthur asked.

"The armory!" Max yelled. The armory was closer to them than the terminal, there were guns there, and armed men for protection on top of that. "I'll be there in a bit, you guys hunker down! And find Eva, make sure she's safe!"

"Take my wife, too, Arthur!" Reverend Miller cried, stomping the man's face again. The man's arms waved about, trying to grab the reverend's leg. "Honey, go with him!"

"He's not stopping! We're going to have to find something… here!" Max yelled, ripping a metal support pole from Sharon's collapsed tent. Gripping it tightly, he bashed it across the attacker's face, sending several teeth skittering across the parking lot.

"Good idea," Reverend Miller said, placing one more well-placed kick to the attacker's ribs before abandoning their assault to find his own weapon from the tent.

Unfazed, their attacker slowly rose to his feet and a growl rumbled from his gap-toothed maw.

All the pent up rage in Max boiled over. He smashed the metal pole into the assailant's head, dropping him to the pavement. The hollow pole bent from the impact. Max wielded it like a spear and rammed it several inches into his opponent's eye socket. The eyeball itself dislodged and hung gruesomely from the exposed optic nerve, and still the man came at them. Max snatched the pole from the man's skull, and with a roar of fear, loathing and rage, rammed it back into the exposed brain through the eye socket. The man fell to the pavement, and Max slammed the pole into him again. And again, the deepest strike yet.

A hand grabbed his arm on a backswing, and Max spun to face his next opponent. It was Reverend Miller.

"Max! Stop it! He's dead!" Reverend Miller's face was pale and he regarded Max with wide, fearful eyes.

Max's chest heaved, drawing deep breaths as he refocused on the scene around him. The attacker's brains were seeping out of his eye socket in a gooey, dark crimson mass. Max looked away and swallowed hard, trying to keep from throwing up at the scene.

The supermarket attacker. Peterson and Rodriguez. All stopped with headshots, Max thought. *And the attacker going after Sharon and the girls, stopped by destroying the brain.*

"It's the brain," Max yelled. "You've got to get the brain!"

"Max, we need to go," Reverend Miller whined taking him by the arm. "To the armory, like you said."

"You go, Reverend," Max said, shaking himself free of the reverend's grasp. He could see Arthur, Mrs. Miller, Sharon and the girls, making their way to the armory with a crowd of several dozen other refugees. "You can catch up to them. I've got something I have to do."

Max ran headlong into the mayhem engulfing the encampment. Gunshots rang out as soldiers arrived on scene from their bivouac area and from the security perimeter, ineffectively firing at center mass of their targets, per their training. Max yelled instructions to aim for their heads. As they heard Max's warning, they slowed their rate of fire, targeting the heads. Attackers began to fall, and Max saw more than a few friendly-fire casualties in the carnage.

Some refugees fought hand to hand with their attackers. Max could see many had been bitten, and at least several appeared to be deceased. His eyes trailed up the stream of attackers coming in from the airfield. He saw Thomas struggling with one, desperately trying to ward off scrabbling hands and snapping jaws. Max grabbed the assailant from behind and snapped his neck, unceremoniously shoving the limp body aside. "Thomas, they're coming from the mass graves," he spat in a rage, "They're coming from the fucking graves!"

†

"Blood pooling shouldn't surprise us, as there is no respiration. No pulse," Dr. Brookings said, examining the captain. "Now the patient has the objective symptom of rigor mortis, which of course, is also attributable to lack of respiratory activity." She sighed and examined the patient monitor. "And our EEG *still* shows brain activity."

"Minimal brain activity," Eva corrected. "The same level of activity recorded before rigor mortis set in. Patient hostility is likely to remain unchanged, just in check due to rigor."

Dr. Brookings tapped her pen against her lips thoughtfully, and grunted in agreement.

"So doctor," Eva continued, "what happens when rigor mortis dissipates?"

"Shh! Do you hear that?" Jake interrupted, his brow furrowed.

Eva listened intently, then shook her head. "I don't hear anything."

"I think there's trouble in the camp," Jake said. "I'm hearing gunshots." He stepped quickly from the room and strode purposefully across the hall, with Eva following. They entered Private Nguyen's room, where the window faced the bivouac area.

The private had been sleeping, and was jarred awake when they entered. "What? What is it?" he asked groggily. "Is that–"

"The camp is under attack," Jake announced.

Eva looked out the window, past Jake, her mouth agape with horror.

The camp was in chaos. Refugees ran haphazardly, fighting or fleeing. Hundreds of attackers were shambling in from the airport runway through an open gate, joining dozens more already attacking the camp. Some of the refugees were in full sprint, taking down other, fleeing refugees, even soldiers.

Eva gasped at the sight. "Oh my God. It's like it was in the Medical District. Jake, It's happening again!"

Private Nguyen struggled against his restraints. Central was taking no chances. "Damn it, untie me! I ain't dead yet, and I can still pull a trigger!"

"Easy there, High Speed," Jake cautioned. "One more swinging dick won't change the situation. You're injured and infected, so you stay here. This isn't your fight, soldier." He stepped into the hallway. "This may take some firepower. I'm going to get my carbine. Eva, you stay here with Dr. Brookings. You're going to have a lot more customers and you two need to get ready for them."

Eva nodded.

There was a sudden crash and a surprised scream from Captain Jenkins' room.

Jake cursed and drew his sidearm. He entered the room and fired one shot. "Eva get in here!"

This is ridiculous, she thought as she ran to help, her pulse pounding.

Captain Jenkins' body lay slumped over the side of the bed, a huge splatter of hair, skull, scalp, and bits of brain sliding down the wall behind him. A large pool of blood was spreading on the floor. Crawling away from it on the floor beside him was Dr. Brookings, cradling her arm. She gazed up at them with a wide-eyed expression of shock.

"I... I broke out his rigor to see what would happen. Just one arm! I had to loosen a restraint. Just a little!" Dr. Brookings swallowed hard. "It broke."

"Did he bite you?" Eva asked, kneeling beside Dr. Brookings.

Brookings didn't respond.

"Doctor, did he bite you?"

She blinked and nodded slightly.

"God damn it!" Jake cursed, slapping the wall hard.

"I just broke out the rigor in his arm. He began... contorting and convulsing. It was as if I started the process, and he continued it. He broke even more rigor out himself and grabbed me!"

"Move your hand, doctor. I need to see your arm." Eva examined Brookings' arm, rolling it gently to check all sides. "I don't see a tear in the suit. We'll need to get it off of you to examine the wound itself."

"I think it's just bruised where he bit me," Brookings announced, regaining her composure.

"Even a microscopic tear in the suit could let the virus in. And if there's an abrasion..."

"I'm sure I'm fine, Eva. Really. It was just a close call."

"Scary close. We'll have to keep you under observation until we know for sure," Eva said, gripping Brookings by her good arm. "Get up, doctor. We can't afford to lose you!" She looked over her shoulder at Jake. "I've got this. You go!"

Jake nodded and darted to the door.

"And Jake? Try to find Max and Arthur!"

He turned as he reached the door. "I've seen Max, but who's—"

"Look for the nerd. He'll be with Max. *Go!* Save everyone you can!"

†

Arthur and his charges were swept along in a crush of survivors fleeing towards the armory. Arthur led, trying to thread his way through the surging crowd. He was followed closely by Sharon carrying Becca while dragging Sarah behind. Mrs. Miller brought up the rear, helping Sarah keep up and shielding the girls from being trampled.

Reverend Miller came huffing and puffing through the crowd to catch up, dripping in sweat.

"Michael! Thank God! Are you okay?" Donna asked her husband, rushing to embrace him.

He nodded and hugged her back.

Arthur spun to see the reverend join the group. "Where's Max?"

"He said he had something to do," Reverend Miller said. "I don't know what. He ran off into the camp."

Through the din, Arthur heard a shrill bark. Scanning through the exodus of fleeing refugees, he saw Lassie. She was still tied to the fence, straining against her chain and biting it as hell broke loose around her. Two shambling attackers that had been pursuing the fleeing refugees broke away and stumbled towards her, groaning in anticipation of a meal. In his mind's eye, Arthur saw Jasper retreating into his doghouse as Arthur's mother cornered him and tore him apart. *Nothing deserves to die like that.* He slowed his pace, letting Sharon and the girls pass him, and grabbed Reverend Miller by the arm to get his attention. "Take them the rest of the way, I've got to do something, too!"

Reverend Miller didn't slow down as he nodded a curt acknowledgement, unwilling to argue. "That's a bad idea, son, but okay!"

Arthur turned and jostled his way against more fleeing refugees until he broke into the open.

The two attackers were approaching Lassie. She had withdrawn to the furthest limit of her chain, alternately barking at her attackers and futilely gnawing at the chain which held her. She shrank in fear, whimpering as the first attacker drew near, a slender girl in a nightshirt, with a stump where her arm should have been.

She never saw Arthur sprinting from behind. He gave her a hard shove, which sent her flying past Lassie. She bounced hard off the fence and spun to the ground. She struggled to rise as Arthur skidded to a stop by Lassie.

He put his arms around her and hugged her tight. She was trembling and whimpering, and Arthur was happy she recognized him through her fear.

"I'm here, girl," he spoke soothingly as his fingers fumbled for the clasp of her chain. "I'm gonna get you out of here."

The chain popped loose and Lassie bolted. The second attacker, a man in a mechanic's uniform, made a clumsy grab for her as she darted past, then shuffled after. Lassie zigzagged through and past the surging crowd, towards the armory.

Arthur turned and saw the female attacker almost to her feet, growling at him with an eerily vacant, yet hungry, stare. Arthur kicked some dirt at her. "Bitch."

He turned and ran to rejoin the fleeing refugees, shoving down the mechanic as he ran past. *That'll slow you down.*

†

The soldiers and melee defenders still battled the horde streaming in from the airfield. Max saw the attackers marching in a seemingly endless parade, and knew he had to do something. "There are thousands of bodies there, Thomas. We've got to try and nip this thing at the source." Max looked around frantically, trying to come up with a plan. "You got your lighter?"

Thomas nodded.

"Then come with me!"

Max and Thomas raced towards the airfield. Bullets from the soldiers snapped through the air past them as they ran, making Max question the wisdom of his course of action and hope for a little luck. The attackers were spread thinly, making awkward grabs at them as they darted between them and onto the runway. Max paused to smash his elbow hard against the head of an intruder wearing a light tee shirt, staggering him for a moment. With a great roar of effort, Max ripped the shirt from his victim. He was grateful they were so plodding and slow; had they been as numerous and fast as they were during the attack on the university, the camp would already have been wiped out.

"What's your plan?" Thomas puffed, running behind Max. "To draw them away? Because it's working! They're following us!"

Max looked over his shoulder. A number of attackers were shambling after them. "Fuel truck!" Max yelled, pointing to a large truck on the tarmac, numbered thirteen. He ran to the terminal and found the key box that Arthur had described. Rifling through it, he quickly found the key and squinted in the darkness to be sure it was labeled correctly.

He couldn't tell in the gloom, and held it out to Thomas. "Is that a three or an eight?"

Thomas sparked his lighter, which flared brightly in the darkness, and read the marking. "That's a three. Let's get a move on, huh?"

They trotted to the truck. Max activated the fuel pump and soaked the shirt, then hopped into the driver's seat.

"Give me your lighter, Thomas. Then get on the back and get ready with the hose. I'm not going to stop, just circle the pits while you spray. Then we light these motherfuckers up!"

"Oh, shit, you're crazy, man! This is fucking insane!" Thomas whined, but did as instructed.

The truck lurched forward and sped down the runway. Max tried to avoid hitting their shambling pursuers as he flew past them, more out of concern for the wellbeing of the truck and Thomas being exposed on the back, than concern for the attackers. He couldn't help but smash the truck into several, as despite the headlights, they seemed to materialize from the darkness in front of him in a strobe effect from the runway lights. He grimaced as their bodies bounced off the truck. The head of one split open, smearing its contents on the windshield. Max winced in disgust and flipped the windshield wipers, but it only smeared the gore and made visibility worse.

They approached the mass grave, and Max slowed the truck. Many bodies in the open burial trench were moving, giving a hellish appearance of a twitching, seething and alien mass. *At least they're not all up yet*, Max thought. *We still have a chance.* He leaned out the window. "Okay! Hose them down!"

In the side view mirror, he saw a long stream of jet fuel spray from the truck, into the pit, as he circled it one, two, three passes. He veered wide to avoid a heavyset man who had crawled from the abominable pit.

The engine suddenly roared and the truck lurched forward, slamming to a dead stop, throwing Max forward. The steering wheel smashed into his solar plexus, knocking the wind out of him. It felt as though there were a crushing weight on his chest as he gasped for air that wouldn't come. He realized he was staring at dirt through the front windshield, and guessed the weight of the truck caused one of the mass graves to collapse beneath it.

The driver's side door opened. A bloody hand reached in, grabbing for Max, trying to pull him from the cab.

It's over, Max thought, slapping away the hand but expecting to see the gnashing teeth of the fat man seeking another meal. A bloodied face with long, stringy blond hair thrust into the cab, and Max managed a weak smile. Thomas, injured from the accident, was nevertheless more mobile than Max, who was still fighting for breath.

"Get up, man!" he yelled, reaching in with his other hand to grab Max. "What the fuck is wrong with you? We gotta go!"

Max slapped his hand away again and reached across the seat, trying to find the lighter. He could see it on the floor of the passenger side, and crawled over to get it. His peripheral vision began to dim, giving him tunnel vision, when air slipped into his lungs again. He drew as deep a breath as he could, and the world brightened, if only a little. He still felt weak and slightly disoriented.

"Max! They're right on top of us! We've got to go, *now!*" Thomas yelled.

Max's fumbling hands found the lighter and the shirt. *Get some distance*, he told himself, as he felt the breath of life returning to his lungs more fully, though he still felt weak. He rolled out the driver's side of the cab and Thomas helped him to his feet. The ground heaved and shifted beneath their feet. Max didn't want to think of what they were stepping on as they scrambled from the trench. They ran to put distance between themselves and the truck, perhaps thirty yards away, dodging the grasping hands of abominations crawling from the pits. The stink of jet fuel weighed heavy in the air.

Reaching the ground torn up by their excavation earlier in the day, Max scooped up a fist-sized rock and wrapped it in the tee shirt, leaving a thin tail of material. He sparked the lighter and set the shirt ablaze, then hurled it in a high arc towards the pit.

"*Run!*" Max screamed, shoving Thomas forward.

The two sprinted as fast as their legs could carry them, and Max's ankle throbbed. A fireball exploded into the night sky, briefly lighting up the airfield behind them as the blast wave knocked them to the ground. Max and Thomas were bathed in scorching heat as the inferno raged in the mass grave and engulfed the fuel truck, which was consumed by the hungry flames.

"Yeah! Yeah! Yeah!" Thomas yelled ecstatically as he bounced back to his feet. "Burn, motherfuckers, *burn!*"

He helped Max to his feet, and after glancing about to see that no more attackers were sneaking up on them, they admired their handiwork. Bodies lay burning all around the edge of the pit.

"That was badass! High five, baby! We're heroes!" Thomas smiled, offering his hand. Max slapped it hard in acknowledgement.

"Here's your lighter. Thanks," Max gasped handing it back to Thomas.

"I always thought the smokes would kill me," Thomas laughed nervously. "It was almost the lighter! Man, did you feel that fucking blast wave?"

One of the burning bodies clambered to its feet and stumbled towards them, emitting a tortured groan as the flames licked about, consuming its clothing and searing its flesh. And another. And yet another. Still more boiled forth from the other, barely covered burial pits, like a colony angry ants, twitching in a grotesque display of unnatural power. Silhouetted against the backdrop of the fiery pit, they marched forth as if the bowels of hell had opened and spilled forth the damned.

Max shuddered at the scene playing out before him.

"No way, man," Thomas whined, transfixed. "No fucking way! They should be dead!"

Max remembered Arthur's comment about zombies, for which he had poked fun. He remembered the red-headed spitfire in the Bate building, and the blood trail showing where she dragged herself. Seeing the hellish figures streaming from the pit, reality sunk in. The spitfire dragged herself to the triage room, but was standing when he entered. *She died, and reanimated. Only rigor kept her from killing me.* "They were dead. And I think they still are," Max said softly. "We'd better move." He grabbed Thomas and pulled him along. "Get to the armory!"

Casualties from the first wave of attackers were on their feet, missing arms, bloody stumps, torn out throats notwithstanding. They were taking down the few remaining refugees with the same speed and ferocity of the killers from the campus. Their numbers were bolstered by the shambling, burning figures streaming in from the runway burial site. Soldiers, unable to score consistent headshots against the newly-risen, fast-moving targets, were overwhelmed as the battle shifted in favor of the dead. Those that escaped the surging horde were forced to retreat.

Max and Thomas ran through the chaos enveloping the refugee camp, towards the armory. Max's ankle was still sore from its injury at the battle of the Bate building, and Thomas quickly pulled away from him. Dr. Banerjee, his throat a ragged and bloody mess, roared and sprinted after Max. Looking over his shoulder, Max saw his snarling attacker closing on him. Max focused on a burst of speed to gain some distance, but his ankle twisted from the effort. He stumbled forward, sprawling hard to the pavement.

"Thomas!" Max shouted, looking for help as he rolled to a stop. Thomas kept running for the airport entrance by the armory without looking back. Max rolled onto his back as his pursuer lunged. Sticking his feet in the air, Max kicked hard, bracing for pain in his ankle as he caught Banerjee in the chest. Momentum did the rest. Fingers groped at thin air as the good doctor sailed over him and skittered across the pavement. Max rolled to his hands and knees, desperately scanning his immediate area for a weapon. Banerjee bounced up to lunge again.

Bullets snapped through the air near Max. Banerjee's head jerked once from a bullet's impact and he sunk to the ground.

"This way Max!"

Max scrambled to his feet and limped towards the unfamiliar

voice. He reached the edge of the parking lot near the airport entrance. About twenty yards away he saw a tall, athletically built man wearing a helmetless hazmat suit, wielding an M4 carbine. Max didn't know who he was, but was happy to entertain the possibility he was a guardian angel. He was expertly laying down cover fire for the last surviving refugees fleeing the carnage of the encampment.

"Get down!" Jake yelled as Max approached.

Max dove onto the grass a few feet from Jake as he let loose with another controlled burst of fire. Max could only imagine how many, or how close his additional pursuers were.

"Get inside the armory! Move!" Jake yelled, unleashing several more shots in rapid succession.

Max scrambled to his feet and bolted for the armory. The commanding crackle of Jake's carbine punctuated the chaos as Max dove inside the armory, joining others who made it inside for shelter.

9

"Are you bit?" a soldier yelled as he dragged Max further inside the building and away from the door. "I said *are you bit!*"

Max shook his head as the soldier aggressively frisked him, lifting his shirt, his pants leg, rolling him over looking for bites. Max was so thankful to have made it inside, he barely noticed or cared what the soldier was doing. Sweat dripped down his forehead and his heart thundered like a jackhammer in his chest. His ankle throbbed.

"Here's another one!" yelled a nearby soldier, a squeaky crack in his voice betraying his near-panic as he searched another refugee. It was Arthur's supervisor, David Wright. "I got one that's bit!"

"Let me go! I'm with Central! They can fix this!" David Wright howled in protest as two more soldiers grabbed him by the arms and quickly dragged him down a hall towards the assembly area. *"They can fix this!"*

Max was reminded of events to which he had been a party, with a similar atmosphere. An Iraqi family crying and begging as loved ones were declared terrorists and dragged from their homes. How certain then he had been that they *were* terrorists, that his team had done the right thing. From the other side – being among the searched and potentially accused – the view was less than clear. He had no doubt these soldiers, like himself in Iraq, had surety of action. While he was no longer a soldier, these men were still his brothers and he understood them; he understood their fear. They *needed* clarity of purpose in separating the bitten from the healthy. Max's stomach twisted in knots.

"This one's clean!" the soldier searching Max announced. He helped Max to his feet and shoved him towards another hallway. "Go down there, you're cool." He turned and began frisking another survivor, assessing her injuries.

Jake slipped into the armory with the last of the surviving refugees, who were immediately lined up by soldiers for their bite assessment. "That's the last of them. Lock it down!" he yelled, shouldering his carbine.

Max pushed through the crush of bodies to thank him for the rescue. He wouldn't have made it to the armory without the assistance, and knew it. Beyond his savior he saw that the soldiers had barricaded the armory entrance with the same type of materials the students had used on campus. They chained the last door and slid a heavy office desk in front of it as a mass of shambling attackers streamed in from the airport grounds. More than a few were still smoldering from Max's fuel truck assault, their scorched clothes burned into their cracked and blackened flesh. Several fresh victims ran full speed through the mob, roaring as they hurled themselves into the doors with a ferocity familiar to Max from the attack on the Bate building. Glass doors bowed, rattling but holding firm. The barricade, flush against them, shuddered from the impact.

"Clear the way!" Several soldiers shouted as they arrived with tables and doors they had removed from their hinges. They also brought wooden boards and power tools, and a deafening whine filled the entrance hall as they built a more cohesive barricade structure in the midst of the rough and tumble triage being administered by their comrades.

Max fought through the last few members of the roiling crowd to reach Jake. "I don't know who you are, but you saved my ass!"

Jake clapped him on the shoulder. "Max. Name's Jake. Eva sent me for you." He jerked his chin in the direction of the hallway. "Come on, we need to join the others. The military is getting nervous."

"They're not the only ones."

As Jake headed down the hallway for civilians who passed the military's cursory examination, Max waited a moment to catch his breath and take in the scene around him.

Panicky refugees argued incoherently with terrified and almost overwhelmed soldiers, pushing, shoving, jostling. The few remaining survivors from the encampment were at a boiling point, with attackers thundering a cacophonous rhythm on the doors, held back by a hastily-built barricade that Max knew would not hold long.

He spotted Sergeant Collins nearby, and fought through the pulsing mayhem to reach him. The big man's face was slack, as if from shock.

"Sergeant? Are you okay?"

After a few moments, Collins blinked, regarding him with pained eyes and slowly shook his head. Max realized he was standing next to, and slightly behind a man with a crew-cut and the golden oak leaf insignia designating him as a major, the highest-ranking officer Max had yet seen with the Greenville operation. Collins leaned toward Max and whispered, "You and your friends need to keep clear of this area, along with anyone else you can keep with you. You don't want to be here."

Max shook his head, confused.

"Just try to keep clear and hope everyone cools down," Collins said without further explanation.

The major growled at his underling. "Sergeant, don't you have something constructive you can be doing other than chatting up the local yokels?"

"Yessir," Collins said, glancing an apology at Max. He darted into the crowd to separate a soldier and a civilian that were getting especially physical and about to come to blows.

Max hobbled down the hall to catch up to Jake.

Jake led him, with a handful of other survivors cleared by the military, to a holding area guarded by a wide-eyed young soldier with the name 'Hall' stenciled on his uniform. He was holding an M16 rifle and grinned nervously, nodding as Jake and Max passed him.

Not long before, the room had been a small office and seemed to Max crowded with survivors, until he did a quick head count. He saw no more than two dozen. With those still waiting to be cleared, he estimated there were perhaps thirty or forty non-military, unbitten survivors from the camp of hundreds, plus an unknown number of bitten survivors. The stink of fear permeated the armory, and Max's blood ran cold as he realized the casualties must be near eighty percent.

Thomas punched Max in the arm. "Man, you made it! I got here and realized you weren't with me."

"Yeah. Yeah I made it," Max mumbled. He didn't know if Thomas had heard him cry out for help, or if he had abandoned Max in the mayhem, but didn't like Thomas anyway and didn't want to respond in such a way that he might think they were friends.

"Max!" Eva yelled, smiling as she pushed her way to him through the milling crowd. "Glad you could make it." She was still wearing her hazmat suit, although the helmet was missing.

He smiled back, his relief in seeing her wiping Thomas from his mind. "Well, I wouldn't have if not for—"

"Jake!" Eva cried, gliding to him and wrapping her arms around his thick neck as his arm encircled her waist. "Thank you for getting them back!"

Max's smile vanished and his gaze drifted to the floor. *When did this happen and where the hell was I?* Then he remembered Aimee. It had only been a couple of days of not knowing her fate. Seeing Eva with Jake and feeling jealous, he questioned his own character and his depth of devotion. He took a deep breath, steeling his resolve. *I've still got Aimee out there, somewhere.* He managed a weak smile that felt plastered and artificial on his face.

There was a slight tug on Max's sleeve. Turning, he saw Arthur.

"What's up, dude?" Arthur said, his face shrouded with concern.

"Arthur, you made it, good," Max said, noting a hint of uncharacteristic seriousness to Arthur's demeanor. *Does he know I like Eva? He must know! No, it's Arthur, I'm good – he doesn't know shit.*

"Hey, Combat."

Max's blood ran cold as he once again heard Riggins' voice. He glanced nervously around the room.

Riggins' disembodied voice chastised him, "You barely escaped a horde of freaks and you're thinking of a girl? Get your head on straight."

"How's everyone doing?" Max asked Arthur, trying to ignore Riggins' voice, while accepting the advice as valid.

"I got the Millers here, and Sharon and the girls. And Lassie."

"Lassie?"

"Er, Clara. The rescue dog. Sarah and Becca kind of renamed her." Arthur looked around the room. "I don't see her now, though."

Eva and Jake joined them. "So what's the plan?" Eva asked.

"Right now, we wait. The military is running the show," Jake said before Max could speak.

"Yeah, but we need a plan of egress," said Max. "Those barricades won't hold for long. We know that from personal experience. They'll get in. They will."

Jake responded, "Agreed, but for now, the military is near panic after being overwhelmed like that. They're jumpy and we need to steer clear. As for egress, it's covered. More or less."

"Covered?" Arthur asked. "Want to clue us in?"

"There's only one option, given the numbers outside. The vehicle yard is fenced in and clear, at least for now. We'll have to grab a ride and smash our way out, so there's your egress. I know where the keys are. Once we have them, we'll get in trucks and roll."

Max wasn't sure of the chances of even large military trucks pushing through a crush of several hundred bodies, but at least it was a plan. "'A good plan today is better than a perfect one tomorrow'," Max said, echoing the words of General George S. Patton. "Okay, so one problem down, although we still need to figure where we're going to go. I hear Central has some nice digs."

Jake smiled. "Defensible and stocked with provisions."

"So we'll blow this joint, go back to Jake's pad, kick back with some beer and wait for all this to blow over," Arthur summarized.

"In a nutshell," Jake replied. "Very soon, any place will be better than here. But some places are better than others, and our facility ranks right up there. I also want to know what the military is doing. Feel out our options."

"Right now, they're separating bite victims," Max replied.

Eva nodded. "That makes sense, given what we've seen so far. Speaking of which, Dr. Br—"

"Dr. Brookings is confident we can find a cure for the bites," Jake interrupted, surreptitiously grabbing Eva's wrist, a move not lost on Max.

Eva's eyes searched Jake's face. She lowered her voice to a whisper and leaned towards Max. "Dr. Brookings was bitten. I don't think she was infected through her suit, but there is a slim possibility."

Jake's face visibly hardened and he released his grip on Eva's wrist.

"That's something the military doesn't need to know right now," he practically growled. "Neither does anyone else."

"I think it's critical, Jake," Eva said. "From what we've seen of bite vic—"

The thunder of a volley of gunfire rumbled down the hall.

"Are they inside?" wailed Donna Miller. "Oh my God, they're in here with us aren't they!"

Reverend Miller tried to calm his wife. "Honey, we have to trust the soldiers and let them do their jobs. They know what they're doing. We'll sit tight and we'll be okay. I promise."

"I didn't hear the barricades fall," Max said. "That should be loud. What the hell are they—"

Another volley.

Jake hissed a curse. "That's no breach. It's a firing squad. Volunteers on me! We've got to find that asshole and stop this!" He shouldered his M4 and rushed towards the assembly hall as a third murderous rumble from the firing squad roared in their ears.

"What asshole?" Max asked as he ran after.

"Major Upton!" Jake yelled back at him without slowing his charge.

Private Hall put his hand up and stepped in front of Jake, who rudely shoved him aside. "Stop! Central and civilians are to remain here," he shouted as he took a step towards Jake. The barrel of his rifle tipped up, as if he might be considering an aggressive posture.

Violence of action. The words rang in Max's ears, but with Riggins' voice. Max didn't think; he just exploded, slamming his fist into Hall's nose, dropping him to the ground. He ripped the rifle away as Hall lay gasping in pain and surprise from the sudden assault, reaching to wipe at the blood streaming from his broken nose.

"Sorry, brother. This is not open for discussion," Max said. As he turned to follow Jake, he saw Eva rush to the soldier's aid and begin ministering to his injury. She glared over her shoulder at Max, with an uncertain, accusing countenance. *Good, she'll keep him secure.*

Jake's small group of volunteers, including Max, Arthur, Reverend Miller, Thomas and four other young men, sprinted through the hallway, past the entrance. They ignored the verbal protests of the four soldiers guarding the entryway against the attacking mob, and continued to the assembly hall as the roar of another murderous volley echoed through the halls. They burst into the room through double doors.

If hell reigned outside, it was something worse in the assembly hall as survivors turned on each other. Against one wall, spattered blood and telltale bullet holes indicated the killing zone. In a nearby corner, nearly a dozen bodies of the executed were heaped in a grisly pile with blood pooling around its base. Max ground his teeth when he saw David Wright's corpse among them. *The kid didn't deserve that end, put down like an animal.* In the opposite corner, bitten survivors were clustered under guard, fruitlessly pleading their cases to soldiers unwilling to listen as they dragged away another group of four.

"Stop! Stop this!" Jake yelled, his face red with rage. "This is insane!"

Teary-eyed soldiers looked uncertainly over their shoulders at the intruders, as if grateful for the intervention. Major Upton approached Max's group, flanked by a sullen-faced Sergeant Collins and several armed soldiers.

"Gentlemen, you all need to leave this area immediately," Upton said calmly. "I know it looks brutal. It *is* brutal. But this has to be done."

"Bullshit!" Max roared, spittle flying.

"Don't you get it? These people have been bitten. They *will* become hostile. They are a dire threat to those around them. We have to protect *you* by killing *them!*"

Arthur rolled his eyes. "Translation: we're going to protect you by killing you. That makes perfect sense coming from the people who brought us Mai Lai, Little Big Horn, the U.S. Postal Service…."

"Look at my men!" Upton exploded, glaring daggers at Arthur.

Taken aback by the intensity of the outburst, Arthur ducked his head and shuffled a step behind Max.

Upton continued to berate him, a vein bulging in his forehead. "They're not enjoying this, you snot-nosed little punk! But it *has* to be done! We have to eliminate these threats to save *your* worthless hide!"

"They're not threats, Major, they're people," Jake said, somehow managing a calm and collected front.

"Son, the greatest threats in history were people."

"We're not going to let you or your men murder any more of them. We're going to give them every chance at life. Do you know why? Because there aren't that many of us left. Because your men could have misdiagnosed a bite wound, or because some people might be immune. And because it's the fucking civilized thing to do, Major."

"At least wait until you hear from the authorities," Reverend Miller pleaded, "this can't be right. They can't mean for you to do this!"

Upton glowered at Jake. "Last chance, Central. Get back to your holding area. Martial law was declared. We *are* the Authority."

"When's the last time you heard from Washington?" Arthur squeaked from behind Max.

Upton hesitated. "What?" he said through clenched teeth.

All eyes moved to Arthur, peeking around Max.

"Or Fort Bragg?" he continued.

Upton's tongue darted, snakelike over his lips. "Come again?"

"Well, you say you're the Authority, but you're not, dude. You're just their representative. And when's the last time you got any instructions? I know you've lost contact with Fort Bragg, or you'd be calling in those helicopters that were buzzing the town that first night. I saw them. Why haven't you called them in?"

Max glared icy darts at Major Upton. "Fuckin-A."

Next to the major, Sergeant Collins' face perked up, the first sign of life in the big man.

"W-we've had a communications glitch—" Upton stammered.

"It's true," Sergeant Collins interrupted.

Upton gave him a hard stare in response to his insubordination.

"I'm sorry, sir, but you're on the wrong path here," Collins apologized to his commanding officer, then faced Jake and his group. "Yes, it's true. We've lost contact with Bragg. We don't know why. It *could* be a glitch. Our last orders were to secure the airport and other select locations, protect civilians and dispose of bodies."

"That is enough, Sergeant!" Upton growled.

Collins continued, "I have every confidence that in his mind, Major Upton is still executing those orders, eliminating infected civilians to protect uninfected ones. Tactically, he may even be right in doing so." He turned to Upton. "Morally, sir, you're dead wrong. We need to regroup. Focus on reestablishing contact with Bragg or the Pentagon, if we can. If Central thinks they can care for the civilians – their care, feeding and protection – they should have that opportunity. It's better than *this*," he said, gesturing to Upton's victims. "Sir, we've lost the airport, but may be able to reclaim it. And there are other elements important to our mission. We can only be successful by getting updated intel and orders, if possible."

Jake nodded at Upton, subtly encouraging him to listen to his sergeant. Max wanted to rip the Major's head off for the murders he'd already ordered, but they couldn't be undone. Jake's cool-headed response, supporting Collins and likely echoing the feelings of most of the soldiers, gave the officer an out. Max hoped he would take it. If Upton ordered executions resumed, Max wondered, would his men support him? If so, could he fire on U.S. soldiers? Would Jake? Would it save anyone or just add to the body count? *Please don't make me choose.*

Upton rubbed the stubble on his head. He turned and squinted at his men, and the nearly two-dozen civilians whose fate rested on his next decision. He turned back to Jake and his group. "We leave in fifteen minutes."

Max breathed a sigh of relief.

"Any uninfected civilians who wish to travel with us to Fort Bragg need to be here in ten." Upton barked orders to his men to cover the blood and the bodies, and to secure weapons and ammunition for the trip. He then approached Jake's group again.

"You win, Central. You may yet live to regret it."

"Thank you, Major," Jake said calmly. Almost politically, Max thought. "What about Private Nguyen?" Jake asked. "He's military, but he's been bitten."

"If he comes with us, I'll put him down for the threat that he is, Billings," Upton said coldly. "You're the ones who think you can get cuddly with a killer virus; I suspect he'd rather take his chances with you."

"And the disposition of guns and ammo stored here?" Max asked.

"It's military gear. Given the circumstances, I'll allow you to take whatever we leave."

"Technically, it's the taxpayer's gear," Max replied.

Upton huffed. "The taxpayers are dead. It's ours."

Max felt his face flush and took a step toward Upton, but Arthur intervened. "Actually, we're what's left of the taxpayers, we're not dead yet, and we want our stuff."

"No," Upton replied simply.

"Dude, that's cold," Arthur grumbled.

"That's acceptable, major," Jake said, turning to Max and his other men. "We've got a lot to do and not much time to do it. Getting in a pissing contest over small arms won't help us."

Upton began organizing his men, then stopped for a moment and looked back. "Good luck, Central."

Jake nodded, then led his group, along with the bite victims, back into the hallway.

"Jake, we need more weapons. We can't let the Army take all of them," Max said, clutching his rifle. He genuinely felt bad for the kid he'd smacked, but liked the results. With a gun in his hands, he didn't feel entirely powerless. More guns on his side would make him feel more powerful still.

"We'll get some. It's not an issue."

"Not an issue?" Arthur interjected. "Dude, maybe you missed the newsflash, but there's a couple thousand freaks banging on the doors. Lack of firepower is a definite issue."

Jake countered, "Only if we plan on fighting them."

"We're running?" Max asked.

"On the heels of the military, if we can get everyone organized fast enough."

"Good to go!" Arthur shouted in approval, standing tall and offering a poorly-formed salute.

Max walked over to the victims of the firing squad and examined them briefly. He ground his teeth, fighting back his rage with Upton. David Wright stared back at Max with empty, dead eyes. Blood soaked his shirt and the right side of his forehead was missing, with bits of skull clinging to the ragged wound. The other bodies bore similar injuries. Max's stomach churned at the sight. *At least they knew to shoot them in the head*, he thought.

"Well what are we standing around for? We gotta get everyone moving! Chop-chop!" Arthur said, sharply clapping his hands.

They wound their way back through the halls of the armory. The unspeakable devilry of which men were capable haunted Max. How well he knew that good men could do bad things. In the bloody birth of the new world they inhabited, it seemed there was no room for good men or bad men. Just living and dead ones. Jake spoke, interrupting his thoughts.

"So the military lost contact with Fort Bragg. They were holding back information from us. Who could have guessed," Jake said sarcastically.

"They're not the only ones, though, are they?" Max said.

Jake cocked his head and looked quizzically at Max. "What do you mean?"

"Dr. Brookings' status, for one. Then there's the inmate situation at the jail, and the fact you have a facility nearby. Central has been less than forthcoming as well. Anything else you guys are hiding? If you want to come clean, now would be a good time."

"Yeah, now that we've put our asses on the line for you guys," Arthur added.

Jake sighed and spoke softly. "Keeping the inmate issue quiet was the military's call, not ours. I'm not saying I disagreed with it, but it wasn't my call. I *am* responsible for Dr. Brookings' safety, however, and after seeing what the military did, I think you can understand why I didn't want to relay her status. Yes, she was bitten. She wasn't infected because her suit protected her, but people panic."

"Where is she now?" Max inquired.

"Tending the bite victims. I think it helps keep her focused."

"Well if we're going to work together, we need to work *together*," Max said. "And if Dr. Brookings should become a threat—"

"If Dr. Brookings becomes a threat I'll deal with her myself," Jake snapped. "Max, we've got a full plate. Can we hold off on the penis wagging until we're secure? We have to get everyone ready to roll."

Max nodded while eyeing Jake warily. "Okay. Sure."

The door to the assembly hall opened behind them, and

Sergeant Collins emerged, flanked by two soldiers. They walked quickly to catch up to the group.

"Coming with Central, I presume?" Jake scoffed.

"No. I'm to explain the situation to the other civilians, from the military's perspective," Collins said, looking at Jake. "Just to make sure they understand *all* of their options here."

†

"We're going to take the military up on their offer, and go with them," Reverend Miller stated flatly. Donna stood meekly by his side as he explained their decision. "They're the United States Army. They're the official voice of the government, the official voice of the nation, and they deserve our loyalty."

"And they have more guns," Donna chimed in. "We feel safer with them."

"Wake up Reverend," Max said. "You didn't think they'd announce the end of civilization on the evening news, did you? I don't think there is a United States. Not anymore. This is a medical war, and it can't be won with guns and bullets. Central has the best chance of finding a solution to this plague, the best chance of restoring some sense of normalcy, or at least providing a platform for recovery."

"The CDC can do that," Donna argued.

"The CDC isn't here," Max countered. "Central is. If the CDC is still active, they're scattered, or being overwhelmed in the larger cities. Look at the devastation in Greenville, North Carolina! Imagine what New York or Philadelphia are like now! Come with us. With Central."

"I've made up my mind, Max." The reverend reached into his pocket and withdrew a small, leather bound volume. "I want you to have this. It's my Bible."

"Reverend," Max grimaced, reaching slowly for the reverend's gift. He wasn't sure about God's existence and the subject made him uncomfortable. Poring over the Bible wasn't how he envisioned spending his time in the dystopian nightmare that had engulfed his world. There was too much to do just to survive. He swallowed hard and took the book anyway, feeling obligated to be polite. "Thank you. But don't you need this?"

"Not as much as you. Don't worry about me, I'll find another one. I know you're not a believer. You're also a smart young man, Max, and you have a curious mind. You're always looking for answers and trying to find the good in the world. Well here it is. All I ask is that you never stop considering the possibility that the Bible is exactly what it purports to be."

"Seek and ye shall find, huh?"

"No, just seek. It's not my job to save your soul, Max. Only Jesus can do that. My job is to let you know salvation is available. Faith is a journey, not a destination."

"Huh. That's how I look at life, Reverend."

Reverend Miller smiled. "Then you have a head start."

They shook hands and parted ways.

All healthy, unbitten survivors were gathered in the assembly hall, where the grim evidence of Major Upton's folly was poorly concealed by blue tarps with blood pooling around them. Max felt that Upton's victims deserved to be buried, deserved to be remembered – deserved justice. *Maybe justice is folly in this dead world*, Max thought. *Or maybe justice must be fought for, pried from the hands of the dead – or the hearts of the living.* He made a vow to himself, never to forget David Wright, or Upton's other victims, and to mete out justice upon Upton if ever the chance presented itself.

The soldiers rolled up the great steel door in the assembly hall. Eight soldiers in two man teams trotted into the vehicle yard to find trucks that matched their keys.

Max heard one groan from the dead on the outside of the fence grow to a chorus. He took a tentative peek at the source. They saw food in the yard and were clawing and biting at the chain link fence. It creaked, rattled and bowed from the weight of their swelling numbers.

Max motioned for his friends to join him. "How many do you think are out there?" he asked.

"I make it anywhere from eight to twelve hundred," Jake replied, looking over the gathering horde.

"Too many for the trucks to move through?" inquired Max.

"Don't know. Regular people, no problem. They have a sense of self-preservation. These aren't regular people. That many hostiles are going to–"

"*Zombies!*" Arthur interrupted. "Call them what they are! They die, they get up, they eat the living. They're not 'freaks', 'psychos', 'headcases' or 'hostiles', they're zombies *of course they're hostile!*"

Jake nodded at Arthur as if to concede the point. "Fair enough. That many *zombies* are going to crowd in on the trucks. I'd think the first truck should have the hardest time, the others should roll through without too much trouble."

"Unless the zombies work together and roll one," Arthur mused.

Zombies. The stuff of movies and costume parties had become brutally, horrifyingly real. Max recalled the utility room in the Bate building, where they had difficulty working together to remove a simple barricade. "I don't think working together is their strong suit, Arthur. Sheer numbers, brute strength, inability to feel pain or fear and single-minded determination are."

Arthur rolled his eyes. "Well that beats the garbage we have in our hand, don't you think? I mean, what have we got?"

"The ability to think," Eva replied simply. "To strategize, to learn, to adapt, to work together."

Arthur cocked his head and grinned at Eva. "We're gonna hose the bastards."

The first two trucks backed up to the armory loading dock and their heavy metal tailgates slammed down like hammers on an anvil.

"Civilians! Load up in the right truck! Military! Alpha team load up in the left, Beta team cover! Move!" Major Upton roared.

The civilian split was predictable to Max. Those with families, or remnants of their families, went with the Army, as their weapons and training promised greater security and stability. The Millers, Sharon and the girls and over a dozen more scurried onto the truck, fear evident in their wide eyes and the silence with which they moved. As Sharon and the girls boarded the truck, Becca looked back and waved.

By contrast, the civilians staying with Central were predominantly younger, singles or couples without children. Some had lost friends or family to Upton's insanity, and couldn't bear to be near the man or his men.

Soldiers loaded ammunition boxes and weapons onto their truck. The soldier Max punched in the face glared at him as he boarded the truck, and Max patted his rifle in response.

Sergeant Collins approached Max.

"Newsome." Why don't you and your friends come with us? We can use you, soldier. You belong with us. You and Jake both."

"I served my time, Sarge. I'm not one of you; not anymore. Sometimes I'm not sure if I ever really was," Max replied. "The Army made me a killer, but it's not my nature. I've paid a price for it."

"We all have, son."

"Why don't you come with us instead?"

Collins smiled wistfully. "I've got to get back to Bragg. My family is there. I have to know what happened to them."

"Come on Sarge, you know damn well what happened. You know what you'll find. Do you really have to see it to…." Max's voice trailed off, and his eyes drifted to the floor in shame. *The same could be said for you searching for Aimee*, he thought. "Yes, I guess you do, Sarge. I'm sorry. I wish you luck. I hope you find your family."

The big man smiled sadly. "You people take care of yourselves. Once we find out what happened at Bragg, we'll try to get back in touch. Communication is key. You guys figured out where Central is going?"

"Jake says they have a defensible location stocked with supplies. An old VOA site outside of town."

"Unfortunately, there aren't a lot of supplies," Jake added quickly. "It was supposed to be a major supply depot for our East Coast operations, but we never got it fully stocked before this all came down."

Collins nodded. "We've got a small team holding VOA Site B," Collins said. "It's the only one of the three that is still active. Like I said, communication is key. Stay safe, Central. Hooah?"

"Hooah!" Max enthusiastically barked in reply. *Old habits die hard.*

Collins offered a salute, returned by both Max and Jake, and he boarded the truck.

The first two trucks pulled away from the docks, lining up to start forming the convoy, and were replaced by the next two backing up to the armory.

"I'm not happy with the interest all this activity is generating," Jake said, peering at the gate from the loading dock. "We should grab our trucks now. Get the bite victims and start loading them up if we're going to follow the military out."

A man's scream erupted from the corner of the assembly hall. Lassie barked ferociously, but backed away, tail between her legs. Max and Jake sprinted to the source of the commotion, rifles in hand.

David Wright and another of Upton's victims lay on top of the major, holding him down as they tore large chunks of flesh from him with their teeth. Shots rang out. David Wright and his zombie friend collapsed again, bits of skull and brain sprayed across the floor of the hall.

"What the hell, man?" Max exclaimed. "They shot those guys in the head earlier! I looked!"

"People can survive being shot in the head, and they use more of their brains than these… *zombies*," Jake shook his head in dismay. "I guess they missed hitting the right bits."

"Damn straight, 'zombies'," Arthur said, clearly pleased that his nomenclature was sticking. "But the 'right bits'?"

"The brainstem. The basic motor of the body."

Upton groaned as he was helped to his feet by two soldiers.

"Oh my God," he whined. Upton looked at the blood soaking his uniform, dripping onto the floor, incredulous. Angry. "I've been bitten!" he roared, his face flushing with rage. The two soldiers took a few steps away, either from fear of his temper, or the virus now certain to be coursing through his veins. *"I've been bitten!"*

The poetry of Upton being bitten, by his own victims no less, was not lost on Max. But there was more. Max took note of Upton standing in his own killing zone, where he had ended so many lives only minutes before.

Max silently raised his rifle and sighted down the barrel, setting the crosshairs on Upton. *It's justice*, he thought. His heart beat faster as he clicked off the safety.

"Max! No!" Eva screamed.

Upton turned to face him. He paused a moment as the realization of what was happening set in. His eyes flicked from Max's face to his rifle and back again. "Do it," he growled.

"No, Max! Please! You can't do this, you're not a murderer!" Eva pleaded.

Memories flooded Max's consciousness, memories of killings and retribution in the war. Memory of an Iraqi child detonating a suicide vest at a checkpoint near him. Memory of Riggins being blown up by an improvised explosive device. Memory of a smooth-faced Iraqi teen in the window, holding a remote detonator. Tears blurred Max's vision as he tried to focus on his target. *I'm not a killer anymore*, he remembered telling Arthur back on the rooftop.

Riggins' voice rang in his head. "You can never go back, Combat. You *are* a killer. You've killed for less than *justice*."

"You're not a murderer!" Eva repeated.

"You don't know shit about me, Eva."

"Do it soldier!" Upton roared.

I am a killer. Max exhaled and slowly, purposefully squeezed the trigger.

"Holy shit," Jake swore incredulously as Upton's lifeless body slumped to the floor. He grabbed Max by the shoulders and spun him to face the door, then gave him a rude shove. *"Fucking run!"*

Max's shoes squeaked and pounded a rhythm on the concrete floor as he ran. He heard yelling and the clatter of weapons being readied echoing in the assembly hall behind him as he ducked into the hallway. He ran to the main entrance, where four soldiers still stood guard.

"Hey man, what's going on? We heard gunshots!" one soldier asked.

"Zombie, or whatever you want to call those things. It got the major. You're needed in the assembly hall. Now," Max said, hoping adrenaline and fear didn't betray him. "Go on, I'll watch the barricade."

"All of us?" said another. They were already moving in the direction of the assembly hall, eager to see what the commotion was about. They needed little prodding.

Max nodded, and the soldiers sprinted past him. He considered the potential problem they could cause for his friends, entering the assembly hall behind them, and raised his rifle, aiming at their backs as they ran down the hall. *No. No, they're not my enemy.* He lowered it again and exhaled a shaky breath. He was concerned that he may have regrets whether or not he pulled the trigger, but regret was a matter of degree. He shouldered his rifle and looked at his hands, shaking with adrenaline and fear. It wouldn't be long before they knew the truth behind the gunshots. He wanted to hide, but knew that with the dead outside he was trapped. It would only be a matter of time before the military found him; they had only to search. He opted instead for a defensible position in the event they came back for him, to make any effort to get him too risky to pursue.

He glanced at the press of dead flesh outside the entrance. *We are so screwed.* Max grunted with effort as he dragged an unused desk from the barricade construction across the tile floor, placing it in the hallway to provide additional cover. He took a position around the wall. He knelt and sighted his rifle down the hallway. *Wish I had a grenade or two.*

Max heard shouts and raised voices. He could hear Jake and Eva making impassioned pleas, but couldn't make out exactly what they were saying. Some yelling in response. A squeal from Arthur. Loud banging, echoing from the cavernous assembly hall. Tires squealing. A crash. Eva screaming, followed by the throaty staccato bark from an automatic rifle firing in quick succession.

Max's heart leapt into his throat. He stood, shifting his weight from one foot to the next, uncertain if he would be a hindrance to his friends if he charged in, or able to help. He made his decision. Gripping his rifle, Max charged down the hall as he heard more loud metallic banging and shouts.

The door to the assembly hall flew open, and Arthur scurried into the hall, followed by Thomas.

"Thanks for that, Max," Arthur said in mock joy upon seeing him. "Seeing you blow that dude away was an enjoyable experience. And staring down gun barrels after was exhilarating. *I peed my fucking pants!*" he gestured to his crotch, where a wet stain had formed.

Jake stormed into the hallway. "*Moron!*" He grabbed Max by the collar and slammed him against the wall. "What the hell were you thinking?"

Max felt his adrenaline spark from the physical contact, but kept himself under control rather than push a bad position with Jake. "Justice," he replied calmly. "For all of those innocent civilians whose only crime was being bitten. Now get your hands off me before I take it personally."

Jake tightened his hold on Max for a moment, sizing him up, boring holes into him with the intense anger in his eyes – then released him.

Eva slunk into the hallway, eyeing Max fearfully. "You murdered that man. Murdered him in cold blood."

"You didn't see what he did to the bite victims, Eva," Max explained, tugging his collar straight. He gestured to Jake, Arthur and Thomas. "We did. What I did was justice for a lot of people. That son of a bitch deserved it."

"Did he, Max?" Jake asked, veins still popping out in his neck. "Who made you God?" Jake bit his lip and continued more calmly, but his hands were shaking with rage. "Look, Upton was bitten. He was a dead man walking. I'd have shot the son of a bitch myself, but goddammit, Max your timing was shit. Killing a major in front of his men? Fucking stupid. He was dead anyway from the bite; there was your justice. We're lucky it didn't turn into a bloodbath in there."

"What happened?" Max softly asked.

"I talked them down. Some of them agreed with what you did. Seems they didn't take kindly to Upton ordering them to kill civies in the first place, and saw it as a justified fragging. Others thought bite victims *should* be shot, no matter if it was Upton. Others wanted to kill you, and even us, but they backed off since they didn't have the support of their mates – lucky for us. There was confusion. They all saddled up and dee-dee'ed. I mean hell, Collins was already on the first truck, so killing Upton decapitated their command and control."

"Almost literally," Arthur added. "And they didn't get the gate closed when they bailed."

Jake nodded, a grim smile on his face. "Zombies flooded the vehicle yard. A couple of the fast movers got into the building before we could close the loading bay doors, but I managed to put them down."

"We're trapped, Max," Thomas said, joining the party berating Max. "Can't even get to a truck now."

Jake shook his head, incredulous, and whispered. "Moron."

"I'm sorry," Max weakly offered. He thought it best to let everyone vent, rather than defend his action, though deep down, in the core of his being, he believed it was the right decision. He felt his only mistake was not consulting others first, making it an individual's act rather than a group decision.

Jake continued. "Half the people who were going to stay with us left with the military after seeing what you did. They didn't want anything to do with you, or us. Do you realize that in this new world, more people means greater strength? *Population is power!*"

Max looked at the phalanx of the dead clawing at the barricaded entryway, vanguard of a fearless army of potentially billions. "If you're right, then a dozen more survivors won't make any difference."

10

Once the survivors with Central calmed down and accepted Upton's murder, their attention turned to their own survival, for the dead did not rest. As they massed against the armory in ever growing numbers, the living huddled in a side office and bickered over their next course of action.

"Isn't there someone we can call?" asked Eva.

"Nine-one-one isn't answering, Eva!" shouted Arthur. "Even the military bugged out! There's no one left to answer!"

"What about Central?" Eva suggested. "There's a whole network designed for communication and response. Surely there's a way to get in touch with your superiors. Dr. Brookings?"

Dr. Brookings looked up from the notes she was studying. Her chubby face had taken on a disturbing hue. Stress and fatigue made her look almost gaunt. "We can't get to the RV. That's our lifeline to COR headquarters in Kansas, but it's surrounded by those... things."

"Zombies," Arthur mumbled, rubbing his brow. "What is so difficult about saying the word?"

"Even if we did get someone to the RV," Dr. Brookings continued, ignoring Arthur, "the value is questionable, because they'd never get back. The horde would close in on whoever went. They'd be trapped out there."

Arthur chimed in. "We still have the Internet, at least until the power plants start going offline. You had us build out that network for a reason, doctor. Let's use it. You've even got video if you want it. Heck, just an email saying 'get us the hell out of here' couldn't hurt."

"Hell yeah, Doc," Jake said. "I say we give it a shot. Let Gray know what we're dealing with, anyway, and get his input. Ring him up. You've got all the info you need, right?"

Dr. Brookings nodded and pocketed her notes, patting them for assurance. "Okay then."

The small group headed down the hall to a makeshift computer room Arthur and David Wright had set up the day before. Dr. Brookings disappeared inside, closing the door behind her. Jake stood guard outside, his arms crossed. His posture communicated perfectly: *you're not getting in.*

"What the hell, Jake?" Max complained. "I thought we were a team here. We've all got skin in this game."

"Trust me, Max, this moment of privacy is as much for you as it is for Brookings. Cyrus Gray can be a bit... odd."

"But we may have something to add," Max argued.

"No."

"Shit, you're just as intractable as Upton," Max sneered.

"Come on, let's just go," Arthur said, tugging at Max's sleeve.

"This is bullshit, Jake," Max griped as he turned to follow.

They rounded the corner and Arthur ducked into what looked to be a sparsely furnished side office, perhaps for the command officer's administrative assistant. Arthur darted smoothly behind a desk and sat at a computer.

Max followed. "Arthur, this isn't the time for solitaire. What are you doing?"

"Breaking the law, but you're not going to tell on me."

"What do you mean?"

"Dude, I built the network here. More specifically, I patched her workstation into the existing network, but it's almost the same thing since I had to give myself administrative rights."

"Don't you need passwords and stuff?" Max asked as he and Eva crowded behind Arthur for a better view of the computer.

Arthur pulled out a drawer nonchalantly and tapped his finger against a slip of paper that had been taped inside. "Some people don't properly appreciate security. They get what they deserve. I'd have gotten in anyway, but they made it easy."

"Okay, so what are you doing?" Max asked.

"Hacking her webcam."

Max scratched his head. "And that will let us… do what exactly?"

"We'll be able to see and hear everything Dr. Brookings is doing."

"You can do that?" asked Eva, wide-eyed in amazement.

Arthur nodded. He looked pleadingly at Eva. "Just don't tell Jake, okay? That dude would totally fuck me up." Arthur's hands were a blur, clacking on the keyboard, and Max's eyes couldn't adjust to what he was seeing on the screen as windows popped open to show what to Max was cryptic information. Arthur would type commands and move to another program.

"I'm uncomfortable with this. It's like eavesdropping," Eva said. "She has a right to privacy."

Max replied, "Hell if she does. What about our rights? Central has been keeping information from us since we got here. What about those evening updates they said we'd get? We never heard squat."

"We were only here one night," Eva defended.

"They've been treating us like mushrooms, keeping us in the dark and feeding us a lot of shit," Arthur added.

"Okay, yeah, you're right. And we might not get another chance."

Max looked at Eva as Arthur sped through windows and programs. She made eye contact but didn't smile, her eyes distrustful, accusing. *Upton is dead. I killed him. Get over it, woman*, Max thought.

"Ladies and gentlemen, boys and girls! Here! We! Go!" Arthur dramatically announced, striking a final key with a flourish.

Dr. Brookings' face appeared in one window. The sallow face of a man appeared in another. He was thin, perhaps in his early fifties, with graying hair slicked back. His sideburns were a blazing white.

"Look, Reed Richards," Arthur commented.

"That's Cyrus Gray," Eva said. "He's the director of Central Outbreak Response."

"Well, he looks like Reed Richards."

"Who's that?" asked Eva.

Arthur rolled his eyes and sighed. "The lack of cultural awareness in this room is astounding."

"What?" Eva whined with feigned offense.

"Mr. Fantastic of the Fantastic Four. You know, Invisible Woman, the Thing, Human Torch.... Dude reminds me of Reed Richards, a.k.a. Mr. Fantastic. But older. And maybe constipated."

"An older, constipated Reed Richards?" Max smiled. "Can Stretch *get* constipated?"

Arthur shrugged. "At least you know his nickname, Max. There's hope for you yet."

Audio, slightly out of synch with the grainy and choppy video, started to play, focusing their attention.

Dr. Brookings was speaking. "-minimal brain activity, but no respiration. No pulse. They exhibit blood pooling and rigor mortis."

The man maintained a steely countenance. "Yes. Fascinating, is it not?"

"It's not fascinating when several thousand are at our door."

"Don't be dramatic, doctor. Your bunker is well-stocked and secure."

"We're not *in* our bunker, Cyrus."

"Why not?" Cyrus spoke in a measured tone, scowling. "Doctor, I told you to grab the civilians and evacuate the airport at the earliest opportunity. It's a deathtrap."

"We were unable to comply. The damned military was in charge and wouldn't let us go, much less 'grab the civilians'. They wanted the airport."

Cyrus steepled his fingers and sat quietly for several seconds. "That is unexpected. And unfortunate. I always liked you, Dr. Brookings. Strong will, dedicated."

"I-I did manage to get a handful of our people out under the pretense of a supply run during the downtime, but the rest of us are trapped in the National Guard armory with the other civilians."

"At least you got a few people out. The Greenville operation isn't a complete loss."

"Not a complete loss? You're giving up on us!"

"You're trapped, doctor. Surrounded by thousands of virally animated corpses. Unless you exaggerated, which is not something to which you are prone. What do you expect me to do?" he asked pointedly.

"Tell me you have an emergency evacuation plan to get us the hell out of here!" Dr. Brookings cried, fear evident in the rising pitch of her voice.

Cyrus maintained his steely monotone. "I would never lie to you, doctor." He leaned closer to the camera. "If you can make it to your bunker, you can survive long enough for most of the animated corpses to rot away. For your immediate predicament, however, you are very much on your own. I am sorry."

"You mean we're dispensable. The entire Greenville staff."

"The survival of our species is at stake. Everyone is dispensable, doctor."

The door to the office opened. Jake entered the room and circled around the desk to view the monitor. He shook his head and scowled. "I thought you gave up a little too easily on our argument. Turn it off."

"Should have had a game of solitaire running, and alt-tabbed to it. Sorry, guys," Arthur mumbled in apology as he clicked off the monitor. Jake escorted the trio from the room. They made their way back down the hall and waited outside the computer room. Max felt like a kid being sent to the principal's office.

"I give you points for creativity, eavesdropping on Dr. Brookings like that," Jake admitted, almost admiringly. "Still, chain of command is necessary. You understand that, Max, better than the others. Groundpounders don't listen to generals talk. They'd have trouble following orders if they did. Like making laws, or sausage — it isn't always pretty."

Max bristled. "Come on, Jake. We didn't sign up to be grunts for Central. We got drafted. And we're still here because we chose to be, remember? We could have gone with the military."

"Until you blew away their commanding officer," Arthur corrected. "That kind of screwed that option for us."

"Can it Arthur," Max hissed over his shoulder before turning back to Jake. "We're working *with* Central, not *for* you. You've got to cut us some slack."

"I am, Max. I'm not going to tell Dr. Brookings what you three did. Mostly for Eva's sake."

Eva clasped her hands in front of her and gazed at the ground.

"But I like the plan that guy laid out," Arthur said cheerfully. "Just like I said earlier; we go to your place, kick back with a few brews and wait for this whole thing to blow over. I just didn't expect your place to be a fortified bunker. That rocks!"

"Why, Jake?" Max questioned. "I mean, a warehouse makes sense, storing medical supplies for distribution. But a bunker?"

"It has certain defensive advantages. 'Bunker' is too strong a word. I prefer 'compound' myself, for stockpiles of supplies, and staging for the entire East Coast of the U.S. Almost six square miles of fenced, cleared land in an area with very few people. We'll be able to see anything coming well before it gets to us, and the buildings we're in are far enough away that we can move around without attracting too much attention."

The group arrived outside the room Brookings was in, and waited.

"And where's that Reed Richards guy?" Arthur asked.

Jake smiled knowingly at the reference. "Cyrus Gray. He's in Kansas, where Central's headquarters is located."

"How many other facilities does Central have?" Max asked. "Where are they located?"

"Anywhere land is cheap. Nearest to us are facilities in Kansas,

Oregon and Panama, but there are a total of twelve Central supply depots scattered around the world."

Dr. Brookings opened the door and joined them in the hallway. She let out a deep, resigned sigh. "I spoke with Cyrus. There's nothing they can do for us here. We're on our own."

"So we're hosed," Arthur dejectedly observed.

"Not necessarily," Brookings said. "I've been thinking. They are drawn to activity. Noise or movement, probably both. So if we stay quiet and away from windows, they may begin to wander off. Then we can slip out of here and drive back to our bunker."

Jake shook his head. "I don't like it, doctor. It relies on our adversaries doing something, which takes the situation out of our control. We don't know enough about them to predict how they'll respond. But since we don't have the firepower to blast our way out of here, I see no other option at this time."

"Remember when I said lack of firepower was an issue?" Arthur clucked. "Take note of this moment. Breathe deep and revel in it. Bottle it up and save some for later."

"Can it, Arthur," Max grumbled. It was only a matter of time before Arthur pressed the wrong button on someone like Jake, and he'd end up a small stain on the floor. "I'll find us another option, Jake. Shit, I'll *make* one if I have to."

"Fine, you do that. Just stay out of sight, away from the windows, and keep quiet," Jake warned.

Max snatched up his rifle and stalked down the hallway with Arthur following close behind.

"You've got something cooking, don't you?" Arthur asked as they walked. "Tell me you've got something cooking. What do you have in mind? It better be good."

"Nothing, Arthur. I'm hoping inspiration will strike," Max said curtly. "I'm not big on sitting around waiting for the inevitable."

The two of them took a seat on the floor near the armory entrance with their backs propped up against the wall.

"You know the barricade will fall, right? Just like at the Bate building," mused Max.

"Of course."

"And instead of preparing for that certainty, we're sitting quietly in a herd – like we did in the Bate building – hoping the zombies get bored and wander off," Max continued.

"Mmm-hmm."

"Is it just me, or does that also strike you as a particularly stupid course of inaction?"

"Yep. Really stupid."

"Do you have any suggestions as to what else we should be doing?"

"Beyond the general and generic 'get the hell out of here', no. But I'm thinking on it."

"Good. *Keep* thinking on it."

In silence, they listened to the cacophonous pounding of the dead against the windows for several minutes. Max idly picked at the strap on his rifle, until the relentless noise started to give him a headache. He decided conversation, even with Arthur, was preferable to the aural torture of the attacking mob.

"I don't think I'll ever find Aimee in all this. I know she's… probably dead," Max said softly.

"Probably," Arthur mumbled in agreement.

"That's not the answer I was looking for."

"What did you want?" Arthur asked.

Max rolled his eyes. "Oh, I don't know, Arthur. Something uplifting? Something to give me hope?"

"Come on, dude. It's me! Look, you knew the odds were against her back on the rooftop, you just couldn't accept it. You've fought it every step of the way, given her every chance. You think if you want it badly enough, fight hard enough, that you'll be good enough to impose your will and make things turn out the way you want. The world doesn't work that way. Not the way things were before, and not the way they are now. How's that old song go? 'Sometimes you're the windshield, sometimes you're the bug.' I always liked that tune.

Well, until now, since we're definitely the bugs in the analogy."

Max ground his teeth in frustration.

Arthur continued, "But if you want my advice, Max, it's that you need to make peace with her being gone, and not just for yourself. Maybe you haven't noticed, but people around you have come to depend on you. I seriously doubt I'd be alive if it weren't for you. So gird up your nutsack and give yourself a reality check, because we're in a jam right now, and we need you here. One-hundred percent *here*, not in la-la land chasing a ghost."

"You have a way with words, Arthur."

Arthur shrugged. "It's a gift."

Max cracked a smile. "Get out of here before I thump you."

"I'm going to see if I can find Lassie. I haven't seen her in a while." Arthur stood up, his knees cracking as if in complaint, and wandered down the hall, leaving Max alone with his thoughts. At length, Max stood and shouldered his rifle. He swallowed hard, choking back the lump in his throat, and looked around the corner at the roiling mass of the dead pounding the windows. *There's no way she survived. She'd have been in the thick of it, trying to help people.* He ducked back behind the corner, and sighing deeply, whispered "Goodbye, Aimee."

A loud pop echoed in the entranceway. Max peered around the corner again, and saw shattered glass sprinkled under the barricade. The glass doors and windows were breaking under the relentless assault, and only the hastily-built barricade the military had erected kept the horde from flooding the armory. The moans of the dead, perhaps energized by the tantalizingly close meals within, rolled loudly into the building.

Max jogged to the communications room to warn the others. He entered and saw Eva snuggled up next to Jake. His arm was around her, comforting her. Arthur was stroking Lassie's golden fur and Thomas was leaning against a wall, dozing.

"They're breaking through," Max announced.

He led Jake, Eva, Arthur and Thomas back to the entryway. Dr.

Brookings was still tending to the bite victims further down the hallway, and Max was happy she wasn't there. Her apparent need to control the group interfered with their ability to enact alternate plans, and her first idea had delayed escape and endangered them all.

"They'll get in, Jake. That barricade can't hold forever. Not against that many. It's only a matter of time," he said.

Jake nodded in agreement. "Waiting them out isn't working. We're going to have to come up with a Plan B soon. Maybe we can thin them out by going to the roof and shooting them?"

"We don't have the ammo, Jake," Max admonished him. The military had taken most of the small arms and ammunition when they left for Fort Bragg, leaving only a handful of M16 rifles and assorted handguns. Max wondered if his group would even have those if the military hadn't been forced to set out quickly after the murder of Major Upton.

The other survivors with Central still regarded Max with suspicion, but given the circumstances did not seem willing to make an issue of it. He hoped to make it up to them and prove his worth as a member of the team. It was Eva, distancing herself from Max and drawing closer to Jake, that bothered him the most. Her furtive, accusing glances and curt replies to him spoke volumes. From his assault on Private Hall, to Upton's murder, she had seen a violent side of Max that she hadn't suspected was there, and was having difficulty coping with it. Her expertise was in healing, trying to save lives, and it made sense to Max that she would resent him. To her, violence was brutish, evil and destructive. To him, it was merely a tool. It was the ends to which it was employed that determined whether it was moral or not.

When the dead rose, the rules changed. Max saw himself and Arthur modifying their behaviors to deal with the new reality. Others, like Reverend Miller and Eva, were having a more difficult time accepting that their world was now a brutal fight for survival, their futures measured by hours, days, and weeks instead of decades.

"Damn, I wish we had more ammo," Jake groaned.

"When I said lack of firepower was an issue, did you bottle up some of my awesome rightness? Because now would be a good time to take another swig." Arthur bragged.

"Yes, yes, you were right," Jake admitted through gritted teeth.

"Just wanted to hear you say it."

Jake glared at Arthur. "Well, genius, do you have any suggestions for another plan?"

"As a matter of fact, I do. We need a distraction," Arthur said. "I like distractions. They work. Like when I used the baggage cart to get by the soldiers. There are just too many zombies out there, and they know we're here. If they think we're somewhere else, they'll go there and we can sneak out."

Max ground his teeth, deep in thought. Arthur had a point. They had been keeping quiet, hoping the dead would wander off, but all they had done was waste time. The dead were as numerous as ever, and every minute that passed brought them closer to sinking their teeth into warm, living flesh.

"What kind of distraction did you have in mind?" Jake asked.

"Well, when I snuck off and went home, I saw piles of bodies around a house where the burglar alarm was going off. I mean *piles*. If they're drawn to noise, then let's give them some. Preferably, like, away from us."

"Go on," Jake encouraged.

"I was thinking about the rent-a-car place on the other side of Memorial. Some of those cars must have alarms. I bet one of you Army-trained marksmen could shoot out a window from the roof here."

"I'm Navy," Jake said defensively.

Arthur shrugged, "Whatever."

Jake rubbed his chin thoughtfully, then shook his head. "The gunshots will draw them here."

"But the alarms go off after the gunshot, and for longer," Arthur defended.

"I like it," Max said. "They're already here, already aware of us. I don't see the gunshot adding fuel to that fire. But every one that Arthur's car alarm plan draws away, is one closer to giving us a fighting chance."

"How long does a car alarm go off?" asked Jake.

"Reformed car thief here," Thomas said, raising his hand like a schoolboy calling for the teacher's attention. "It depends on the alarm. Some will run until the battery gives out. Others only go a few minutes before resetting." He chuckled. "They're more nuisance than deterrent. I mean, they never deterred me. They're so common that no one pays any attention to them."

Arthur's face lit up. He was clearly pleased with the group taking his plan seriously, and continued, "The one advantage I see to our following Brookings' plan – namely, sitting around with our thumbs up our asses – is that the fast-moving zombies from casualties at the camp are probably slowing down from rigor mortis."

Eva checked her watch and nodded. "He's got a point. Even if they're not in full rigor, they should be slowed by it. On top of everything else, we don't need to have turbo-zombies running us down."

Arthur smiled. "Turbo-zombies! I like that!"

"That could give us an edge in getting to a truck," said Jake. "But we need to have our truck already selected, and have everyone ready to move."

"Our patients are in worse shape also, though," Eva cautioned. "Many of them aren't fit to travel. What do we do with them? We can't just leave them."

"The hell we can't," Arthur countered. "They're bitten. They're dead anyway. I don't see a need for us to die with them."

"Can it, Arthur," Max growled.

"Arthur!" Eve shouted. "We're *not* leaving them!"

Jake rubbed his chin thoughtfully. "We'll have to risk them traveling. Move them to the assembly hall. Get them ready to load up on a truck as soon as we can get the loading dock clear. We're going to give those people every chance we can."

Eva smiled at Jake and stroked his muscular arm in thanks for his support.

Arthur rolled his eyes and sighed.

"Everything is dependent on Arthur's plan working and drawing them away," Thomas said.

The loud crack of wood splintering indicated the barricade itself was beginning to fail.

"That's our play," Jake said, picking up his carbine. "We're out of time."

"Jake, if you're going to take the shot, use my M16. It's got better range than your M4," said Max, offering his rifle. "But I want her back; we've grown fond of each other."

Jake found the roof access ladder in a storage room next to the assembly hall and climbed stealthily onto the roof while the others readied the bite victims to move. There was a single report from the rifle, and a car alarm blared in the distance. He slipped quietly back into the armory and returned Max's rifle.

It took them thirty minutes to move the patients to the assembly hall. Fourteen were sick but still mobile. Eight were unconscious or otherwise unable to walk, even with assistance, and had to be carried. Dr. Brookings and Eva laid each on their own blanket or sheet, to be used as a stretcher if needed, for quick loading. Thomas rifled through the armory's key cabinet, locating one for a large transport truck nearest the loading dock, the logic being to limit exposure.

The steady banging of fists on the metal doors echoed in the assembly hall, making everyone nervous as they waited quietly for the car alarm to draw the zombies away. Ten minutes passed. Fifteen. Four more bite victims lost consciousness as the disease progressed.

Arthur worried. "The noise isn't letting up. Maybe they can't hear the alarm on this side of the building. Or maybe the noise they're making, beating on the doors, is covering it up. Whatever the reason, it's not working."

"Max, go check the front barricade," Jake said. "Make sure it's still holding. We're going to have to come up with a... what is it now,

Plan C? Plan D?"

Max picked up his M16 and trotted out of the assembly hall, happy to have something to do. The agony of waiting had once again worked over his nerves, leaving them frayed, putting him on a short fuse. He walked down the darkened hallway and crept up to the corner of the entranceway. Moans of the dead still drifted in, but Max noted they weren't as loud. He peered around the corner.

Through slats in the barricade, Max could see a half dozen zombies still bashing on the barricades, but the majority were either attacking the car rental lot, or on their way to it. The first zombies to the car lot had bumped into other vehicles in the lot, setting off more alarms, making more noise and drawing still more zombies away. There were only about a dozen zombies in total between the armory and Central's RV.

Max smiled as he ducked his head back around the corner and trotted to the others in the assembly hall.

"Get ready to be happy," he announced, grinning as he entered.

Jake and Dr. Brookings accompanied Max for another look at the barricade, and to formulate a plan.

Brookings breathed a sigh of relief. "We can make it to the RV, can't we Mr. Billings?"

Jake grunted. "Those of us who are healthy can probably squeeze in. But what about the bite victims? We can't take them all. They won't fit."

"We can't take *any*," Max corrected. "They're bitten. They're dead anyway, and we all know it. So do they. We haven't saved one bite victim. Not one. We have no idea how passable the roads are, if there are roadblocks, so we can't even guess how long it could take to reach your little slice of heaven. They could die and resurrect while we're driving, in cramped quarters. Our situation is beyond critical, and we can't risk it."

"Doctor? What's your take?" Jake asked, turning to his superior. Dr. Brookings' jaw twitched.

"I agree with him, Jake," said Dr. Brookings. "I'd love to get the patients out of here, if not for medical care then for… for study."

Max glared at her. "Study?"

"We can't cure them, but we can still learn from them. They can help us cure others we are almost certain to encounter, possibly bite victims from among our own ranks. Maybe even you, or your friends. But we'll have to pass on these victims. Mr. Newsome is correct; they're too dangerous to transport. But we still have people who can be saved, people who aren't compromised as of yet."

Jake's brow furrowed and he shook his head. "That's some cold shit. I'm not leaving them. You can count me out, doctor."

Brookings' face flushed with anger and she snapped at Jake. "Mr. Billings, you were brought on board with Central to make difficult decisions, to help ensure the safety of our personnel."

"Great, but that doesn't include leaving innocents to die at the hands of these freaks. That's fucking inhuman."

"We won't, Jake," Max said somberly. He took a deep breath. *God help me.* "We're going to finish what Upton started."

†

Max and Jake strolled into the assembly hall, trying to appear casual despite their pulses pounding in fear of what was to come. Jake was worried about how to get everyone away from the bite victims, how to get them all into the hall at the same time. Max told him not to worry; he would handle it. *You deal with getting everyone to the RV,* he told Jake, and suggested that he may have to carry Eva if she didn't go readily.

Max poked around the side storage room with roof access, and emerged with a long chain. He didn't want to waste time explaining, or coming up with some elaborate lie. *Keep it simple,* he told himself.

"Everyone out," he announced. "To the hallway. There's something you all need to see."

"What is that?" asked Eva.

"A way out."

Buzzing with excitement, the unbitten survivors leapt eagerly to their feet and paraded out of the assembly hall with Jake leading the way. Arthur, Thomas and eight more survivors Max hadn't had the time or the inclination to meet walked past Max, but Eva remained.

"I'm not leaving my patients," she announced.

Max approached her calmly. "I'll look after them, Eva. You need to go with Jake now."

"Why? Why now? Why do you have that chain?"

"Eva, there's a possible way out through the front door. Arthur's plan has drawn enough of them away from there, that we can make it to Central's RV. But we need everyone's opinions on the risks, and your expertise in particular, to determine how best to move the patients."

"There are still too many here by the loading dock?" she asked, glancing at the loading bay doors still thundering from the banging fists of the dead.

"Yes. But not at the front door. Can we stop with the twenty questions and move?"

Eva nodded, convinced at last, and left the assembly hall. As she left, Max closed the doors and lashed them shut with the chain. Eva immediately tried the door from the other side.

"Max?" she cried, slapping her hand on the door. "Damn it, Max, what are you doing?"

Max turned his back on her pleas, and looked towards the bite victims. *It's all on you now, Combat.* He heard arguing as Jake tried to coax Eva to the entryway – and the possibility of safety.

Eva was Jake's problem; Max had his own mission. His targets lay on the floor, on blankets in neat, orderly rows, waiting for a transport truck that would never come. Buckets or bowls of bloody puke lay next to each. Most were unconscious, for which Max was thankful. Eva had rolled them onto their sides so they wouldn't choke to death on their own vomitus. He took a deep breath, focusing on the task at hand.

Private Nguyen rolled to one elbow and looked at Max with

bloodshot eyes. His skin was pale and sweaty, and a small rivulet of bloody spew trailed from his mouth. "What's going on?" he asked weakly.

Max bit his lip and considered the consequences of lying, versus telling the truth. If he were in their position, he would want the truth, and quickly decided that they deserved the same. "There's a possible way out of here, but we can't take you with us."

"You're just going to leave us here?" Nguyen asked doubtfully as he sat up, alarmed, his eyes locking on Max's rifle.

"No."

Nguyen licked his lips nervously as he considered the implications of Max's denial. "You're here to kill us. You're the one who killed the major, and now you're going to kill us." Three more bite victims struggled weakly to crane their heads around after hearing Nguyen's assessment.

"Being eaten alive is no way for a man to die. If the horde outside doesn't get you, then the first one in here to die from the virus will. I'm so sorry. It's the only merciful thing we can do."

"Tell that to God," Nguyen whispered quietly.

The sound of gunfire echoed faintly into the assembly hall. Max surmised the other survivors were fighting their way to the RV.

"That's my cue."

"You know, as a soldier, you accept death as a possibility on the battlefield," he laughed weakly. "When it comes, it must be a surprise. Suicide is dying on one's own terms. Can't you give us each a pistol or something, so we can go out on our own terms?"

Max pursed his lips shook his head sadly. "I don't have one to give."

"I'd have killed you with it anyway, and figured it as self-defense," Nguyen said, disappointment in his voice as he turned his back on Max. "Well, waiting to be executed is scary as hell, man. Get on with it already. Mercy killing or no, it's still an execution. I hope it gives you nightmares."

Max stood and took aim at the back of Nguyen's head. He took a deep breath the calm his nerves. *A few seconds of courage, Combat. Four quick shots, take the conscious ones first*, he thought. "Brother, it already does." Max's rifle thundered in the assembly hall and sent Private Nguyen slumping to the floor. He pivoted to his left and hit his second target in the temple as she turned away, then aimed beyond her to kill the third, who was desperately trying to crawl away. Spinning back to his right, he saw his final victim sitting peacefully, facing him, eyes closed and hands in the air, and dispatched him as well with a shot dead center to the forehead.

Two more bite victims stirred from the commotion and Max put them down quickly. He then methodically put a round in the head of each of the unconscious bite victims, his M16 announcing his guilt to the universe with every pull of the trigger. He moved robotically, as if he were watching someone else commit the evil deed, moving from victim to victim. His task completed, Max sank slowly to his knees and gasped. He felt queasy as the realization of what he had just done sank in, and he knew he would never again be the same. Self-loathing took hold, and Max threw up on the floor, already slick with the blood of his victims. "God help me!" he cried, wishing God would strike him down and end his suffering.

Max's hands shook and he wept openly. He had killed Upton for doing precisely what he had just done. *Better to have let Upton finish his task, and let him bear this burden.* In this hellish new world in which he lived, the inhumane had become humane. His heart pounded a rhythm along with the thundering fists of the dead on the metal loading bay doors, and his vision blurred. He didn't have the strength to go on fighting, and collapsed, succumbing to a tidal wave of memories and emotions.

†

Something clicked or snapped near Riggins, and the alley exploded in a blinding flash of light and heat. Max felt himself airborne, landing hard on concrete and sliding. He cried out as pain lanced through his shoulder, and his rifle was wrenched from his grasp. Reaching back to his shoulder, he felt something wet. Withdrawing his hand, saw thick crimson blood covering his fingers. He brushed bits of Riggins off of himself in revulsion.

Max looked around in confusion, trying to get his bearings. He saw pieces of bodies strewn about. His squad mates screamed a silent chorus, their cries overwhelmed by the ringing in his own ears. Shadowy figures of insurgents moved in the windows above him, taking potshots at the Americans. Max's hands scrabbled desperately for his rifle amid the shattered glass and concrete. His fingers found purchase, and he snatched it from the rubble.

A young Iraqi boy of about ten poked his head from a window, his face partially hidden in shadow. He was holding a wireless controller in one hand, and some small item in the other. Horrified, Max again witnessed his actions that day in the war as he drew a bead on the child and fired. A fine red mist spattered the wall behind his target, who was thrown back into the room from the round's impact, dropping the controller and a blue remote-controlled car into the alley below.

Bullets ricocheted angrily around Max as the din of battle penetrated the ringing in his ears. A pair of hands grabbed Max from behind and roughly pulled him into cover in a doorway, out of the line of fire. Max looked up to see Sergeant Sommers, wide-eyed and splattered with blood.

"What the fuck are you doing, soldier! For Christ's sake, that was a kid!"

†

The wailing sound of a mother crying for her dead child still rang in Max's ears as he drifted back into consciousness. He found himself laying on the cold concrete floor of the assembly hall, surrounded by bloody lumps of his victims. Max grasped his sides and wept still more.

He slowly became aware a horn honking faintly in the distance, and struggled to his feet. *The RV. How long was I out?* "Get your ass in gear, Combat," he growled, forcing his unwilling limbs to move as he clambered to his feet. "Move it, soldier!"

Max shouldered his rifle and stumbled to the exit. Unlashing the chain, he threw open the door and bolted down the hall, still wiping tears from his eyes, thankful the nightmare was behind him. He rounded the corner from the hallway and ran to the entrance. One section of the barricade had been dismantled by Central on their way out. Through the slats in the still-intact portions of the barricade, he could see Central's RV trying to force its way through a throng of what looked like hundreds of zombies that had encircled it. A huddle of zombies, similar to what Max had witnessed on campus, indicated that not everyone had made it to the RV. He could see shadowy shapes of people inside the vehicle, and heard the crackle of gunfire from the windows as they tried to clear a path. The RV was rocking violently, dangerously from the assault, unable to get up to speed against the press of flesh closing in on it. Its engine lacked the power of a military transport.

They're not going to make it, Max realized, and knew he had to act quickly.

Enraged at the prospect of seeing all his friends torn apart, Max roared a battle cry and fired controlled bursts at the zombies near the front of the RV, trying to thin them out while drawing attention to himself. Several zombies on the fringe of the attacking mob turned and staggered toward him. Then a few more. Max pressed his attack to draw still more, emptying the rest of his magazine. He hurled his empty M16 at the oncoming horde.

The RV lurched forward and through the smaller number of zombies in front of it, bouncing over and crushing struggling, twitching bodies as it pulled out into the street. Max saw the driver roll down his window and look back at the armory. The shock of long, dirty blond hair blew in the breeze as the RV gained a head of steam.

Thomas. Max pointed to the sky, hoping Thomas would get the message, that he wouldn't just abandon him. The zombies closed in on Max, and he retreated back inside the armory. Racing to the assembly hall, he heard the cracking of the barricade as the horde surged inside. They were slow, and Max easily outpaced them, but they were relentless in their pursuit and powerful in their numbers. He slipped inside the assembly hall and quickly chained the door again.

Max was halfway to the storage room when the chained door shook once, then twice, and a loud, metallic creaking and popping sound exploded from it as the door was ripped from its hinges. Zombies poured into the assembly hall. Some headed for the still-warm flesh of the deceased bite victims. Others shambled after him, moaning loudly in anticipation of a fresher meal. He retreated into the storage room and scrambled up the ladder to the roof, slamming the hatch after him as the first several zombies crowded into the small room.

He ignored the desperate groaning below him as he trotted across the roof to check on the RV's situation. It was on Memorial, driving away.

Max sank to his knees. He remembered how Thomas abandoned him when he fell on the run to the armory, and realized the dread he felt when he saw Thomas driving the RV. The man was a coward. "God damn you, Thomas." *Maybe this is my justice. As I laid judgment upon Upton, maybe this is God's judgment upon me for what I've done.*

The RV stopped on Memorial. The horn honked a cacophonous rhythm of long and short blasts.

"What the hell are you doing, honking in Morse code?" Max mumbled. He picked up a little Morse code during the war, but was never very good at it. He listened intently and identified a few letters amidst the gibberish, but decided the honking was too haphazard to be an attempt at communication. Zombies lurched towards the noise, spreading out. *Unless you're ringing the dinner bell*, Max thought, smiling. After several minutes, the first zombies drew near to the RV, which began slowly rolling forward, still honking, stringing them along. At length, the big vehicle made a sweeping U-turn and threaded its way back past its pursuers, spread out over almost a quarter of a mile. A few zombies rolled under the RV's crushing wheels as it passed the car rental lot, where zombies were thick, but most merely banged their fists ineffectually against its sides. Thomas maneuvered the behemoth admirably across the grass next to the armory, and right up to the building. The roof hatch popped open and Jake stuck his head out, motioning to Max.

Max leapt to the roof of the RV and slipped inside to a chorus of cheering as the RV pulled back out onto Memorial and away from the nightmare of the airport.

"We weren't going to make it until you thinned them out!" Thomas yelled back from the driver's seat. "We owed you, man!"

Max did a quick headcount to see who was missing. He knew Jake and Thomas were there. Dr. Brookings sat in the passenger seat to direct Thomas, nodding once curtly to acknowledge Max.

Arthur tugged on his shirt, a somber expression on his face.

"Arthur, you made it, good. I saw that little zombie huddle in front of the armory and was worried. Who did we lose?"

"Lassie. The rescue dog. We were running in a tight formation, but a bunch of zombies came around from the backside of the RV and cut us off. It's my fault she's dead." Arthur wiped his nose on his sleeve. "I had her on a leash. I had control – responsibility for her – and practically fed her to them as a distraction."

"I'm sorry."

Arthur nodded sadly.

"Do you think your action saved human lives?"

"Yes."

"She was just a dog, Arthur. You did the right thing. You may have saved everyone by doing that, no matter how hard it was for you to do." He gripped his friend's shoulder in a supportive gesture. "That took guts, and I'm proud of you."

"Just a dog," Arthur whispered, as if trying to convince himself.

"Where's Eva?" Max asked.

Arthur motioned to a small table where Eva was sitting alone. She was gazing out the window with a vacant, expressionless stare.

"Take it easy with her, Max," Jake whispered. "I think she's in shock from all the shit that just went down. What we had to do with the patients...."

We. Not 'you'. Yes, Max had been the trigger man, but Jake acknowledged his own role in massacring the bite victims, acknowledged that his own hands weren't devoid of guilt. He wasn't laying blame solely on Max, as others might have. Here was a man of honor, of tenacity, a man with heart, a man he might one day call 'friend'.

Max slipped over to Eva and knelt beside her, placing his hand over hers. She ignored his touch and continued to stare blankly out the window. "Eva," he whispered, gently squeezing her hand.

She slowly turned her head to face him, and he saw tears streaming down her cheeks.

"It's okay, Eva. You're going to be okay," Max said reassuringly.

She shook her head slowly and whispered, "No, Max. I'm not."

A chill ran up Max's spine. "Were you bitten in the escape?"

Eva cackled a nervous laugh. "If I were, would you murder me, too? Like you did that soldier and all those people in the armory? Just what kind of devil are you, Max? Tell me, because I *thought* you were a good man."

"After all we've been through, Eva – you, me and Arthur – you guys are like family to me. I've never really had a family until now. I'd do anything to keep you safe, anything at all."

Eva slipped her hand from his. "It's not your job to protect me, Max. *You* can't. You need to worry about yourself and get right with God after what you've done."

Max felt his heart sink and his pulse quicken. The blame game was getting old, and he couldn't take it much longer. "I couldn't leave those people to be torn apart, screaming. To be eaten alive. That was a merciful thing I did, and one of the hardest I've ever done. It will haunt me the rest of my life, Eva, but I have no doubt – *no doubt* that it was the right thing to do. If we tried to take them with us, we all would have died."

"You keep telling yourself that, Max. Maybe one day you'll believe it."

Max felt his cheeks burning and stood over her, fists clenched with rage. "No, Eva. Maybe one day *you* will. You need to recognize that this is no longer the world we knew. We saw it die over the past few days. All we have left is each other, and I'm not going to let you withdraw like this. Like I said – you're family now.

"There are people out there, survivors like us. People like Sergeant Collins and his men, or the people at other Central facilities. We need to find them. We can use Central's compound as a base. It's defensible and stocked with supplies, food and medicine. It's a place from which we can learn about our enemy, both the zombies and the virus itself. A place where we can learn how to beat them. A place to call home, a place to start rebuilding. We will find other survivors, bring them under our protection, and I swear to you… no, I swear to *God*, together we *will* reclaim our world from the dead!"

ABOUT THE AUTHOR

RJ Kennett is originally from Houston, Texas. He has lived in Virginia, Oklahoma and Colorado at varying times, but is currently back in his home state of Texas. He is a graduate of the University of Oklahoma in Norman.

In previous lives, he has been a political consultant, a one-man marketing department and a web programmer.

RJ Kennett enjoys connecting with his readers, and can be contacted in several ways:

<u>Website</u>
www.rjkennett.com

<u>Facebook</u>
facebook.com/richard.j.kennett
facebook.com/central.outbreak.response

<u>Twitter</u>
@rj_kennett